When Worlds Collide

AMY LAURENS

OTHER WORKS

Find other works by the author at
http://www.amylaurens.com/books/

SANCTUARY

Where Shadows Rise
Through Roads Between
When Worlds Collide

When Worlds Collide

AMY LAURENS

AUSTRALIA

Copyright © 2018 Amy Laurens
2 4 6 8 10 9 7 5 3 1

ISBN: 978-0-9945238-2-2

www.inkprintpress.com

National Library of Australia Cataloguing-in-Publication Data
Laurens, Amy 1985 –
When Worlds Collide
350 p.   cm.
ISBN: 978-0-9945238-2-2
Inkprint Press, Canberra, Australia
        1. Fantasy Fiction 2. Fairies 3. Shadows 4. Juvenile
        Fiction

Summary: Sanctuary is breaking apart and it's up to Edge to fix
it.

First Edition: August 2018
Printed in Australia.

Cover design © Clare Williams.

For Michelle, who taught me the way.

1

THREE WEEKS.

Three. long. weeks, as long as the trails of raindrops that streaked down the smudgy windows of the old school bus, racing each other on and on and on until it seemed impossible there was any rain left in the drop.

I picked at a worn patch on the corner of the once-bright-blue bus seat, where the fabric had worn away and the yellowed foam was showing. Three weeks. That's how long it had been since I'd healed my best friend Gemma, since Scott (bizarrely, now also someone I could sort of call a friend) had destroyed Sanctuary.

Well, the magical, multi-dimensional home of the fairies was a little more robust than that. He hadn't *destroyed* it, but he *had* severely damaged it. Using death magic in a place where you're only ever supposed to use life magic will—apparently—do that.

I shrugged as the tag of my uniform dress itched my clammy back. Behind me, kids shouted and hooted, and someone way down the back of the bus had music blaring from their phone, only half-audible from the front over the chatter and the pattering rain. I leaned against the window as a car shushed past, its tyre kicking up spray that still managed to glitter, even though neither it nor I had seen the sun in two days.

The traffic in front of us eased, and the bus hauled itself around the corner onto the main road just a couple of minutes away from school, indicator clicking time as we went. Outside, the grass had shot up to nearly mid-calf on the side of the road, vivid green in the wet, grey light, exactly the kind of lush that would snap and crunch when you snatched a handful of it. Even the gum trees seemed livelier, their usually dull grey-green more vibrant, deeper, the orange-brown sap stains down their trunks bright—almost as bright as the one broad-leafed street tree that was starting to think about winter, the very topmost leaves tinging reddy-orange around the edges.

I glanced up as someone across the row from me clunked the bus's top window open to let in some air; the windows were starting to fog, even though the aircon was blasting. The smell of wet dirt and wet asphalt percolated through the bus, and I inhaled deeply as we turned the final corner into the school, bottle-green gates pegged wide open for the day. The smell reminded me of Sanctuary—not because it was similar, but because it was almost the opposite of Sanctuary's salty, jasmine-scented air—and my stomach twanged with longing.

The bus juddered to a halt, hydraulics hissing as it tilted, the left side lowering to minimise the step to the footpath. The student horde around me rose as one, chattering, waving, school bags slinging onto backs and shoulders and in other people's faces, squashing toes in their careless stampede.

I sighed heavily and slung my navy backpack over my shoulder.

Three weeks.

I schlepped off the school bus with the horde, girls in our blue-and-white summer dresses, boys in their crisp white shirts, and made my way up the footpath to school, once again cursing myself for trusting Mrs Caro, Gemma's mum.

Not that she was an untrustworthy sort of person, of course, but she was an adult, so her sense of priorities was... different. I wanted Sanctuary fixed— *needed* it fixed, because it was my second home and the thing that had taught me to love small-town Nowra after being dragged here unwillingly from big-city Melbourne. But Mrs Caro was more concerned about keeping everyone safe.

Which, yeah, okay, I admitted as the student horde thinned, clusters heading in different directions to the lockers spread throughout the school buildings, safety was pretty important. Been there, learned that one the hard way.

But Sanctuary was important.

Sanctuary was home.

And Mrs Caro had promised we'd try to fix it. And in the last three weeks, she—and we—had done nothing.

I turned the corner around the orangey bricks of H block and glanced ahead to the bay where my locker lived, an alcove of laminated sky-blue lockers stacked double high, the concrete floor stained by decades of locker detritus.

My stomach twisted. Gemma stood in front of my locker, books already clutched to her chest, lip between her teeth as she held her ground against the tide of students swooping in and out to visit their own lockers. Her dark hair seemed even darker in the overcast light, like a cap of shadows pulled back into a ponytail, her thick, sweeping fringe nearly hiding her equally dark eyes.

But as I scanned her with my road mastery—the special ability I had to read and manipulate people's soulprints, a kind of multi-sensory aura unique to each person—I breathed.

Three weeks ago, the connection she'd accidentally developed with the Valley, Sanctuary's bloodthirsty counterpart, had started growing, consuming Gemma's soulprint in an attempt to take over her body. There had been no way to break the connection without risking her life—I'd managed it for Scott before that, but he'd been nearly dead anyway. So for Gemma, I'd gone the safer route: with Scott's help, I'd connected her to Sanctuary, and the two connections balanced out, holding her soulprint steady in between.

I still got a wave of anxiety every time she seemed particularly serious or sad.

Right now, though, the Valley was behaving itself, and Gemma's soulprint was perfectly fine: the same midnight blue, studded with stars and with the texture of velvet, all accompanied by a faint, high-pitched whine and the feeling of being about to remember something important.

I hesitated for a second, wondering if I could avoid her for a little longer. I missed Sanctuary. I needed to get back there and *do* something, and I didn't think I could stand another day of ignoring it, pretending everything was alright. But she saw me and tension melted from her shoulders.

Sighing, I wound my way through the throng of kids to my bottom-tier locker and gave Gem a weary smile as I dumped my bag on the concrete next to it. "Hey."

"Edge!" she said, practically bouncing on her toes. "You'll never believe what's happened!"

I glanced sharply at her. "Sanctuary?"

She deflated a little as pity filled her eyes. "No. You know Mum said we have to wait."

"Mm." I rolled the combination on my school-issue lock, popped it open, and busied myself prepping my books for the day. Gem hesitated a second before launching into some meaningless chatter about a kid named Sally, but I mostly tuned her out. There'd been a time when Gem would have been just as eager as me to fix Sanctuary, and her mother's instructions to wait wouldn't have bothered her a bit. Would have made her *more* eager, even.

It wasn't like I missed the old Gemma, or didn't appreciate this new one who wasn't trying to convince me to break the rules every five seconds, but... I shook my head as I gathered my English and art books into my arms. I kicked my locker shut with my bag inside, snapped the lock closed, and nodded vaguely as Gemma paused for my input. "Uh huh."

She beamed at me and tucked my free arm into hers. "Oh, Edge! Thank you! I knew you'd understand! Come on," she added as the warning bell rang.

Great. Now I'd just agreed to something she'd obviously thought I wouldn't, and I couldn't ask what it was without admitting I hadn't been listening at all.

Something bumped my other shoulder.

I glanced over to see Scott falling into stride with us, blond hair up in its usual ruffled spikes, black-rimmed knock-off designer glasses in place, and—yup, tie-knot loosened to the precise balance between getting in trouble, and making a statement. "Hey," I said.

He didn't look at me. "Hey."

It still felt a little weird to be walking around the school with Scott like this. I'd moved to Nowra at the end of the last school year, mid-November with only three weeks of school remaining before summer break. The first week had been okay—but then Scott had decided he liked me, and that the most appropriate way to try to get my attention was to tease me in front of his mates.

School had started up again in February after the holidays, and it seemed like I'd be in for more of the same—until Gem and I discovered that Scott had gotten himself tangled up with the power of the Valley, Sanctuary's magical counterpart—the one you used death magic to get to, the one that had been leaking awful, soul-sucking shadows all over the place and destroying Sanctuary.

The only way to save Sanctuary at the time had been to fight Scott—but then Gemma had gotten tangled up in the Valley too, kind of accidentally, and a few weeks later—three weeks ago, in fact—Scott had helped me save Gem. In the process, I'd learned that it had been his mother who'd introduced him to death magic—and who he'd been trying to save when he'd gotten connected to the power of the Valley.

I gave my head a little shake as we neared the science block where Gemma and I had roll call first thing every morning.

After I'd convinced him to help me save Gemma, and he'd revealed that he'd only become entangled with the Valley in a last-ditch effort to save his mum's life (an effort which failed, and nearly led to his own death), Scott had demonstrated that he actually had the capacity to act like a decent human being.

And since healing Gemma had involved Scott connecting with the heart of Sanctuary (saving *my* life in the process), he now had a vested interest in its wellbeing. Besides. When there were only three of you who could travel to a secret, magical land, some sort of group bonding was inevitable.

So Scott had ditched his old mates to become a third member of our friendship group. I still wasn't one hundred percent sure I could trust him though.

We slowed to a halt behind the small crowd of my roll call, and I glanced over at Scott to ask if he'd been switched into our class or if he just didn't care about being late to his own—a rhetorical question, of course, since I knew he didn't care, and he tended to shepherd us to our roll call most mornings anyway.

I blinked. He seemed fainter than usual, faded somehow.

I turned to Gemma—but she was the same, slightly faded—and, I realised abruptly, not moving.

Neither was Scott.

My heart raced and the edges of my books dug into my fingers. The last time Gem had vagued out like this, it had been the Valley's connection with her strengthening—prompting the rescue mission that had resulted in Scott kind-of-sort-of mostly breaking Sanctuary.

I bit my lip and leaned close to Gem.

This seemed different, though. The faint fadedness... That was new. And, I realised, looking around more carefully, it applied to everyone. The whole walkway of students seemed faded... and I could smell jasmine, and salt water.

My pulse leapt again, this time in anticipation. Sanctuary! The hall was fading away and everything smelled like Sanctuary.

I stared eagerly around, waiting for it to materialise—but it didn't, and I realised that no one else was moving at all, it was just me, and I hadn't planted a seed to power the crossing to Sanctuary anyway.

I slumped, exhaling heavily.

The world returned to full colour and people began to move again.

"Did either of you feel that?" I asked softly.

Scott and Gemma stared at me.

"Feel what?" Gemma said.

"Sanctuary," I murmured. "Everything just... faded. For a moment. I could smell Sanctuary."

Scott and Gem exchanged glances over my head. I tried not to let it bother me.

"Edge," Gem said carefully, and now I *was* bothered, though I tried to keep the irritation from my face. "Are you sure you weren't just imagining it?"

I tossed my head. "Oh, yeah, you're right, I have no clue at all what Sanctuary really feels like and I was totally hallucinating."

"Edge!" Gem said reproachfully. "You know that's not what I meant." She glanced at Scott again, who gave a tiny shrug.

"What?" I said. "What are you both not telling me?"

"Nothing," Scott said, holding Gemma's eye.

Gem sighed and bumped my shoulder. "He's right. We're not hiding anything. It's just... Well, I know you're impatient to try to fix Sanctuary, but Scott and I can sense it. It's not safe to be there right now. If we crossed over—"

"Then maybe we'd have a chance of figuring out what's going wrong," I snapped. "And fixing it before there isn't a Sanctuary left to fix."

Gem shook her head calmly. "If Sanctuary had been here just now, however that might be, we'd have felt it," she said. "The connection."

I ground my teeth. I knew I was the only one in this party not boasting a magical connection to a magical land. She didn't have to rub my nose in it.

"I'd better go, I'll be late to class," Scott said.

I rolled my eyes. "Yeah, because being on time is *so* important to you, we know."

He patted the top of my head and I was tempted to growl and snap at his fingers. *This* little doggy was not tame. "See you round," he said.

He disappeared into the crowd and I rolled my eyes again. "I really think—" I turned to Gem as the teacher opened the door to our roll call room and students began to file in.

"Later," she murmured as students packed close. "There's no rush."

I clenched my books in my arms. Easy for her to say. I was tired of being the only one who couldn't get answers just by closing my eyes and weighing up a magical connection, tired of people telling me to wait, to not worry about the best home I'd ever known, about the fact that it had been fractured, decimated, last time I'd seen it.

And now they were trying to convince me I'd imagined feeling it just now.

That was it. Everyone else could like it or not; I was going to Sanctuary this afternoon without anyone else, and I was getting some answers.

2

I WALKED UP the driveway with my backpack
straps heavy on my shoulders and the sound of traffic
humming out on the main road. The clouds were
finally starting to sweep away, and the air closed in
like a damp rag. I'd always thought Melbourne
summers were bad, but man, they had nothing on
Nowra, where the humid days seemed to go on and
on and on. Urgh.

I dragged the back of my index finger over my
temple to wipe away some sweat. Nearby, a few
shrieking cockatoos provided a discordant melody to
the baseline of the traffic, punctuated by the
slamming of a door somewhere.

The sound that was distinctly lacking, however, as
I tromped up the stencilled-concrete driveway
toward the old brick house, was Veve's barking.

Usually our chocolate Labrador couldn't wait for me to get home. But today, there were no frantically excited barks and yips and whines greeting me as I let myself in through the front door.

Frowning, I listened carefully for the sound of anyone else who might be home. "Anna? Mum? Dad?" But it was still too early for Mum and Dad to be home—Dad never got home before six, and Mum had been working back late this week. And it was Wednesday, so Anna would have stayed back at school for maths tutoring.

And yet, no Veve. Weird.

I dumped my bag, then crossed through the house to the glass sliding door in the family room. Maybe she was asleep in her kennel, dreaming so deeply of swimming and chasing rabbits that she hadn't heard me.

I grinned. There was one thing that was sure to wake her up, no matter how deeply asleep she was. I clicked the lock of the door.

Nothing. I frowned again.

I slid the door open and stepped out into the yard. The splintered, grey-wood fence pails were beginning to turn gold in the afternoon light and the lawn was cooling as the shadow of the house stretched over it. Somewhere, someone was mowing their own grass, and the smell of it drifted over the yard. Ants scurried across the pale apricot-beige paving to my left in a rush to get stocked up before the weather started to cool off for the year, and cicadas screeped in the tall, scraggle-footed gum trees down in the reserve behind the house.

But there was still a distinct lack of furry brown Labrador in the yard.

I checked her kennel. Empty.

Anxiety clawed at my chest and I circled around to the left of the house, peering behind the hot water cylinder, under the old pailings, and around the back of the compost bin to make sure Veve hadn't gotten stuck. Nothing, except some old, matted fur and damp dirt. Biting my lip, I headed to the other side of the yard, where it opened up to a raggedy lawn bordered by various small yard trees and ugly, lanky shrubs crouched atop silvering bark chips. Still nothing.

I turned away, thinking that I might give Mum a call and see if she knew anything.

A low noise sounded. I stopped, craning my neck, and listened for it again. There: a low, groaning sort of whine, coming from the awful prickly bushes that grew against the side fence where it met the front one—the same bushes where the Valley's shadows had once dragged Gem and Veve away in the middle of the night.

Heart in my throat, I hurried over and crouched.

Veve gazed back at me, eyes wide, tongue lolling. She tried to stand, tugging backwards, but she couldn't move—some of the lower branches had twisted through her collar, tangling her so tightly she couldn't get out. She'd obviously tried; the collar was up around her ears and thick salvia glopped to the ground as she panted.

I exhaled loudly through my nose. "Frogging elephants, Veve." She must have crawled under there trying to keep cool. You'd have thought she'd know better than to try to hide right where the stinking Valley had captured her.

"Alrighty then," I said as I got down on my knees. "Let's get you out of there, beastie."

Veve's tail flopped twice, as though she was too exhausted to wag it any more.

"Aww, poor Vevey-skin," I crooned as I belly-crawled in next to her. "It's okay. You'll be out in just a sec."

She took the opportunity to plaster some of her salivary goo to my cheek and I screwed up my eyes.

"Thanks, mutt-brain."

Sticks scraped at the skin on my arms as, wincing, I wound my hand up over Veve's head. The branch that had hooked her collar was gnarled and spikey, and I gasped as a thorn pricked the soft flesh between my thumb and forefinger. Gritting my teeth at the awkward angle, I squeezed the branch tight, exhaling in relief as it snapped. I fed it back through Veve's collar and dropped it.

"Come on," I said. "All done."

I wriggled backwards, one hand twined in Veve's collar, the other pressing into the cool mud. My legs, bare in my school dress, fried in the sun, and for a second I thought I could understand the appeal of this prickly underworld. Then a stick stabbed me behind the ear. "Urgh!" I said, clutching the offended ear. "Frogging elephants. What *possessed* you, Veve? Seriously!"

Her tail thumped again as she crawled towards me, claws digging into the dirt as she sought purchase.

The smell of rotten fruit and stagnant water drifted past, and I gagged, heart racing. That was the smell of the Valley, and this was where Gemma and Veve had been stolen by the Valley's shadows in the middle of the night.

But as I lay frozen in the mud, the smell drifted away. I shrugged my shoulders, trying to ignore the unease. The Valley had been quiet ever since we'd connected Gemma to Sanctuary. It was Sanctuary that was leaking all over the place this time, not the Valley. Of course it smelled rotten; who knew what disgusting things had rolled under here and been trapped and rotted away. Probably mice.

Urgh. I shuddered.

Veve lolloped her tongue all over my face again. Whatever. I could think about this later. After a cold shower, for preference.

Everything was perfectly fine.

At last, both Veve and I were extricated from the awful bushes, and I scowled at them—right as Veve collapsed on the grass, eyes rolling, and saliva frothing at the corners of her mouth. My heart raced into overdrive as I flung myself down next to her. "Veve? Veve, what's wrong?"

Her breathing was thick and heavy, and as I stroked her head I noticed that her ears were hotter than I'd ever felt them before. Heat exhaustion, maybe?

I glanced up at the sun, finally showing amid the tattered rags of clouds. Surely it hadn't been that hot today. Muggy, yes. Gross and sweaty, sure. But... heat stroke?

If the Valley had done anything to my dog, someone was going to pay.

"Come on, beastie," I said, shooting a glare at the bushes again. "Let's get you inside." Crouching, I drew her to me and hauled her upwards. She moaned, but I couldn't help it. "It's not my fault you're a heffalump," I told her. As quickly as I could manage while carrying a dog that weighed more than a third of my body weight, I made my way to the sliding door, kicked it open, and got inside. I set Veve down on the tiled floor and switched the air conditioning on just in case before heading to the kitchen.

I snatched up the house phone and hit speed dial, tucking it between my shoulder and ear as I grabbed an old ice cream container from under the sink and filled it with water. "Mum? Hi, it's me. Listen, there's something wrong with Veve." Carefully balancing the container of water, I described what had happened as I made my way back to Veve.

"Call the vet right away," she said when I was finished. "I can't make it home for at least another forty minutes, but call me back and let me know what the vet says."

I agreed and hung up, dropping the phone on the floor for a moment as I put the container of water by Veve's head.

She stretched to sniff at it, nostrils flaring slightly, but didn't move.

Her nose was dry and leathery. I blinked back tears as I scooped up some water in my fingers and let it dribble into the corner of her mouth. She licked feebly and swallowed, tail twitching in the shadow of a wag.

Eyes prickling, I hurried back to the kitchen with the phone and swiped the vet's business card off the fridge. Even if it was the Valley's fault, a vet could probably help me treat her.

My gaze lit on the old towel lying on the kitchen floor that Anna had used to wipe the tiles yesterday, and I snatched it up, wetting it in the sink while I dialled the vet.

"Hello? Yes, hi, it's Emma Tanning here, there's something wrong with my dog Veve." I listed off the symptoms as I carried the wet towel back to Veve and laid it over her belly.

"Do me a favour," said the vet's nurse. "Can you check the colour of Veve's tongue and gums, please?"

I lifted up a flap of jowl and peeked inside Veve's mouth. "Her gums are pretty pale," I said. "But her tongue's really bright."

"Okay. But she hasn't vomited or lost consciousness?"

"No, I don't think so." A tear broke loose and streaked down my cheek.

"Okay, that's good. It sounds like Veve has heat stroke," the nurse said. "It's really important you cool her down as quickly as you can, but not so quickly she goes into shock. Do you know how long she's been like this for?"

"No," I said, struggling to steady my voice. "I got home and she was stuck under the bushes outside. It... It wasn't *very* hot under them, but I guess she'd been stuck for a while, and..." I trailed off as a sob rose in my throat. Veve was five and a half, and one of the only constants I had left from my old life after our sudden interstate move. If she died...

"Hey, Emma, it's going to be okay. Tell me what you've done so far."

I knelt beside Veve and let her lick some more water off my fingers. "Um, I brought her inside to the air conditioning, and she's lying on the cold tiles.

I tried giving her some water but she won't drink, so I'm just letting her lick it off my fingers. I have a wet towel on her, too."

"Okay, that's really good, Emma, you did the right thing. Make sure you don't leave the towel on her for too long or her body will think it needs to try to stay warm, okay? How's her breathing?"

I moved the towel and ran my hand down Veve's side, dislodging dust and fur in the process. "Um, actually, I think she's breathing a bit more steadily than she was," I said.

"Good, that's really good. You can probably leave the towel off now. See if she'll have some more water."

I scooped some more water into Veve's mouth and she licked and swallowed, this time her tail giving a good solid thump-thump-thump on the tiles.

"She wagged her tail," I said. "She wasn't doing that before."

"Okay, that's really good, Emma. It sounds like she's doing better. Now," the nurse continued. "Do you have a thermometer in the house at all?"

I thought for a second. "Yeah, I think we have one somewhere."

"Do you know how to take her temperature?" said the nurse.

I nodded, then realised she couldn't see me. "Yeah, I know how to do it."

"Okay. I'll wait while you do that. Let me know what it is."

I nodded again and didn't bother to correct myself this time as I put down the phone and headed to the laundry. I rummaged around in the cupboard below the sink. Why couldn't Mum keep the thermometer somewhere sensible, like with the bandaids or something? But after a minute or so I found it, and ran back to the lounge room.

I grabbed the phone as I uncapped the thermometer. "I have it," I said into the phone. "I'm just taking her temp now."

Veve winced as the thermometer invaded her private places, but I soothed her with a shush and waited with my breath held for it to beep.

It beeped.

I whipped it out and stared at the numbers. "Thirty-nine point three," I said, hoping it would mean more to her than to me.

The nurse sighed in unmistakeable relief. "She's fine, Emma. Her temperature's borderline where we'd usually be worried, but it sounds like you've got it coming down. Good job."

My voice shook as I spoke. "So she'll be okay?"

"Yes, it sounds like it. Bring her in for a check-up as soon as you can just to make sure, but I think she'll be fine. Just keep doing what you've been doing until she feels well enough to get up, and call us back if anything changes or if she seems worse."

"Thank you," I whispered, then said goodbye and hung up. I burst into tears and buried my face in Veve's neck. Her tail flopped and she strained her head to reach me, sniffing.

"I'm okay," I said as I sat up, fur clinging to my tear-dampened cheeks. "You're okay." I squeezed her front paw and noted that it felt hot.

I moved the water container around and dipped Veve's foot in it. "Everything's okay." I hugged her gently, laughing softly as she licked my cheek. "Yeah, yeah," I told her. "I love you too."

3

AFTER DINNER, AS the sun began its drop toward the horizon, I hurried down to the glade by the creek that ran through the reserve out the back of my house, all senses on high alert. The chances of Gem or Scott being down here right now were slim-to-none, but my ears still strained for the crack of twig or rustle of leaves that might mean someone else was coming, and my road mastery senses scanned the bush around me.

But the little clearing amid tall, straight gums and scraggly tea tree thickets remained quiet and empty under the still-overcast skies, the tea-coloured creek burbling along, fat, swollen and happy after all the rain.

I took a packet of seeds out of my pocket: everlasting paper daisies, this week.

In the first month of school we'd been crossing to Sanctuary practically every day, and between us we'd managed to plant a veritable garden. A row of sunflowers bobbed their sunny heads just before the edge of the no-grow zone at the gum trees' feet, and below them the feather-fronds of carrots waved. After three weeks of neglect, I was surprised they were all still thriving—it looked like most of the carrots were ready for harvest.

We'd been talking about introduced species in science class this week, though, and I'd decided the glade needed some natives to balance things out—hence back to the paper daisies.

So I pulled the packet out, tore it open, and gently shook a seed out onto my palm. I tucked the packet away and pinched the seed in the tips of my fingers.

Closing my eyes, I visualised the Sanctuary entrance alcove in as much detail as I could: soft, thick, emerald grass with a circle of gleaming glass wishstones marking the arrival point; rough, white wall enclosing an area the shape of a jellybean about thirty paces end to end, with the archway leading out to the meadow halfway along the scoopy side; the little rockery over to the right inside the wall, with dark grey boulders the size of wombats dotted through a field of smooth, white pebbles and studded with fire-red bushes with long, leathery leaves that smelled like cinnamon.

Once I was confident I had it exactly right, I pushed the seed down deep into the soft dirt of the glade. As I did, my genetic ability to travel kicked in, harnessing the energy stored in the seed to transport me across into Sanctuary—and leaving behind a flower that would grow to almost full maturity in a matter of minutes.

A soft, salt-water breeze kissed my cheeks, and I inhaled joyfully. Sanctuary.

Then I opened my eyes.

When I'd left here last time, a giant rift had been slashed across the middle of the meadow beyond the alcove wall, and the pines along the left edge that separated the meadow from the beach had stood at crazy angles, some snapped in half and some uprooted completely like a drunken giant had passed through. But then, the entrance alcove itself had been perfectly intact.

Now? Not so much. Cracks snaked over the white walls; in places the white had chipped away, showing dark rock underneath. The grass was tipped with yellow, and the little rockery was in disarray, the careful swirling patterns disrupted. It was a wonder I'd been able to get here at all, with it looking so different from what I'd imagined.

A snort interrupted me, and I glanced towards the entrance to see Aphros's white equine head peering around the corner, golden horn glimmering softly in the dusk light.

Instantly, my chest felt lighter and I rushed toward Sanctuary's resident unicorn. "Aphros! I've missed you."

She put her nose over my shoulder and hugged me close. "And I you."

"It's been three weeks since I saw you last," I said. "How long has it been for you?"

Aphros drew back, grave. "Three weeks? But that is not typical." She snorted and tossed her mane. *Here it has been two months*, she sent through our magical, non-verbal connection, the one we had because we'd once joined soulprints in order to save the world—and my life.

Is that normal, I wanted to ask, but she'd already answered that. I'd only been visiting Sanctuary for the last couple of months, but I'd never yet known time to slip that randomly. The worst I'd ever experienced was a couple of hours, and that had been crossing out from Sanctuary back to Earth (although a few times I'd had random side effects that lasted up to a couple of days, like seeing my own body doubled, offset to my left by a few inches). "What's causing it?" I said instead, and she tossed her mane again, indicating the meadow with her gleaming horn.

I glanced out at the meadow that ought to have been gently sloping up to the fairies' Lodge at the top of the hill, and adrenalin twanged in my stomach. The fissure across the meadow had almost doubled in width, now something like five or six metres across. The pines still stood drunkenly about, and a strange kind of shimmery steam seemed to be coming from the fissure, blurring the air and making it hard to see the Lodge, or Aphros's stable.

"What *is* that?" I asked.

The blur intensified for a fraction of a moment, and I glanced back at Aphros—only she was gone.

My eyebrows knotted and I peered around for her. "Aphros?" *Aphros?*

Edge? Is that you?

I turned to my right, and there she was, appearing around the outside curve of the alcove's wall.

It is good to see you! she sent as she approached. *It has been a long time. Are you well?* She neared and drew me into a hug under her chin, just as she had when I'd arrived.

"Um, what just happened?" I asked, face pressed against her soft cheek, hands pressed firmly against the strength of her neck.

Her mane fell over my right wrist, the coarse hair tickling.

"What do you mean?" she said, stepping back so she could eye me.

"You were just here," I said. "I was talking to you. Asking how everything was. Then I blinked and you vanished, and then you were coming out from behind the wall again."

Aphros stamped her hind foot. "Oh dear," she said. "I had hoped that they would not affect you."

I opened my mouth—and the ground rumbled. I darted a glance back up the slope at the fissure, distracted. "The quakes haven't stopped?"

"No," said Aphros sadly.

My hands fisted by my sides. When we'd been here last, Scott had used death magic to protect us against the life magic the fairies were using—but the two magics had clashed, and the ground had rocked—and apparently, it hadn't stopped since.

I still had no idea whether the giant fissure in the meadow was a result of the earthquakes, or if it was something I'd done when I'd been in the heart of Sanctuary—the physical source of all Sanctuary's magic, and the birthplace of—

My lips twitched as a giant, golden pegasus swooped into view over the trees.

The heart of Sanctuary, birthplace of Helios, the great golden pegasus who was the embodiment of Sanctuary and its magic.

He glided toward the ground and landed at a run, cantering toward us before propping to a stop, huge wings flaring to slow him. My breath hitched a little in my throat at the sight.

Helios bowed. "Greetings, Road Master."

I nodded back. "Hi, Helios."

A hiss like steam caught my attention for a second, and my gaze flicked over the fissure—more of the pearly, shimmering fog erupted from it, and the world flickered again.

Nerves thrilled through my stomach, and sure enough, when I turned back, Aphros had gone. Helios, though, had remained. He stood stock still, regarding me gravely. "You see," he said simply.

Throat dry, I nodded.

"The fairies are trying to fix it," he continued. "Well. Some of them. But they too are fractured, just as the land is. It must be fixed."

His gaze bored through me, even as I nodded. "Of course. That's why I'm here." Obviously I was going to fix it. I'd fixed it before, I'd fixed Gem, and now I'd fix Sanctuary again.

Helios tossed his head, great wings half flapping before he resettled them over his back. "No."

My stomach dropped. "No? What do you mean no?" Anger stirred in the depths of my chest. The fairies had tried to stop me once, too, but with a little illicit help from Quoise, my favourite fairy, I'd done it anyway. I was totally prepared to fight the fairies again—though knowing what they were capable of now, this time I'd be a lot more careful. I hadn't expected Helios to stand in my way, though. My nails bit into my palms.

"It is not for you alone to fix," he said, as though pronouncing a weighty blessing—or a curse.

My nails bit harder and I jutted up my chin. "I fixed it all last time."

"No." He shook his head gently and ruffled his wing feathers. "But this time you must."

"That's why I'm here," I ground out. "I already said that."

He nodded. "You must. But you cannot do this alone."

Scott and Gemma's faces as we'd waited outside the classroom swam to mind, skeptical and cautious, sharing information over my head that only they knew. I shrugged. "I'm the only one who wants it fixed," I said. "There isn't anyone else."

The steam from the fissure hissed again, but I kept my gaze firmly fixed on Helios, determined that he wouldn't get away so easily. But despite that, he began to fade. "It is possible, of course," he said, "to follow good rules badly. But it is just as possible to follow bad rules all too well."

Riddles! I didn't need riddles, I needed *answers*.

But before I'd even opened my mouth, Helios had gone. Instead, midway down the slope, on the close side of the fissure, a small flock of fairies had appeared—led by a green-dressed, emerald-winged fairy slightly taller than the rest.

I spun around back into the welcome alcove and headed to the circle of wishstones. I needed answers, and I needed to figure out what in the world was going on with Sanctuary—but I couldn't face a confrontation with the Keeper right now. And besides, I needed to get home.

I slipped back into the yard while the crickets screeped and the dying light of dusk lingered on the horizon. Veve met me, tail now wafting gently and gums no longer deathly-pale. I tussled her ears, my chest tight. "No more getting stuck, okay Veve?"

She licked my arm with enthusiasm, and I didn't even flinch at the slime.

I headed around to the side of the house where the awful prickly bushes skulked in the dying light. My skin crawled as though covered with tiny spiders and Veve leaned up against my leg. "Yeah. Maybe we'll just look from here," I told her.

Pressing my back firmly against the bricks of the house, I closed my eyes. The bricks' warmth seeped into me, a steadying, calming presence. In front of me, though...

I flicked my eyes open again to check that what I was seeing hadn't suddenly come to life. Still just a bunch of shadowed prickly bushes by the fence. Good.

I closed my eyes again, controlling my breathing carefully to keep it even, digging my fingers into Veve's warm fur. A patch of darkness darker than the rest floated in front of me, and a fetid stink of overripe fruit and rotten leaf litter smogged past, something unsensed by my nostrils but perfectly real nonetheless.

Veve sneezed.

I chewed twitchily on the inside of my lip and stared at the bushes until dusk faded to twilight, considering my options. I had a few, and none of them involved standing around in the dark with probably-malicious bushes, so I headed back inside. Sanctuary had done something a lot like leaking earlier today, and was suffering through random time skips—and now it looked the Valley might be too.

I made a fist with my non-Veve hand. Helios had said I couldn't fix this alone—but how was I going to convince the others to help?

4

I THOUGHT MY biggest problem on Thursday morning was going to be facing Scott and Gemma again at school and trying to convince them that they really, really needed to help me figure out what was going on with Sanctuary.

When the alarm rang at seven, I left the dim comforting cocoon of my bedroom, and headed into the kitchen for breakfast. Here, sunlight splashed across the walls and over the glossy white floor tiles, turning the pale grey of the laminate benchtop to something slightly gold.

Mum and Dad stood together at the sink, Dad's arms wrapped tightly around Mum as she nestled into his shoulder.

I barely glanced at them as I stooped to grab a bowl from under the bench—but something made me look again, and I saw the tear tracks down Mum's face.

"What's wrong?" I said immediately, straightening, white Corel bowl clutched in the tips of my fingers.

Mum inhaled deeply as Dad smoothed her wispy, light brown hair back off her face, making her seem even more wild than before, like she was trying her best to impersonate a dandelion.

But it was Dad who turned to me, dark eyes sombre, shoulders tense—or was that just from holding Mum still?—and said, "The police from Melbourne called."

In my head, the bowl I was holding crashed to the ground and shattered. Shards spiralled across the shiny floor, spinning under the fridge, up against the skirting, out into the hall.

In reality, I just swallowed hard and placed it carefully on the bench by a scarred, dark-wood chopping board. "Why's that?"

It could have been for something good. It *should* have been. It had been four months since we'd been whipped away into hiding—nearly two since the police had arrested one of the major players in the case my father had been a witness for and told us we didn't have to be quite so secretive anymore.

It could have been something good.

But Mum was wringing the tears out of her eyes with the tips of her fingers, slowly, deliberately, as she leaned back from Dad against the sink, and his shoulders were still tight, and my stomach danced like spiders.

In my head, the face of a random girl—I swallowed again—Georgia, her name was Georgia, I couldn't let myself shy away from that, not if I wanted to move on, the police psych had been crystal clear about that—a face crusted with blood, blackened by fresh bruises, lay on the white tiles of the train station bathroom floor where I'd found her on my way home.

"What's wrong?" I whispered.

Dad calmed himself visibly, flowing in an instant to the crinkle-eyed joker that was the only face of his most people ever saw. "It's okay," he said. "It's all going to be okay." He scooped me into a hug.

I resisted, stiff and straight armed. "Tell me what they said."

"What who said?"

As one, we pivoted to my older sister Anna, who had just walked into the family room. Dark-haired and light-eyed, she looked as different from me as two siblings could get—but just like Georgia, the girl who was dead. My gut clenched.

She read the situation in an instant, hands fisting at her sides, eyes tightening. "What did the police say, Dad?" Her voice came out low, quiet—the deliberate tone of someone used to moving mountains.

Dad stopped trying to hug me, ran a hand over his head and smiled a smile that didn't reach his eyes.

"Just tell them, David," Mum said, gripping the sink behind her with white knuckles. "It's not like they won't find out eventually." She met my eyes with something knowing.

I resisted the urge to toss my head.

Dad sighed, and finally looked like himself. "The police called," he clarified for Anna. "It seems that they've intercepted a threat to us, something that suggested to the police that Romano knows where I am."

Bile rose in my throat.

Last year, back in Melbourne, Dad had witnessed something shady going down—he still wouldn't tell us exactly what—and had been called on to testify. The police had been hoping it would be enough to let them finally get to Antonio Romano, a mob boss, or whatever the proper word was. Did we even have mobs like that in Australia? I had no idea.

But alack. They'd rounded up some important middlemen, but Romano had remained, as ever, untouchable—and a couple of weeks later, I'd been on my way home from school, and Anna had had to hang back at school for something and I'd gone into the public bathrooms which should have been teeming at that time of day—only they weren't, and there was the girl Georgia on the floor, dead and broken and looking so, so much like Anna.

My hand slipped off the edge of the bench from where I'd been leaning, cutting against the corner of the cupboard handle. I winced and lifted my hand up heel first, inspecting the line of chafed skin on the inside of my wrist. Tiny beads of blood were forming along it, like dewdrops along the jagged edge of a rose's leaf.

Two days after I'd found Georgia, we'd been moved to Nowra under witness protection.

I sucked at my wrist.

"So, what," Anna said, crossing into the kitchen with the rest of us. "We have to move again?"

My stomach fell through the floor. I hadn't thought of that.

"I don't know," Dad said. "The police are investigating still."

Anna folded her arms, shrugged, then swung her arms down by her sides again. "Nice of them to get their info sorted before calling us, then."

"Anna." Mum cut a sharp glance at her then took a deep breath. "Look, we're all a bit freaked out by this, I know."

She straightened, shoulder to shoulder with Dad. "But we don't know too much yet, so there's no point worrying. We just have to keep doing what we've been doing, lying low and keeping our heads down. Unfortunately," she added, this time glancing at me for just a fraction of a second, "it means we're back to the old rules, which means straight home from school every day, no wandering around, and no excursions on weekends unless they're strictly necessary."

"What?!" Anna shrilled, exactly as I bolted upright and said, "But *Sanctuary*!"

Ignoring Anna, I ploughed on. "Mum, you *know* there's something weird going on with Sanctuary, you know I have to help Aphros and Quoise fix it, and—"

"No, actually, I don't know that," she said, turning to me with her arms folded tightly across her ribs. "And to be honest, knowing that something strange is going on there, I'd be happier all round if you stayed away anyhow. I'm sorry. I know that's not the answer you want to hear, but I refuse to believe that you are the single only person on the planet capable of saving Sanctuary." She lifted her chin, amber eyes fixed and determined.

"But Mum—"

"No."

It was stifling in here, like someone had turned the heating on prematurely, and my heart was thudding in my ears, and my stomach clenching in on itself.

I might not be the only person *capable* of saving Sanctuary, but it seemed a whole lot like I was the only one who cared to.

"What about maths tutoring?" Anna chimed in. "And my art classes at tech? How long is this going to go on for, what do they mean they *think* he might know where we are, what are they *doing* about it?"

Dad shook his head like a horse irritably dislodging a fly. "I told you, Anna, they didn't say much. I'm not holding out on you. I don't know how long this will last, no one does, but you're not the only one it impacts and the family would have it a darn sight easier if you'd grow up and keep your theatrics to yourself." He threw his hands in the air and stomped out of the room.

Anna opened her mouth as he passed, but thought better and closed it again.

I stared at the spot where Dad had vanished into the hallway. I'd never heard him speak to Anna like that before, not even back in February when Anna had gotten a parcel from her Melbourne boyfriend, the one who wasn't supposed to have our address.

That made my throat go dry, and I looked carefully at Anna, hair twisted up in a messy bun, one strap of her baby pink pyjama singlet slipping from her shoulder as she shrugged and headed to the fridge.

Anna, the one who didn't care about what anyone else thought or said or did.

She'd given Kade our postal address. Granted, that was a couple of months ago now, but… How long would it take Romano to make the connections, to track Kade down and—I swallowed—apply some pressure?

Something inside me crumbled, and adrenalin followed hot behind it. We couldn't spend the rest of our lives running. We just couldn't.

5

MUM HAD GIVEN Anna and me a lift to school, something she hadn't done since we'd first moved up here last year. I guess in the long term it made her feel better or safer or something, but in the short term all it did was make all three of us cranky—and late.

I edged open the door to my homeroom (a science lab-slash-classroom the rest of the day, with bays around the outside for experiments and rows of two-person desks in the middle), scowling and clutching my books—and my late pass. Frogging elephants. Of *course* Mrs Johnston had picked today to be actually engaging with the class, some sort of obligatory-fun, rather than mostly ignoring us for the fifteen minutes of roll call like usual.

Gritting my teeth, I headed toward my usual seat near the front with Gemma, making sure my bright yellow late slip was clearly visible.

Mrs Johnston nodded curtly as I sat, piling my books on the pale-wood laminate desk.

"What's up?" Gemma murmured, barely moving her lips.

"Later," I said, still scowling.

She nodded, and nudged my shoulder affectionately.

Later, as it turned out, wasn't until recess. Scott found us in our usual corner of lawn, tucked between two bricked garden beds just off the footpath in the walkway between the senior common room and the Maths building.

I cracked the top on my banana and peeled the skin down in four equal strips as Scott folded himself down to a cross-legged sit. He leaned back against the bricked edge of the garden bed and tipped his chin up to the sky, this morning a deep blue with clouds scudding across it, the sun playing hide and seek as they did.

Gemma was already sitting to my right, legs curled up under her school dress, carefully plucking purple grapes from their stems with tiny little popping sounds.

We hadn't had grapes around home for nearly a month now; summer was over and they were all overpriced and mostly past their best.

Scott, of course, didn't have a snack, but his butt had hardly touched the ground before the unpeeled half of my banana and a little cluster of Gemma's grapes landed in his lap. He lifted them with his eyes closed and picked the grapes off the stem with his teeth, stuffing them into his cheeks like a cartoon chipmunk. He didn't say thanks, but that was how it went: we pretended he didn't really need our food, he pretended he wasn't really grateful.

A light breeze wound around the buildings, setting the leaves of the creeping, vining ground cover in the planter boxes shivering, and the drier leaves of the dark-trunked gum tree rattling. I grabbed up a fallen leaf from the ground and folded it in my fingers, lifting it up to smell the eucalyptus scent. They were always stronger in hot weather; it was nearly the end of term, and after the Easter holidays the temperatures would cool off, the days would turn grey and short, and even though there'd be plenty of eucalypt leaves whenever I wanted them, they just didn't quite smell the same when they hadn't been baked by thirty-degree heat for weeks on end.

"So why were you late this morning?" Gemma asked, tipping the grape stems off her skirt then picking up the biggest pieces and tossing them into the garden bed.

I frowned as she did. She raised her eyebrows, prompting.

This morning's nerves flooded back, ice settling in my stomach, and I lowered my gaze again and shoved the last mouthful of banana in. I chewed slowly, as slow as I could, but she never took her eyes off me all the while.

"The police called this morning," I said when the banana had gone and I'd licked my slightly sticky fingertips and wiped them on the grass.

In my peripheral vision, Scott tensed, though he kept his head tipped back and his eyes closed as he chewed (banana now), and an outsider wouldn't have caught anything wrong.

On my other side, Gemma was frowning. "The police? Why? Did Anna do something?"

I sniffed. Of the four of us in my family, Anna was definitely the most likely to be in trouble with the police—but in the end, I was pretty sure she was more stubborn than stupid. "No. Not the Nowra police, the Melbourne police."

Something electric ran through me, and both Scott and Gemma caught it. Gem leaned in closer, reaching for my hand, while Scott sat bolt upright, fixing me with his assessing gaze.

"The mob boss..." I swallowed through a suddenly-dry throat. "They think the mob boss guy might know where we are, or something. We're back to school-and-home-only rules. No Sanctuary."

"Oh, Edge!" Gemma launched herself at me, practically landing in my lap as she clasped her arms around my neck. "Is everything alright? What are you going to do?"

"It's fine," I said, Dad's words echoing in my thoughts: *I don't know how long this will last, no one does … you're not the only one it impacts and the family would have it a darn sight easier if you'd keep your theatrics to yourself.*

I breathed deeply. "We're all fine. It's just a bummer, right? And I have no clue how we're supposed to fix Sanctuary now, since I can't go and—" *And you two won't.* I sighed and gave Gem a squishy hug.

Accidentally, I caught Scott eye: his look was all too knowing, and I narrowed my eyes back at him. So what if he knew I wasn't saying everything. Neither were he and Gem.

"Anyway," Gem said, righting herself and pushing hair out of her face where it had come loose from her ponytail, "it's not like you're *supposed* to be going to Sanctuary at the moment. I know, I *know*," she said, waving her hands as I tried to interrupt. "But I've told you. We've told you," she added with a quick glance at Scott. "It's not safe to be there right now."

I stilled. Okay, so the time skips had been weird, and there was always the Keeper to contend with since she was utterly determined that the three of us were still banned from Sanctuary, even though Gem and Scott practically *were* Sanctuary now, what with their magical bond with the pegasus Helios and all, but… it hadn't seemed *dangerous*, as such. And Helios himself had said I needed to fix things—that *we* needed to fix things. "Please," I said quietly. "Please just tell me what you know." I buried my face in my hands. They still smelled faintly of eucalyptus.

In the silence—which of course wasn't silence so much as awkwardness; the sounds of other students chatting and laughing and shouting still ebbed and flowed around us—I remembered something else I hadn't told them.

"Veve," I said, rubbing at my face before looking up. "You know how I said yesterday that it felt like Sanctuary had, like, faded in on top of us or something?"

Gemma made as if to protest, but Scott silenced her with a tilt of his head and a cutting look.

"Well," I said, ignoring them both, "I got home and, you know those awful prickly bushes around the side of the house?" I raised my eyebrows at Gem and she nodded. "That's where the Valley snatched Gem and Veve," I added for Scott's benefit, oddly gratified when his eyes widened, knuckles blanching as he made fists at the mention of the Valley. "Well, I got home yesterday and Veve was stuck under them. She had heat stroke, and…" I shrugged uncomfortably, as though the Valley's shadows were lurking behind me. "I'm pretty sure she'd been taken by the Valley."

"Taken?" Gemma's voice was thick with scepticism, and she rocked back, lifting one knee and wrapping her arms around it. "Edge, the Valley doesn't just give things back once it's taken them. You know that."

I did—we *all* did—but I also knew what I'd felt.

"And anyway, how do you know it was the Valley? She might've just been stuck. Goodness knows it was hot enough yesterday."

"Not really," I said. "And I'm *pretty sure* I know the Valley when I sense it." My sarcasm could have cut steel. I was used to people questioning me, questioning my abilities—road mastery was rare, so rare that even Gemma's mother and father, who had been visiting Sanctuary for a really long time, didn't know any road masters as strong as I was—but Gem was my best friend, the one who'd always believed me. I busied myself staring at the grey-green leaves of the gum so I had the excuse to look up and blink rapidly a few times.

Something bumped my knee.

Scott. Or his knee, anyway. I stared at it. Somehow, it had never struck me how hairy boy's knees were before—or maybe that was a new thing, because we were all growing up.

"I believe you," Scott said in a low voice, as though he didn't even want Gemma to hear—which was ridiculous, of course, she was right there. Right... there.

I inhaled deeply, and salt water and jasmine filled my lungs while the world around me faded to foggy grey, Scott and Gemma and the plants and the clouds all unmoving. And underneath it all, a different smell, something sweet and sharp that made me want to sneeze, something like sugar and pepper, or fairy floss and sulphur.

I climbed to my feet, peering around through the fog.

But abruptly, the world returned to normal, colour and sound snapping back into place within the space of a heartbeat. I touched the vine leaves in the planter box, heart-shaped, yellow-green leaves on a plant that flowered lilac in the spring: real, cool and slick and waxy to the touch.

"What are you doing there?"

I turned, and saw on Gem's face an expression that was probably a dead match for my own confusion when Aphros had disappeared in Sanctuary. "The time skips in Sanctuary," I murmured to myself.

The Valley had leaked shadows, once. Could Sanctuary be leaking time skips? Urgh. I'd give my right foot to know whether this was just because Scott had used shadow magic in Sanctuary, or because the shadow magic had actually touched the fairies' life magic, or because of something else altogether—maybe something I'd done in Sanctuary's heart.

"What do you mean, time skips in Sanctuary?" Gemma said, quietly, stiffly.

There was a trail of ants just inside the rim of the planter box. You couldn't see them unless you looked closely; they blended in with the dirt and the bark, and were mostly hidden by the viney plant, but they were there, scurrying in their messy row, on their way to who-knew-where.

"Have you been into Sanctuary?" Gem added quietly when I didn't answer.

"Just leave it," Scott murmured, and a burst of good-feeling toward him swelled in my chest.

"No," she said, and I heard her get to her feet. "I want to know. Did you go to Sanctuary alone, Edge? After we'd told you not to? After we'd told you it was dangerous?"

A tendril of vine waved up in the air. I yanked it, and the tip snapped off. "I didn't realise I needed your permission to visit Sanctuary, Gemma. Or," I continued, turning toward her, "did Quoise finally manage to unseat the Keeper, and you convinced them to make you the replacement?"

She paled, but she didn't back down, or look away. "Edge, we told you. Why didn't you trust us? Why didn't you tell me?"

"I'm telling you now, aren't I? Yes, I went to Sanctuary, on Wednesday, after school, and it's a good thing I did, because Sanctuary is breaking, and Helios himself said we need to fix it." I stripped the leaves from my stretch of vine in a single movement and let them drop to the ground. "And besides, why should I trust you when you guys clearly don't trust me? I told you Sanctuary had appeared yesterday, I told you! And it did it again just now, that's why you thought I'd suddenly reappeared over here"—subconscious alarms sounded—*remember this, remember this*—"and inside it time keeps skipping, and the Valley *is* leaking again, and it took Veve, I know it did. So why"—I threw the vine on the ground, snatched up my banana peel from where Scott had discarded it, and prepared to walk away—"won't *you* trust *me*?"

6

I'D AVOIDED GEMMA for the rest of the day, and honestly, it hadn't even been hard. We'd only had one class together, and given it was English in the final period on a Thursday, the teacher just let us read for the lesson. Gem hadn't even come to find me at my locker at lunchtime, so I'd headed out and sat at the edge of the playground alone, trying to look like I'd chosen to deliberately.

Scott, in his defence, did come to find me, but talking to him civilly without Gemma around as backup still felt weird—so as soon as I spotted his blond head weaving toward me through the playground throng, I gathered up the last quarter of my sandwich and ducked around the back of H block, which was *tech*nically out of bounds, all dry, wild, yellowed grass and scrubby bushes and tall scraggly gum trees that were mostly smooth and white trunked, except for the skirt of orangey-brown rough bark around their feet. But here, I could hunker down against the orange, sun-warmed bricks of the humanities building and eat my sandwich in peace. The wind had picked up from recess, too, and it rustled the trees loudly enough that the shouts and cries of the playground faded to white noise. My own little world.

Which would have been super comforting, had I not already *had* my own little world, a.k.a. Sanctuary, and had that particular 'own little world' not been in danger of self-destruction. Or me-destruction. Or Scott-destruction. Whichever.

But I did at least manage to get through the rest of the day uneventfully, and Mum was giving in to her paranoia (okay that wasn't *entirely* fair, it wasn't paranoia if she had a really good reason to be worried) and drove me and Anna home before she went back to work—so I didn't even have to sit with Gemma on the bus.

I mean, I'd have to talk to her soon. She was my best friend. Fighting with her was like, like... Actually, I didn't know what it was like, I thought as scraggy suburban homes with roofs in shades of brown flashed past, their gardens gone leggy and wild from all the rain we'd been having. I'd never been close enough to Anna to fight that badly with her, and my friends back in Melbourne... Well, I'd kind of been conditioned to just go along with whatever they wanted. So no fighting there, either.

Fighting with Gemma sucked, though, that much was sure.

I laid my head against the car's window, which was cold from the air conditioning and buzzing from the thrum of the engine so that my cheek vibrated along with it. More than anything, I wanted to go see Aphros, to talk to her and ask her advice—about Gemma, about Sanctuary, about the police, all of it. But even if Sanctuary had been perfectly safe, I wasn't allowed outside the yard.

Which is how I ended up in the backyard, sitting on the concrete path with Veve, in an old, sky-blue t-shirt and my favourite denim shorts, worn to softness because I'd barely grown in the last two years anyway, staring at the ugly, prickly bushes that skulked against the fence.

Veve lay next to me, face smooshed against my thigh as I idly rubbed the base of her ear between my fingertips, groaning and grunting occasionally as I hit the right spot.

"What do you think?" I asked her, still contemplating the bushes. They stood about chin-height on me, which was to say about a foot-and-a-half shorter than the palings of the fence, and took up about four metres of space along the eastern side of the yard—rather a lot of room for the world's ugliest plant. From here, with my back to the side of the house, I could see the street to my right through the metal railings of the front fence—but we lived in a quiet cul-de-sac; the chances of anyone wandering past and seeing what I was doing—if I did it—were slim. "It's not like we'd be leaving the yard," I added.

Veve sneezed on me and rolled onto her back, wriggling for a moment before tipping her head back, tongue lolling out and flapping drool onto the ground.

"You're equal parts gross and no help at all," I told her, scritching her elbow where the skin was loose and the shape of her bones showed through. "I'm glad you're feeling okay again. But," I continued, "that's exactly why I need to go. I have no one to ask for advice, Vevey. I can't just do nothing. I know it's the Valley, but we've survived it before, right?"

I considered the bushes again with my lips bunched to one side. They had tiny, eye-shaped leaves that tinged to dark red—burgundy, really—on the edges and down the veins, and wicked thorns, some nearly half as long as my thumb and thick as a house nail. Just the kind of place you'd expect a portal to the Valley.

Of *course* I couldn't have a connection to Sanctuary in my yard. Of frogging course.

But... there were no shadows that I could sense. And our excursion into the Valley while trying to save Gem a few weeks ago had suggested that maybe it was just the shadows that were dangerous, not the actually Valley—and that maybe, just maybe, the Valley wasn't *actually* the same thing as the evil, soul-sucking shadows like everyone had thought.

The whole relationship between the shadows and the Valley and the Valley and Sanctuary was kind of murky, and I was pretty sure there was a good story there that the fairies weren't telling—and I was also pretty sure that the Valley wasn't as evil as the fairies tried to claim.

Aphros could cross there, for a start; and Quoise hadn't died when I'd accidentally dragged her there three weeks ago, even though everyone said that fairies would basically spontaneously combust if they went into the Valley.

And I'd used death (Shadow? Death? I couldn't settle on a term that felt right) magic a couple of times now, and nothing terrible seemed to have happened to me so far because of it.

I mean, there was the fact that the sentient power at the heart of the Valley had killed Scott's mother, possessed *him* nearly to the point of death, and worked hard at trying to do the same thing to Gemma... But they had all had to agree to accept the bargain of the Valley's power for that to happen: a soul for power, power for a soul.

"It's not like I'm actually using death, though," I told Veve as she snapped at a passing fly.

The wind exhaled through the garden, and the soft-leaved garden plants wafted happily. Even the lawn rippled a little—but the stiff-branched, waxy-leafed prickle bushes that covered the portal to the Valley didn't stir.

All at once, I sighed. "I'm practically becoming Scott," I muttered as I scrambled to my feet and moved over to the bushes.

Veve leapt up to follow me, tail wagging frantically, making her whole butt wiggle.

"Yeah, yeah, Hairbrain," I said fondly. "Of course I'll take you with me." I made her sit on the ground next to the bushes.

I wriggled my toes in my sneakers—at least I had decent shoes for this trip for a change—and opened the pair of kitchen scissors I'd borrowed from the drawers. This particular pair had three sets of blades to chop herbs into small pieces, and they were super sharp—I'd sliced my fingers on them a couple of times trying to get stuck bits of herb out from between the blades.

I might not have spent the last three weeks planning this exact moment—honestly, I'd hoped never to have to visit the Valley again.

Well, that wasn't quite true; a teeny part of me was actually dying of curiosity over here: rumours that Sanctuary and the Valley had once been part of the same place? Suggestions that the shadows weren't actually a natural result of the Valley? Quoise living through the experience? Urgh. So much curiosity.

So yeah, okay, fine: I'd thought about crossing over to the Valley again. And there were only two ways to do that: one, procure a unicorn-hair ward, because unicorns were the only creatures who could freely cross the border between Sanctuary and the Valley, and walk over from Sanctuary; or two, offer a death sacrifice, which usually meant the literal death of a small animal...

Only I'd figured out a way to make it work by offering my own blood instead.

And in contemplating a theoretical return to the Valley, I'd also thought a lot about how hard it actually was to draw blood on purpose when you wanted it sometimes, and about how the resulting injury tended to sting quite a lot, and how it would be best to have that in as practical a place as possible.

So I opened the scissors, took a deep breath, grabbed Veve's collar with my left hand, and with my right, drew the blades of the scissors over the back of my left shoulder muscle, just about where they jab you with immunisations.

People seriously underestimate the willpower it takes to hurt yourself deliberately. It took a second go before I actually broke the skin, and when I did, I inhaled sharply. Tears sprang into my eyes, but I closed the scissors and laid them carefully on the ground before squishing the tears away with my index knuckle. It didn't really hurt any more than a paper cut—the scissors were razor sharp—but it felt like a shocking thing to have done, and that made the pain seem worse.

"If there was any way but this," I told Veve. "I'd do it." I closed my eyes, imagined the smell and feel of the Valley, and the world slipped sideways.

7

I GASPED, AND fell to the ground, wincing as my palms hit the dry, spiky, straws of dead grass. A wave of nausea crested over me and I swayed on all fours for a moment, waiting for the tussocks and fallen leaf litter to come into focus. The nausea was mostly a by-product of using death magic, but the sudden, overwhelming stench of rotting, overripe fruit, sickly sweet and thick, accompanied by the smell of fetid drains definitely didn't help.

You had to love the Valley. Ha.

Veve slurped at my ear, wet snuffling noises of concern.

I sat up, shielding my face with one hand and wiping slobber out of my ear with my shoulder. Around us, trees that looked almost like some of the shorter types of gum trees gnarled and twisted their way to the sky, their leaves a little less long, a little less dry and grey-toned than any gums I'd seen before. Some had dark red stains down their dark bark, like old blood—and on some, sap still bubbled out, looking an awful lot like new blood.

I'd begun to sweat the second I'd arrived, beads popping out on my forehead and running down my temples, and I winced as sweat made its way into the small cuts on my shoulder. I fished around in my shorts pocket for the bandaid I'd brought and ripped it open. Carefully, I ran my thumb over the cuts, then licked off the smear of blood.

Salty, from the sweat. Ick. I wiped away the sweat with the sleeve of my t-shirt so the bandaid would actually stick, then pressed it on and carefully tucked the tiny bits of rubbish back into my pockets.

The heat pressed down like a wet blanket, thick and stifling. By my side, Veve panted, huffing like a steam train as her tongue lolled. I tussled her ears. "So, how far away is Sanctuary, do you think?" I asked her.

I closed my eyes and looked around with my road mastery, but either I was too far away from Sanctuary to feel it, or the border between it and the Valley blocked my road mastery.

Urgh. There was still so much about the magics of Sanctuary and the Valley that we didn't know. Or, well, that *I* didn't know. The fairies obviously knew a lot more than they were saying, and who knew what Gemma and Scott could now tell through their special connection.

I sighed.

Edge, is that you? Aphros's voice drifted toward me, inaudible but clear as mint nonetheless.

I smiled. *Yeah, I'm in the Valley.*

I could practically see her tossing her mane impatiently. *Stay there, I will come to you.*

Yeah, okay.

I sighed, glancing around at the hot, bright sky that always seemed to feel like midday even though this place had no sun. Not exactly my favourite place to hang out, I'd be honest. But Aphros was right: at least here we wouldn't get interrupted by the Keeper or her lackeys. And Aphros was quick: I wouldn't have to wait too long.

I found a log to perch on, Veve flopped down in the shade right behind me, and we settled in to wait.

Sure enough, before too long—although it was long enough that I'd begun to wish I'd thought about water, not just a bandaid—Aphros's voice flashed into my head again. *I am nearly there.*

I stilled, listening with all my might, and after a moment caught the rhythmic drumming of her hooves somewhere away to my left and a little behind me. I closed my eyes and cast outward with my road mastery; she should be within the fifty-or-so metre range of my ability to detect people any moment now.

And there she was, her soulprint a bright flare of gold and pale green, suffused with the smell of mint—and with her, another soulprint I recognised: deep turquoise blue, rippling in the exact way that sunlight would if you looked up at it from underwater, the smell of rain, and the sound of soft, tinkling fairybells.

Quoise. I grinned so wide my dry lower lip threatened to crack, then pushed my fingers and palms over my cheeks as though I might be able to hold my happiness in.

Veve fish-flopped to her feet in the manner of all startled sleeping dogs, barking delightedly as Aphros appeared.

I hurried over and wrapped my arms around Aphros's neck, inhaling the equine-and-hay smell of her, wiping my face against her neck to get the thick, tickley wisps of her mane out of my eyes and holding tight in case she vanished at any second.

Are you well? she sent.

I'm great. Truth, because I was completely great *now*.

Above me, Quoise giggled. I held my wrist up above my head for the handspan-sized fairy to alight, and brought her in close to my face so she could join in the snuggle. She laughed and wrapped her arms as far around my neck as she could, deep blue wings edged in black and matching her wafty, gauzy dress, fluttering in excitement.

"How did you get here?" I said when the hug-fest finally quit. Although Quoise hadn't been affected when I'd travelled us all to the Valley a month ago, as far as I knew no one but Aphros could walk across from Sanctuary into the Valley—well, Aphros and anyone with a unicorn-hair ward.

"I came with Aphros," she said. "Her presence allowed me to cross from Sanctuary."

"That's great!" I said. "How *is* Sanctuary? What's been happening?"

Aphros tossed her head and stamped a hind foot absently. "You saw how the crevice is affecting things, I think."

"The time skips?"

She nodded.

Quoise held her chin in both hands, heels of her palms meeting in a neat V under her face. "Oh, Edge," she said, eyes wide. "It's terrible. Viri's trying to play things down as much as she can, of course," she continued, referring to the Keeper and ruler of Sanctuary, "but it's hard not to notice that things are getting worse when you can barely finish a sentence these days without the person you're talking to suddenly vanishing."

I frowned. "But that's not happening here?" I waved at the Valley around us.

Quoise and Aphros exchanged glances. "Not as badly," Quoise said. "The main crevice is in Sanctuary, and although the Valley is getting some of the effects, like the quakes and things, overall it seems to be holding up alright. Only..." She bit her lower lip.

There were any number of ways that sentence could plausibly end. "Only Viri still says you all can't come over here without dying?" I said, picking the most obvious.

For as long as the fairies could remember, they'd been told unconditionally that to set foot in the Valley was to die; even the Valley itself had believed that. But for reasons none of us had yet figured out, Quoise hadn't spontaneously combusted when she'd ended up in the Valley nearly a month ago, and if her appearance here today was anything to go by, she'd come over again more than once in the interim.

Quoise nodded. "Of course. She won't let them listen to anything I have to say." She scowled, and it was so adorable I nearly laughed. "But, there are other problems. I might not be dead from being here in the Valley, but it's still dangerous. The shado—"

In the space of a syllable, both Quoise and Aphros disappeared—and Veve. Panic gripped at my chest for a moment before I cast around and spotted her sleeping behind the log, right where she'd been before Aphros and Quoise had arrived.

Aphros, there was a time skip. Where are you?

Coming to you in the Valley, she responded. *We are nearly there.*

I sighed heavily, shoulders dropping, and folded myself down to the ground to wait.

"Things are definitely getting worse," Quoise said as soon as she arrived this time. "Aphros said there was a time skip?"

I nodded. "Let's skip the polite stuff and list out the important things, in case it skips again."

Aphros tossed her mane, exactly as before. "The fissure is widening. The time skips are getting worse and, obviously, are now spreading to the Valley. Shadows have been sighted. Quoise has a small but loyal core of fairies who believe her and are willing to move against the Keeper should circumstances allow."

She cast a questioning glance at Quoise, who nodded.

"I think that about covers it," Quoise said, hovering near me. She tugged on her dark braid. "I need that Book of Laws. You know the one," she said, flicking a glance at me.

I nodded. "The one you found before following us through to the heart of Sanctuary."

"Yes. Only, of course, Viri's locked up the Forbidden Chamber again so no one can get at the book." Another tug on her braid. "If I had it, I think I could persuade the others to join me. It would answer so many—"

I blinked, and they'd vanished again. Rubbing at my face, I sat back down on the log next to Veve and tipped my head back against the tree behind me, closing my eyes. *Aphros? Are you there?*

No answer.

I sighed. Shadows. That definitely wasn't good. Might explain why Veve had been pulled through to the Valley though, I thought, reaching out to run my fingertips through her fur. The shadows had done that last time, at the start of the year, when both Veve and Gem had been sucked through. But that time, the Valley had been strengthening. This time... I glanced around. This time the Valley was quiet.

Still. I shuddered as adrenalin pulsed through my body. Shadows. Not good. Not good at all.

A strange noise, rhythmic, whoomping, sounded over the clearing where I sat.

I frowned and looked around, and then, when I couldn't see anything through the trees, up.

My tension melted away as I spotted Helios, glowing golden in the sky like a horse-shaped sun, great, pale gold wings beating the air as he angled himself to land.

He dropped fast, legs windmilling, wings spread wide—and at the last second before his hooves touched the ground, he flared his wings with another feathery noise, and landed at a trot.

I watched through slitted eyes, his mane and tail rippling out light bright enough to cast sharp shadows behind everything, my hand over my forehead to shield my face.

"Hi," I said as the physical embodiment of Sanctuary's power drew close and halted beside me. "What else has broken?"

Helios snorted and flicked his tail, nearly blinding me in the process. "The fairies have closed the ways to the circle," he said. "Quoise does not yet know, nor Aphros."

"The ways?" I wrinkled my brow as Veve yawned to her feet, saw Helios, and lay back down so she could belly-crawl toward him adoringly. Cute.

"The ways." He tossed his head impatiently. "To the circle. Where those who travel to Sanctuary may enter."

My frown deepened. "What, you mean… the alcove? The… circle?" In the white-walled alcove where everyone who travelled to Sanctuary began, clear-glass wishstones drew a circle in the thick, emerald grass: the place where everyone arrived in Sanctuary, no matter where they'd travelled from (unlike the Valley, where travelling over at different crossing points meant you arrived at the corresponding point in the Valley, wherever that might be). "You mean… no one can cross to Sanctuary right now?"

Helios nodded. "That is correct. The fissure grows worse, and Sanctuary is beginning to fracture. The fairies do not want to risk the lives of anyone else."

I snorted. "Big of them." They didn't seem to care too much about other people's lives when the shadows were roaming around trying to devour everything.

Helios stamped suddenly, firmly, and I jerked away a little. "You must find a way to fix this. If Sanctuary fragments, the middle worlds will die."

The middle worlds. *You can get to anywhere from Sanctuary*—Quosie had told me that on my very first visit. I guessed the 'middle worlds' must be Sanctuary and the Valley, then, the worlds in the middle of all the others.

Helios could barely hold still, flitting his wings, rustling feathers, swishing his tail, stamping... His ears flickered up and down, constantly alert.

Another thought took hold. "Helios, if Sanctuary fragments..." I took in a long breath, right as Veve rolled onto her back, offering her belly to the great pegasus. "What will happen to you?"

He stilled, as instantly and completely as though he'd been turned to stone. "I will be torn apart also."

"Oh," I said softly, so softly. "I'm sorry." I rubbed my hands over my face again, fingers sliding up my cheekbones until my palms covered my eyes. "I don't suppose you have *any* idea where to start with this, do you?"

"Only that you might look in the one place where time does not matter."

I blinked. "The roads? You want me to go on the roads again?"

He made a movement that could have been a nod, or could have been tossing his head.

I narrowed my eyes and leaned forward over my knees. "Helios, how much do you really know about what's going on? Is there more that you could just *tell* me? It would save a lot of trouble, you know."

His back feet danced sideways. "I have not the words, and here, I cannot show you."

I straightened, lighter. "You want me to meet you in the heart so you can show me what's wrong? Okay. Okay, that I can do." I stood, wiping sweaty hands on my shorts, shrugging away the trickle of sweat behind my ear. "Roads. No worries. I can do roads."

Veve did her fish-flop movement to her feet again, and trotted to me, tongue still flapping like a wet, pink flag, tail wafting vaguely.

"No, Vevey-pup," I said, rubbing her ears, "you can't come with me on the roads."

Urgh. Which, problem: who was I going to get to come on the roads with me? Gemma definitely wouldn't approve, and Scott... My stomach flipped. There had to be another option.

I ran my lip through my teeth. There *was* one other option. It was totally crazy, utterly bizarre, but... maybe. Maybe it would work.

"I'll get there as soon as I can," I told Helios. "How will you know I'm there?"

"I will feel it," he said, bowing his golden head. "Hurry, Edge. The world is cracking, and you and your friends are needed."

I sniffed. Me and my friends. Yeah. All those hordes of friends. Never mind. I gave my head a shake and wound my fingers through Veve's collar. The other option would work. It had to.

8

"SO REMIND ME what we're doing again?" Anna said, shifting her weight as we stood in the yard staring at the prickly bushes.

I'd managed to convince her to change, but even wearing almost exactly the same outfit as me (old, fitted jeans and a loose tee—she'd foregone shorts when I'd emphasised how much walking would be involved), with her hair pulled up in a messy bun trailing wisps of untameable hair all over her shoulders and round her face, she still managed to look glamorous.

It was something in the way she carried herself, I decided, something that transmitted loudly that she didn't care for your opinion, that she was perfectly happy rocking her own thing, thanks very much.

I rubbed my hands down the front of my shorts—they weren't sweaty, but the feel of the denim against my palms steadied me a little. The sun was inching its way ever closer to the treetops, and although Mum and Dad wouldn't be home until well after dark (apparently the cinemas were still considered safe if you were over twenty, ha), I had no idea how long it might take to get to the heart of Sanctuary and back again.

"Magic," I said, nudging Veve away with my knee. "We're doing magic. It's complicated."

"Yeah I got that by the lack of logical explanation, thanks."

I squinted at her in a mock glare, then inhaled and exhaled firmly. "Okay. Look. How much do you trust me?"

She shrugged. "I dunno, a lot?"

My eyes widened. "Really?"

"Uh, yeah?" She flung her head exaggeratedly to one side and raised an eyebrow at me. "Miss Goody-Two-Shoes? Never been in trouble at school," she said, checking off on her fingers, "barely ever in trouble with the parentals, most organised student on the planet, probably not even human… uh, *yeah* I trust you. Besides. I wanna know what kind of weird crap you and that Gemma kid have been getting up to. I haven't forgotten you 'falling down the boulders', you know," she added, putting actual air quotes around the words.

I squirmed a little. That had been the day I'd been dragged into the Valley by a mysterious force I'd later learned was Aphros. I'd set Aphros free from the shadows, but the Valley's trees had sprung to life and attacked me when I'd tried to escape.

Quoise had patched up the worst of it, but I hadn't exactly been in mint condition when Gemma had finally brought me home.

It occurred to me that tonight might end with me bringing Anna home in exactly that state.

Urgh. "Look," I said, rubbing my forehead with the back of my hand, "maybe this isn't such a great idea. This is dangerous, An, and you really have no clue what I'm getting you into, and..." I took a step back so I could flop against the bricks of the house. "Urgh."

Anna surveyed me with her arms folded, one hip cocked, lips pursed, while Veve gave up on us both and headed back to the main part of the yard. The sloshing noise of her drinking sounded a moment later.

Traffic whooshed past on the main road one street over to the right; to the left, the last few cicadas of summer were enjoying the reprieve from the rain, singing their hearts out in the bush reserve that stretched all the way down to the creek and up the other side, nearly to my school.

"So why isn't Gemma doing this with you, by the by?" Anna quirked that eyebrow again. "You two were inseparable for a hot minute there, but you've been moping for the last couple of weeks. Did you break up?"

Something anxious leapt in my chest. I scowled. "No, we did not 'break up'." My turn to do air quotes. "It's just actually dangerous, is all, and she..." I cut off and sighed, pressing two fingers over my right eye. "She's had enough of danger for now."

And, frog it all, that was probably fair enough. I'd been attacked by zombie trees and chased by soul-sucking shadows, sure—but Gemma had been *caught* by the shadows, and possessed by the sentient magic of the Valley.

Urgh. Of course she didn't want to rush to go fix Sanctuary, not when she could kind of tell how it was anyway through her connection to Helios.

Frog it. Frogging frog it all.

"Look," I said, raising my gaze to Anna as though it were weighed down by lead, "I need you. Sanctuary is breaking—they've shut everyone out—and the only way I can talk to Helios to figure out what's going on is by travelling the roads, and to do that, I need another person. If you don't want to help me, I can't make you. But I literally have no other options right now."

Anna's jaw worked, but after a moment she exhaled huffily and swung her arms loose by her sides. "Great. Nice to know I'm the bottom of the barrel."

"I didn't—"

"It's fine." Her mouth smiled without her eyes. "I get it. Let's just get this done, okay?"

"Yeah." I inhaled. "Let's."

I pushed off the wall and walked to the bushes, with Anna following at my side.

Once I was close enough that my hip brushed the spiky tendrils of the bushes, I gave her a brief recap of what to expect—she'd get to skip the momentary nausea and dizziness that went along with using your own blood to travel between Earth and the Valley (which, interestingly, was the exact opposite if you killed something else and used *its* blood instead of your own: *you'd* be perfectly fine, but any passengers you took with you would be treated to some good ol' fashioned bone-crushing pain and agony, *thanks* for that experience, Scott)—took her hand firmly, and broke out the scissors.

I figured a second injury was wasteful, and used one of the blades to pick the new scab off the cut I'd made earlier—but even so, Anna tensed, white around the lips and knuckles as I squeezed my shoulder to make it bleed a little more.

"I know," I said, flicking her a brief glance and an attempt at a reassuring smile. "It's gross. But I'm not going to kill an innocent animal instead, so..." I twitched both shoulders in the tiniest impersonation of a shrug. "Eyes closed."

In an instant, we were in the Valley.

I leaned down over my knees, breathing slowing through my mouth to calm the nausea, staring unfocusedly at the ground.

"Whoa." Anna let go of my hand and out of the corner of my eye I watched her do a slow circle. "You weren't wrong."

I eased myself upright, cradling my stomach.

"This place *stinks*." She grinned.

I rolled my eyes and wiped hair out of my face. "Yeah." I inhaled deeply to steady myself, and wrinkled my nose at the rotten-fruit-and-stagnant-water smell. "It does."

Anna wandered a couple of steps away, eyes wide, face tilted upwards. Even in her denim-and-tee, even at five-foot-seven, you could have strapped a pair of wings on and mistaken her for one of the fairies, like travelling had sparked something inside her—like she belonged.

In thirteen years of living, I couldn't remember Anna looking like she belonged anywhere. People looked at her, were drawn to her, precisely *because* she stood out. Being Anna was the opposite of belonging.

I tilted my head, brow wrinkling as I tried to pinpoint what had changed. It was more than just her blissed-out expression, or the wonder in her eyes. Something, something else... I blinked, a normal blink, only a fraction of a second long—but it was enough to catch the change with my road mastery.

Her soulprint was different.

Usually, her soulprint looked and smelled like strawberries-and-cream, a faint blush of berry pink and cream the colour of the palest skin, accompanied by the sound of clacking keys, like a spider running over a laptop keyboard—and equally as squicky and neck-pricklingly unpleasant as the one time I actually *had* heard a spider running over Mum's laptop keyboard.

The strawberries-and-cream-ness of her soulprint was still there, but the sound had changed; instead of being slightly uncomfortable, it seemed... purposeful.

"You're a freak, you know that?" Anna said, turning back to me with her arms and smile almost equally wide. "I can't believe this is what you've been doing all those times. This is ridiculous! This is absurd! You're supposed to be the good little human who never breaks any rules!"

I folded my arms and raised my chin, my heart pounding at my ribcage. "Name one rule I've broken so far." Yes, okay, I'd broken some over the last few months, but I'd been literally saving the world, so I figured I deserved a little leeway there, and it wasn't like I'd suddenly morphed into some careless rebel who smashed rules left, right and centre for the fun of it. Rules were there for a reason. I liked rules. Good ones, anyway. They made life sure, and predictable, and safe.

Anna laughed. "Uh, the rules of physics, maybe? Oh my gosh, I can't believe this. I can't believe it! My sister is a freaking magician!" She rubbed at her arms like maybe she had goosebumps, still shaking her head wide-eyed and laughing to herself.

I rolled my eyes. "Come on." I took her hand and began walking; it had taken some quick map-sketching on some scrap paper at home, but I was pretty sure the entrance to the roads was about fifteen minutes ahead and to the left.

I glanced around at the twisted, ghost-trunked trees and wiped a bead of sweat from my temple with a free finger. "This is just the Valley. Wait till you see the roads."

9

"OKAY," I TOLD Anna as we stood at the entrance to the roads—totally invisible to Anna, and nothing more than a faint but persistent drift of out-of-place sensations for me. "So remember what I said: just keep me moving. That's all you have to do. Especially if you see something scary."

She narrowed her eyes at me. "Is that likely?"

"Truthfully?" I said, looking up at her. "Yes."

Her jaw worked for a moment, lips twisting to one side until she nodded curtly. "Okay."

"Just keep me moving."

"Yeah, you said that." She shifted her weight from foot to foot, avoiding eye contact. "Are we going or not?"

I exhaled. "We're going." I put my hand on her shoulder, closed my eyes to get rid of distractions, and felt for the roads with my road mastery.

The faint drift of sensations strengthened, sights and smells and sounds that didn't belong here in the physical world, and I imagined myself catching hold of them and tugging.

The visualisation helped, and the faint sensations immediately became a steady tension as energy coursed through me. I held on tightly, and the energy grew, power billowing to life inside me, a growing lightning storm in my chest. Energy crackled and snapped, and my body strained at the edges; my skin hurt, as though something was trying to explode through it in every direction, and my ribs ached as the centre of power settled in my heart, my pulse ringing my body like a gong with every beat.

Hold it, hold it...

A cry escaped my mouth—and the tension snapped, leaving my body twanging.

I opened my eyes, and my face melted into a smile: the roads.

If a single person's soulprint was like a multi-sensory aura around them, the roads were like everybody's auras combined into one: a massive scramble of sounds and colours and smells and textures, all drifting through time and space.

If you were patient, if you were persistent, you could pick out the threads of related sensory information, piece together something like a person's soulprint, and follow it through the chaos—if you could remember to keep moving, which you couldn't, because it was total sensory bombardment, sight after sound after smell after touch, hot sunset orange like when smoke is in the air, followed by birdsong and rustling leaves, overlaid with the smell of wood varnish and the feel of a minky blanket against your skin.

And that was only one split instant: the next it might be deep, dark, oceanic blue, the sound of keys clacking, the smell of toast, and the feel left behind by a kiss that was too wet on your skin, followed by pale, strawberry pink, the quiet whoosh of traffic on a lazy afternoon, the smell of dirt and hot concrete after summer rain, sand between your toes...

I blinked slowly, and realised that a couple of those things were familiar: sure enough, beside me and a little behind, I could see Anna's soulprint: cream blushed with pale strawberry pink, the sound of keys quietly clacking. I squeezed her hand, and she squeezed back, tightly, a little desperately.

I never could get a straight answer from a non-Road Master as to what the roads looked like to them, but I'd heard it was nearly as overwhelming, and not half so pleasant.

Trying hard to shut out the constant sensory bombardment that could befuddle me even with my road mastery shut right down, I tugged on Anna's hand.

It sprang to life immediately, and I could picture the raised eyebrows that went with it, her expression as she came back to herself and remembered what she was meant to be doing. Four squeezes. *Are you okay?*

Two quick squeezes back from me, then three quick squeezes: *Yes. I see something non-dangerous, let me look a second.*

Gold. Anything gold. I scanned around me. Hot pink, magenta, baby blue, water falling against the back of my hands, the smell of pine trees, polished concrete under bare feet, the startling blink of a projector firing up right as you're looking at it, the background whirr of a fridge, my very favourite hoodie hugging my body, the exact taste of Mum's chocolate chip cookies—and I knew they were Mum's, because I could taste the pepper and the lavender, and who the frog else put pepper and lavender in double chocolate cookies?

Wait.

I reeled. My hoodie. Mum's cookies. They were *my* sensations. But how...?

A loop of anxiety coiled in my stomach, cold and heavy. Scott's diary. He'd said the roads had stolen memories from him, made him forget more and more every time he went on them.

I looked around, the anxiety rising to my chest. All these sensations—water and cars and fridges and rain, synthetic blankets, kisses, my hoodie—did every one of these sensations belong to someone real, a person? Had the roads stolen them all?

Adrenalin crackled out to my fingertips. And, when I got back—would I remember what Mum's cookies tasted like?

Four squeezes from Anna's hand.

I gasped. I was supposedly protected on the roads by my road mastery; it was Anna who was totally exposed. She might have worn my hoodie before, and she definitely knew the taste of Mum's cookies—but now, she might not remember either.

Gold. Find the gold, so I could follow it to Sanctuary's heart.

I turned frantically back to the roads, searching, sifting through the sensations as quickly as I could.

Emerald green—no.

Sausages sizzling—no.

Soft lounge leather under my fingertips—no.

A seam of gold snaking through quartz.

It wasn't how the gold of Sanctuary had appeared before, but I'd take it. Now all I had to do was remember to keep following it. Five firm squeezes to Anna's hand, the most complicated message of all, but one I'd only have to use once: *I'm ready, let's get going, don't let me stop moving for anything.*

Two squeezes back. *Yes.*

I stepped forward, road mastery wound tightly around that impression of gold in white rock as it slipped and flitted between all the other sensations, left, right, up, down—upside down. Like last time, it wouldn't do to think too hard about which way was up—but I didn't have much spare brain power left over anyway.

Canary yellow feathers on my cheek; lime green; the scent of white vinegar; something that might have been octopus tentacles twining around my hands.

A flash of darkness; the shush of the ocean against a gentle shore; a prickle up the back of my neck.

Anna squeezed my hand—four squeezes. *Are you okay?*

I'd stopped. I shook the daze from my head and kept walking.

The rim of a glass, a perfect circle under my fingertips; a gold-leafed wedding cake; the crisp smell of snow; the colour of deepest night; my neck popping; hungry whispers.

Four squeezes.

Concentrate, Edge. Follow the gold.

The sound of a zip. Golden sunlight streaming through a window. The feel of a pencil moving across heavy cartridge paper. The heat of an explosion. *"Come. Come to us."*

I froze.

Four more squeezes.

I sent her three back—looking at something, no danger, hold on—but my pulse rushed at my ears.

It might be the guardians, nightmarish creatures that looked like fire and darkness to my road mastery, creatures who protected the roads from intruders.

Anna sent four more squeezes, and the pressure of her hand against mine made it clear she was keen to keep moving.

Reluctantly, I sought out the seam of gold again and followed after it.

I *hoped* it was guardians I was sensing.

We followed the gold seam further and further, until my feet were heavy and my tongue stuck drily to the roof of my mouth, like I'd been sleeping. Anna reminded me to keep moving every minute or so, and the prickly, slow-moving dread of being followed remained. In all the sensory stimulus, it was easy to forget the whispers, though—and who knew? Maybe they were just a sensation plucked from the head of someone who'd walked the roads, like all the others.

It didn't have to mean there were shadows here on the roads.

Of course it didn't.

In the distance, something gold blossomed, a slow explosion unfolding like bright petals. It hung, motionless at full height, easily several times taller than me—and the thread of gold led to it.

My shoulders relaxed. The heart. It had to be.

Last time, I'd approached it from above, and it had been like seeing something through a glass floor. Obviously this time I was approaching it from ground level, as it were, and—I cocked my head and listened hard—yes, I could hear a rhythmic pulsing that might be the beating of a heart.

Darkness flickered around the edges of my vision.

Anxiety stirred.

My grip on Anna's hand grew suddenly sweaty, and I awkwardly switched hands across my body for a moment so I could wipe my hand dry on my shirt.

My neck prickled.

Colours and sounds still shifted around me, but they'd been random before, and now... Long, echoing pipe noises. The smell of decay. The hiss and pop of a crackling fire. A sense of vast distance, of exposure. Footsteps right behind me, even though— of course I looked—there was no one.

My pulse pitter-pattered. *Just get to the heart. Just get to the heart.*

Swallowing hard, I took a cautious step forward.

Whispers stirred around me. *"Blood. Want to drink your blood."*

I clenched Anna's hand. *Run.*

I had no frogging clue how shadows could be on the roads, but I'd heard those whispers before, and I'd recognise them anywhere, even in my nightmares.

"Your life, want your life, so sweet, so sweet your blood."

Run. The heart couldn't be that far ahead; I knew it was bigger than it looked right now, but it couldn't be that far.

My back broke out in chills, and I risked a glance behind.

My heart leapt against my chest. Shadows raced each other in the middle distance, a pack of hounds gaining quickly and baying for blood. My blood. I squeezed Anna's hand again, hard.

The golden, glowing heart loomed over us, surrounded by a sheer wall, like glass, or perspex, but finely textured.

Oh, frogs. I'd forgotten about the shield.

Last time, I'd needed blood to get through it, and maybe that had only been because I'd been with Gemma, who'd been connected to the dark magic of the Valley, but this wasn't exactly the time to stop and experiment.

I couldn't let go of Anna. And I really, really needed blood.

"Sweet, so sweet your blood. Want your blood."

I actually snorted at the irony of it all. *You and me both, shadows.*

I tried biting down on my cheek as we ran, but I just couldn't convince myself to do it hard enough, even though the shadows were gaining, maybe a scant ten metres behind.

Anna tripped. My arm wrenched backward. I cried out at the pain in my shoulder.

"Want your life. Come, come to us."

My shoulder. I needed to open the cut on my shoulder. My heart pounded, fear electric and bright.

I jerked Anna along—she followed smoothly. I put my head down and ran.

We approached the shield. I tore at the thin scab on the fleshy part between my shoulder and bicep and squeezed.

My fingers came away with a small smear of blood; I had to hope it would be enough.

Three paces.

I held my fingers out in front of us.

Two.

A shadow leapt, catching my heel.

I kicked it away, lunged for the shield.

My fingers made contact; the blood sizzled.

I fell, rolling onto my shoulder, dragging Anna after me.

10

"ARE WE DEAD?" Anna lay on the smooth, golden floor beside me, still clutching my hand.

I lowered my own head back to the floor and worked on catching my breath, staring at the roof above us that seemed to be made out of light the colour of the sun. "No," I said. "Not dead."

My ankle hurt though, the one the shadows had caught, and my shoulder was going to have a bruise the size of Tasmania from where I'd landed on the floor.

Still. Not dead.

I exhaled loudly.

A flutter of wings responded. I let go of Anna's hand and rolled awkwardly to a sit, cradling my sore shoulder. The walls curved around us, forming a perfectly circular chamber that glowed like we'd found the heart of the sun, instead of the heart of Sanctuary.

I squinted a bit as my eyes adjusted, already breathing more deeply and evenly. Just like Sanctuary itself, the heart contained some magical property that worked to calm you down; minor aches and pains fell away, my chest lifted, my lungs filled right to the bottom with pure, clean air.

In the middle of the chamber stood a small dais, round, like the room, and about five paces across. My stomach twisted. Last time I'd been here, Viri, the Keeper of Sanctuary, had appeared on that platform and tried to kill us.

I scrubbed my eyes with my fingers, not wanting to see Scott slumped deathlike between me and the platform, or Gemma huddled next to me, breathing raggedly, unevenly, like each one might be her last.

Long, slow inhale, smooth, controlled exhale.

Scott and Gem weren't here. Neither was Viri.

I felt more than heard the flutter of feathery wings again, and hauled myself to my feet. "Helios? Are you here?"

"Who's Helios?" Anna dragged herself semi-upright, crossing her legs and leaning back against the wall.

"The..." I waved my hands. "The embodiment of Sanctuary's magic. He *is* Sanctuary's magic. Kind of. It's complicated."

"Sounds like."

My pulse quickened. "But he told me to meet him here, because he can show me what's happening, so he'd better frogging be here or else..." Or else I had no idea what to do. I chewed on the inside of my lip.

The flutter of wings came again, and I turned toward it, eyes closed, road mastery opened.

I relaxed into a smile: the great, golden pegasus was definitely here: I could sense his soulprint, even if I couldn't see his body. *Hello?*

A breath of wind across my face. *Greetings.*

"This is probably going to take a sec," I said, turning back to Anna. "And it might look really weird. But we're pretty much safe here, so feel free to, like, rest or something."

"Sure thing," she said, and tipped her head back against the wall, eyes closing. "Take your time."

So can you show me? Can you show me what's wrong now I'm here? I sent to Helios.

A snort. The sense of something pulling at me, at my road mastery.

Carefully, I spooled it out, a tiny thread of energy that came from either my head or my chest—I couldn't tell which—and extended toward Helios.

He took it, redirected it—and the world exploded into light. In front of me, I saw the great, seething ball that Aphros had shown me once, immense, hanging like the moon in an empty space. Gold and black intertwined with one another, writhing and twisting and flashing, surrounded by a minty green glow. Aphros had told me it represented the balance between Sanctuary's life magic and the Valley's death magic, and at that time, there'd been a lot more darkness than light.

The image changed, and I had the sense of falling backwards—not through space, I suddenly realised, but through time. And the further I fell, the lighter the darkness in the ball in front of me became, until eventually, it was actually a ball of wriggling, flashing green and gold. Not a trace of black to be seen.

I fell a little further, and the wriggling and flashing stopped: the ball was a uniform colour, mostly gold but with that same minty glow around it, and deep inside it, kind of like the way new leaves glow in the sunlight.

What is this? I sent to Helios. *What am I seeing?*

This time, I felt like I was falling forward; I flung my hands out to protect my face from impact—but I hadn't actually moved. The massive ball of light changed, green and gold separating first, and then gradually, the green turning darker and darker, until it was black. The black began to grow, overtaking the gold, until it looked like it had when Aphros had first shown it to me—exactly like it, I realised: Helios was showing me the history of the magics of Sanctuary and the Valley.

A blinding flash engulfed the ball for a fraction of an instant, and the black began to recede until it occupied about half the space again, and I thought that would be it; we'd rebalanced the magics after saving Scott from the Valley, cutting away the extra power from the Valley and forcing it to diminish. But the falling sensation persisted, and the ball continued to change: an extremely slow outward explosion, black and gold separating entirely as the ball ballooned in size, cracks appearing all over it, nothing but void inside.

Abruptly, the connection snapped and I regained my usual senses, blinking rapidly at the sudden change to the round chamber of the heart.

"Whoa."

"What?" Anna shifted against the wall, looking up at me.

I pinched my forehead between my thumb and two fingers, screwing up my face and blinking, trying to make sense of what I'd seen. "Okay," I said. "So. I think what I've just seen is that once, the Valley was green, and not black—I guess that's where the mintiness comes from?—only hang on, back at the beginning they were both the same, which fits with what the book suggested, only then the green went dark somehow?" I slumped. "And now it's all just fracturing."

But I hadn't needed to see the magics to know that. So it must be the other stuff that Helios thought was important?

"Okay in English, this time?" Anna quirked an eyebrow. "Unless, you know, you don't actually want me to know, because you're doing a super job of being incoherently cryptic right now, just saying."

I scrubbed at my forehead with two fingers and winced. "Right. English. So. If I'm interpreting this correctly, which honestly, I don't see how else you could interpret it, so I have to assume that I am—"

Anna cleared her throat pointedly.

"Right. Yes. Okay. There are two places, right? Sanctuary and the Valley? Sanctuary is the home of the fairies, you use life magic to get to it."

"Life magic?"

"Plant magic. You plant a seed."

Anna nodded. "Sure, seems legit."

"And then there's the Valley, which you use death magic—blood magic—to get to, which we did earlier."

She nodded again.

"For as long as most people know, the two places have been... like... opposites of each other. Life versus death, happiness versus terror, good versus evil, that kind of opposite."

"Antithetical."

I furrowed my brow. "Anti-what?"

Anna grinned. "Antithetical. The word you want is 'antithetical'. Not just opposites, but, like, totally incompatible opposites, absolutely contrary, that kind of thing. Antithetical."

I stared at her. "First of all, who are you and what have you done with my sister, second of all why on

98

earth don't you actually use your brain at school, and thirdly, yes, antithetical, sure."

She turned her grin up by several notches, blazing with smugness. "You're welcome."

I rolled my eyes. "Okay *anyway*, Sanctuary, Valley, antithetical," I said, barely stumbling over the new word. "But. There are rumours that they used to be the same place. And we discovered last month that even though everyone *thought* the shadows were coming from the Valley, like, a natural result of it or something, actually they're two separate things: Valley," I said, waggling my left hand, "and shadows." I waggled my right.

Anna frowned. "Shadows like the things that chased us out there?" She gestured roughly to where we'd entered through the wall of the heart.

"Yeah." I stretched my mouth in a frown without moving my eyebrows. "Shadows like those."

Rubbing her upper arms, Anna got to her feet. "You were saying something about colours."

I nodded. "So, Sanctuary's magic is gold. Obviously." I twirled a finger at the glowing gold chamber around us. "And the Valley's has always been black when I've encountered it. But there's always been this weird thread of green everywhere too, pale, like mint green, on everything to do with Sanctuary, and it's there when you look at the combined magics." And, I realised with a jolt, in Aphros's soulprint.

Anna shook her head a little. "I'm going to pretend like 'combined magics' made sense. But I get Sanctuary gold, Valley black, mysterious green."

I nodded again. "Helios, the physical body that holds Sanctuary's magic, showed me a vision just now, backwards and forwards in time. The two magics are usually just intertwined, in a great big ball." I meshed my fingers together and held my hands in a ball shape. "But from what I could see, it didn't always used to be that way. Firstly, there was originally only one colour, which suggests that the theory that Sanctuary and the Valley used to be the same place is right—which the book on road mastery agrees with, so that's cool. But the other weird thing is that the black of the Valley used to be green—that minty green that keeps showing up everywhere."

"Okay," Anna said slowly, drawing the word out. "And this information is useful to you somehow, I assume? We, like, risked our lives and now you got the info you need and all's well that ends well, etc?"

I screwed up my face. "Sure. Let's run with that theory."

"Edge?" Suspicion laced Anna's voice.

I sighed. "I'm sure it's useful information," I said. "I just have no idea what to do with it." I slumped to the floor and buried my face in my hands. "I wish Aphros was here." She *sort of* was, in that I could reach her through our internal connection so long as

I was in the heart—but the communication was faint, distant. Not great for trying to have a technical discussion.

She's green and gold, just like the Valley and Sanctuary used to be. There has to be something in that. I wished I could talk to her *now*, while this was all still fresh. Not that I was likely to forget any of it, but just... I sighed again.

"Uh, Edge?"

I lowered my hands. My eyebrows twitched downward as I saw the concern on Anna's face. "What?"

"I, um, I know you said we're safe in here, but... is that normal?" She tilted her head toward the wall, eyes wide.

Adrenalin spiked through my stomach. The circular wall of the chamber glowed gold everywhere else, but where Anna had gestured... I swallowed, fingers gripping my knees whitely as I stared at the patch of darkness that pressed and roamed against the wall. The shadows, looking for a way into the heart. "No," I said, heart pounding in my ears. "No, that's not normal."

"Right, yeah, I thought so. And..." She licked her lips, hands fisted at her sides. "It's not good, is it."

Shadows on the roads, Sanctuary and the Valley fracturing... No. No, it was all very *ungood*.

"What will happen if they get in?" Her voice was barely audible.

I stood up, strode over, and took her hand. "If they get in—"

Frogging elephants. If they got in, they could corrupt Sanctuary's magic entirely. Was that what had happened to the Valley? Was that why it had gone from green to black? Fear erupted in my chest and I fought to keep my breathing level.

"If they get in it will be bad," I said briskly, squeezing her hand. "But they're not going to get in, so it's fine."

A faint, barely-heard crackling punctuated my words—and fine lines appeared in a fracture pattern across the wall of Sanctuary where the shadows pressed.

I swallowed. "But just to be on the safe side... I think it's time to go."

The instant we reappeared in the Valley, I took off, heading toward Sanctuary. *Aphros!* I called, tugging on the connection between our soulprints. *Aphros!*

"Wait, where are we going?" Anna said, jogging to catch up. The sweltering heat of the Valley had already closed down on us, and Anna looked damp and sweaty. "I thought we were going home now."

I glanced up to my left, back in the direction of the connection with home. "We are. But there's something I need to get first."

Edge? Is that you?

Aphros, I need you. I need some things from you. And I think I'm going to need a few of them.

I am coming, she sent back. *I will see you soon.*

11

WE TUMBLED BACK into the yard a fraction of a second before Mum came around the corner, Veve skipping at her heels. Hastily, I pressed my forefinger over the cut on my upper arm, while Anna tugged her shirt straight.

The sun had vanished behind the treeline, dusk lighting the sky in pink and orange. The pungent smell of the Valley faded away, replaced by the more mundane smells of the suburb: distant smoggy smells from the main road, eucalypts still hot from the day, clean grass and warm pavers from the yard.

Even though it was still warm and a little humid, it was nothing compared to the dripping, cloying closeness of the Valley's heat, and in the light breeze the sweat on my forehead began to dry.

Mum narrowed her eyes. "What have you two been up to?"

Anna shrugged. "Nothing much."

Mum turned her gaze to me, eyebrow lifted.

"Mum, I swear, we haven't left the yard." *It's not a lie,* I told myself. *It's not a lie.*

Mum pursed her lips, scrutinising us.

I forced myself to breathe. We hadn't left the yard, and the only reason we were on lock-down was because of the stupid mob business, and they weren't exactly going to follow us over to the Valley—or, even more ludicrous, the roads—so we really hadn't done anything wrong. We'd been totally safe.

Well. Apart from the shadows.

"Come inside," Mum said at length. "I had a call from the police on the way home."

Anna and I exchanged glances and followed Mum. Veve pranced along beside me and I ruffled her ears. "Hey, Hairbrain."

She licked my fingers and I gave her a half smile, awfully glad she was okay. Impulsively, I reached down and hugged her around her middle as Mum and Anna disappeared inside. She thrashed in protest, and I released her, straightening and blinking furiously. "Love you, puppy."

Inside, Dad had melted into one of the armchairs in the family room, lines of his body shouting fatigue, his fingers barely gripping the glass bottle of expensive soda water whose top tilted precariously.

Mum leaned a hip against the kitchen bench, arms tightly folded.

"So, the police?" Anna said, sliding onto one of the wooden barstools at the bench near Mum.

I stayed near the sliding door, hands behind the small of my back, gripping the door handle, shoulders pressed against the cool glass.

"There's been a reported sighting of some men known to be intimately connected with Romano in Canberra." Mum flicked a glance at Dad. "There's no confirmation of why they were there, of course, and it could be anything. It's probably not related to us."

"But it could be," Anna said, nodding.

"It could be."

I swallowed, tightening my grip on the door handle. "If they're in Canberra," I said carefully. "Then it's only a two or three hour drive to here. They could be here literally at any moment."

Dad raised his bottle at me in a silent salute, then chugged down half the soda water.

"Yes," Mum said, nails bloodless at the tips as she gripped her arm. "The police officer I talked to doesn't think they're aware of our specific location yet, only that we moved north. They seem to be setting up some kind of base in Canberra and the police there have placed them under constant surveillance. But unless they do anything wrong, there's no legal reason to arrest them at this point. The police will call us immediately if it looks like they are moving our way," she added as something of an afterthought, releasing her arms dramatically and striding to the pantry. Jerking the door open, she crouched, then rummaged in the vegetable box.

"There's nothing we can do?" I said softly.

"Are we going to have to move again?" asked Anna.

Mum reappeared with a handful of potatoes, snagged a knife from the magnetic strip above the bench, and started chopping a little more vigorously than necessary.

"No," Dad said when it became clear that Mum wasn't saying anything else. "And possibly."

Mum snorted at that, and Dad cut her a sharp glance. "Liv, it *is* 'possibly'. The police are well trained, and they have them under surveillance. For all we know, they could do something stupid and get themselves arrested in the next hour. We don't know."

And that was the clincher, really, wasn't it: we didn't know. Our whole world could come crumbling down again in the space of a heartbeat—and we just didn't know.

12

MUM DROVE US to school again on Friday morning. Instead of letting us out in the drop-off zone, she turned right into the carpark, found a spot down the far end where the asphalt turned to grey gravel and pale, washed-out dirt, and parked the car.

We walked back up to the main entrance together, Anna towering half a foot over either of us.

I clutched the straps of my backpack so tight I knew I'd have red creases in my fingers for a good while afterwards.

Mum parted from us at the front office, heading in to make an emergency meeting with the principal.

Anna and I walked through the grassy quad together as the breeze rustled the leaves of the huge gum that towered over it, branches tossing, loose strips of bark flapping.

Overhead, misshapen clouds chased each other across the sky. I glanced at them, jealous of their ability to simply disappear. Something heavy curled in my chest, my stomach, and Anna nudging my shoulder with hers in farewell as she split off toward the senior common room did nothing to help.

Everything seemed too bright; even the bushes that lined the hall on the right glinted, with their thick, glossy leaves that felt like palm leaves, but that were long and thin, growing straight out of the ground like a giant's grass tussock—or a clump of swords.

Sun chased shade chased sun as the clouds raced over the sky; the flickering quality of the light and the way the wind snatched people's voices away, muffling them even though the quad wasn't more than about twenty metres across, made the whole school seem slightly unreal, out of place somehow.

I tried to shake it off as I neared H block and headed for my locker—but the sense of unreality only heightened as I realised it was Scott hovering by my locker, instead of Gem.

"Hey," I said, giving him a fraction of a second of eye contact before dumping my bag and crouching over it. "Where's Gem?"

"Geography trip, remember?"

Right. Half the year studied geography in first semester, while the other half—my half, Scott's half—studied history. Midway through the year, we switched. That explained why the quad had seemed a little empty.

I shoved the books I'd used for homework back into my locker and pulled out what I'd need for the first few classes, before cramming my bag into the bottom half. I stood, kicking the blue door closed, and stared at Scott, hugging my books to my chest.

"Uh, what?" he said, taking half a step back and rubbing awkwardly at his nose. "Is there something on my face?"

I exhaled, closing my eyes and hugging my books even tighter for just a second, curling around them. I couldn't do a thing about my family's safety right now. But I could do something about the safety of Sanctuary. If I had time. "Look." I opened my eyes again and straightened. "Gemma won't listen to me, for whatever reason, but you said you believe me, so you have to believe me about this. I've been on the roads again—"

Scott's eyes widened. "You what?"

"I took my sister, it was fine—"

"Your sister? Edge, what the hell?" He ran a hand through his hair, tugging up the spikes. "Are you insane?"

I narrowed my eyes at him. "Look, shut up, okay. Stop freaking out: it was fine. But, well, it's not fine, that's the point." I sighed and let my face drop to my books for a moment. "Scott, I talked to Helios in the heart of Sanctuary. Mrs Caro was right: Sanctuary

110

and the Valley *did* used to be one place, and not only that, but the Valley was corrupted somehow. I'm guessing that's where the shadows come in, given…" I swallowed. "Given there are shadows on the roads right now."

Scott's eyes widened even further, practically owl-like. "*What*?"

"I need to investigate that somehow, try to figure out how and why they got there. They were trying to break into Sanctuary's heart too, but…" I pressed my forehead into the heel of my hand. "I can't take Anna for that. If there are shadows on the roads, I need…"

I let my hand drop to my side, and mentally listed off all the reasons why Scott didn't have to help, why he wouldn't want to help, why it would be stupid for him to offer. I sighed. "You know what? Never mind. I'll figure it out." I turned away.

Before I'd gone two steps, Scott caught my elbow. "Hey, where are you going?"

I shook my head, staring at the white plastic buttons on his school shirt. "You don't have to come," I mumbled. "It's fine. I'll figure it out."

"Don't be ridiculous."

Inside of my lip between my teeth, I looked up.

"Of course I'll come," he said, gaze flicking back and forth between my eyes. "I owe you, anyway. I was a complete ass to you last year, and at the beginning of the year, and I can't pretend that all of it was the Valley. I… I'm sorry."

He had a tiny fleck of yellow in each of his otherwise brown irises.

"Yeah," I said. "You were."

"Sorry." His voice was barely audible this time.

I shrugged, sighing. "So you owe me. You'll help, then?"

He nodded. "Of course. Least I can do. You want me to meet you after school?"

I stared at him for a second longer before it clicked: Scott believed me. He was going to help.

And I was *not* going to cry about that, urgh.

"I can't leave the house, remember?" I said. "You'll have to come over."

His hand dropped away from my elbow as he straightened. "What, to your house?"

"Is that a problem?" I jutted my chin up and lifted my eyebrows. "There's a crossing point to the Valley in my backyard, remember."

His gaze raked my face again, left eye, right eye, back to the left again. "No," he said. "That's not a problem at all."

"Good." I gave him one quick, jerky nod, and turned. "See you after school," I said over my shoulder as I headed off to class.

He didn't reply.

Which was good, because then I didn't have to think about whether to turn and look at him again or not, or whether to try trusting my voice again or not, and meant I was free to inhale dramatically like I'd just been about to drown, and blink furiously as my body decided it was tears that I should drown in.

We'd fix this. Somehow, we'd find a way. I might not have a say in protecting my Nowra home, but Sanctuary? That was my home too, and that one, I could definitely try to protect.

13

SCOTT ARRIVED BEFORE Mum and Dad got home, but just in case I thought I'd managed to escape any awkward questions, Anna decided to step into parent role for them.

"Who's this?" she said with narrowed eyes as I let him in the front door.

I turned to where her head was poking out from her room down the end of the apricot-tiled hall. "Scott."

Her fingers appeared around the wooden door-frame, followed by the rest of her. "Is he your boyfriend?"

"No, Anna." I rolled my eyes, pretending I hadn't noticed the way Scott had gone rigid where he stood, not two paces from the front door. "He's a friend. He's..." Urgh. While I totally approved of honesty in theory, the whole talking-to-my-family-about-Sanctuary thing was still weird: first Mum, now Anna.

Magic. Totally messed your head up.

"He's here to help with the roads."

Anna's gaze sharpened. "You're going on the roads again?"

I nodded, brow furrowed, lips slightly pursed. "I have to." *Please, Anna. I have to do this. Please understand. Please.*

She sighed explosively. "I suppose there's no point telling you to take your phone."

I shook my head. "No reception."

"Or telling you to be careful." She folded her arms and leaned against her doorframe.

"Of course I'll be careful."

She sniffed. "Yeah. Right." She rubbed at her chin with one shoulder, spreading the lock of hair that had fallen there over her ear. "Going anywhere near those shadows isn't being careful, Edge, it's verging on suicidal."

I stared at her, hands fisting by my sides. "It's not. You know I have the ward."

Scott moved to my shoulder. "Ward? Is this something I should know about?"

"I got a couple of unicorn-hair wards from Aphros. They have limited use, but they can protect us from the shadows in a pinch."

"Nice of you to tell me this now."

I raised an eyebrow at him. "You said yes anyway, didn't you?"

"Well sure, but—"

"Pssh." Anna rolled her eyes. "If you two are done, I'm pretty sure you have, like, a world to save or something." She tilted her head meaningfully to the family room.

"Right." I exchanged glances with Scott. "Yeah. Let's do that."

I led him through the family room and out the sliding door to the yard.

Veve greeted us both with her usual buoyant enthusiasm, licking and slurping and pushing through Scott's legs in an effort to get him to scritch her back. He staggered, arms flung wide, and I grabbed his forearm to steady him. He laughed, shook me off, and bent over to snuggle Veve's face in between his hands, running his thumbs over her ears.

It was easy to forget sometimes that his mother had basically made him her slave in her quest for darkness and power, that he'd watched her die, that he'd been possessed by the Valley as a literal agent of darkness and had nearly been taken fully to be used as the Valley's body.

Mostly, that made him kind of wary or haughty, depending on the company, and prone to using the fastest means to get what he wanted, moral or not.

Occasionally, just occasionally, moments like this reminded me of exactly how much he'd missed by not having a normal childhood.

"Okay, I'm sure Veve would follow you to the end of the world and back now," I said all of a sudden, wanting to stop thinking about Scott's Tragic Past™, "but can we get going?" I worked the moisture back into my mouth and rubbed self-consciously at my left shoulder where the cut (and bruise) was. Scott had done some pretty horrible things in his past, some of them directed at me, and I didn't particularly feel like hosting a pity party for him right now.

"Lead on, boss," Scott said, straightening and gesturing at me.

I rolled my eyes, but led him around to the side of the yard where the prickly bushes skulked. "Portal of darkness," I said, waving at them. "As advertised. Here," I added, fishing a braid of thick, wiry, cream hair out of my pocket and passing it to him. "Tie it on." I stooped to tie my own unicorn ward around my right ankle, and Scott, after hesitating for just a second, copied. Veve, naturally, was delighted that we were getting down to her level, and shoved herself into my face, demanding attention. I nudged her away and stood back up. "I don't think you'll be able to activate it yourself," I said to Scott, "but I'm pretty sure I can activate it for you with my road mastery if you get into trouble."

He nodded curtly, and held out his hand.

With just the tiniest bit of my inner lip between my front teeth, I took it, dragged him closer to the bushes, and reached up to peel away the scab on my shoulder.

Man. This was seriously going to leave a scar.

I ignored Scott focusing intently on my shoulder, closed my eyes, and made the crossing.

We tumbled out into the Valley and I squished my face up, swallowing repeatedly to fight down the nausea. I leaned over my knees, resting on my forearms, and forced myself to breathe slowly.

"I could have done it, you know," Scott said quietly.

I glanced at him. He'd barely moved from where he'd entered, which, if I'd been in the mood to be impressed, might have been impressive. The crossing was smooth, but most people still staggered on re-entry. "What," I said, my voice thin and gaspy. "And killed another mouse for me? Thanks. I'm good."

His jaw twitched. "I didn't mean that. I meant—"

"I know what you meant." I straightened, inhaled, stretched my arms up, and exhaled firmly. "I'm fine. Really," I added, making the fleetingest eye contact I could manage. "I am. Fifteen minutes that way." I pointed ahead and to the left.

He looked like he wanted to say something, but I turned to go and he thought better of it, following me silently through the twisted, blood-stained trees.

Within minutes, we were both dripping with sweat. "So why did you agree to come?" I asked to take my mind off the humidity. "I thought it wasn't 'safe'." I sketched air quotes around the word.

"Gemma and I have slightly different definitions of 'safe'," Scott said, copying my intonation.

I glanced over my shoulder at him. "So why didn't you come before? Or say something? When Gemma was going on?"

He shrugged awkwardly. "Sanctuary is your guys' place. What would I do to help? Kill another mouse?" He smiled wryly.

I got the feeling that that wasn't the entire story, but I let it drop and plodded on, ducking under a low branch that tangled in my hair for just long enough to send adrenalin pulsing through me.

I shoved the anxiety aside. No zombie trees. Just normal twigs and branches. Well, normal for the Valley, anyway. I exhaled heavily and rolled my neck.

"Edge?" Scott's voice was funny, a cautious note it didn't usually hold, a little higher than usual.

"Mmm?" I said without looking back.

"Edge?" he said again, and it seemed like he'd fallen a bit behind. "You know that unicorn ward?"

I turned, bracing myself for melodrama, and eyed him where he stood still in the shade of the trees. "What about it?"

He swallowed heavily and tilted his head at the ground. "Might be a good time to use it."

My brain finally caught up with what I was seeing: that wasn't just any old shade pooled around his feet. "Shadows," I hissed. *Crap*, I thought as adrenalin flooded back again. *Crap crap frogging elephants crap.* "Hold on. Don't move."

"Wasn't planning on it," he said shortly.

I closed my eyes. My stomach flipped as the soulprint of the shadows hit my senses, dark and terrifying. I extended my road mastery out, just as I'd done in the heart of Sanctuary, aiming for the tiny sliver of green and gold wrapped around Scott's ankle. But to get there, I had to dodge through the shadows without touching *their* soulprints, or who knew what might happen.

Slowly, slowly…

"Eat you, drink you, give us your life…"

"You doing something there, Princess?" His voice sounded steady, but he hadn't called me Princess in a very long time.

"Working on it."

Closer, closer…

"Sometime today might be nice."

"It'll be faster if you stop interrupting me."

"Come, come to us, give us your blood, your life…"

Urgh, I'd lost about a foot by stopping to answer Scott. I squinched my face up tighter—as though it might help me concentrate—and wove my way through the shadows again. Left, right, left again, over that bit, under through there…

The shadows shifted, constricting the thread of connection I had with my road mastery. *"So sweet, so sweet your blood, your power, your life…"*

I gasped as though someone had thrown a bucket of cold water over my head; it was suddenly hard to breathe.

I gritted my teeth. Just a little bit further.

I forced my senses onward. Closer, closer… There! I snagged the ward, feeding my road mastery into it.

Nothing happened.

Panic squeezed my chest even tighter.

What had I done last time to activate it? I couldn't remember, I couldn't remember…

"Edge?" Scott whispered. "Please hurry."

The shadows had twined around his legs and hips, and were reaching for his chest. *"Sweet, sweet life, sweet power, drink your blood, your life."*

How do I do it, how do I do it? I fed more of my road mastery into the ward. *Come on, work!*

I had a vague memory of silver light and discomfort, drawing on some deep part of myself that wasn't road mastery.

My soulprint. I had to feed out my soulprint.

A burst of silver light momentarily drowned out the soulprint of the ward. Nausea heaved in my guts and I doubled over, pressing my fingers against my mouth.

Frogging elephants, it was like looking at my own body opened out on the ground in front of me. No wonder we weren't supposed to know our own soulprints.

The smell of roses. Another blinding flash of silver. Soft bells tinkling in an unearthly melody. The ward flared to life, green and gold billowing through the dark.

The shadows screamed.

More power, more.

They screeched, a high-pitched noise that grated against my ears.

More power.

The shadows began to retreat.

I kept up the flow of power, hands knotted, sweat pouring down my face.

The shadows backed away. Further, further...

I collapsed to the ground, knees too weak to hold me up any longer.

But the shadows had fled; Scott was safe.

I closed my eyes and curled up on the ground, planning to sleep for a short eternity.

"Thanks," Scott said, settling on the ground beside me.

"No worries," I said, and my voice hardly shook at all.

"This," he said, and I waited patiently for the rest of the sentence—only it never came.

"This what?"

"This," he said, waving his hand in a vaguely circular motion. "You asked me why I didn't come before."

Suddenly the grass in front of him was utterly absorbing, and he stared at it like he might die if he blinked. "You saved my life just now," he said in a voice so low I hardly heard it. "I was waiting to come with you."

Ten minutes later I could move without feeling like I was dragging my limbs through concrete, and I forced myself to sit up. "Okay," I said, screwing up my face and shaking my head. "Roads."

Scott pursed his lips. "I'll be honest, I'm not sure that's such a great idea right now."

"What?" I cut him a filthy look. "That's the entire reason we're here! I have to investigate the shadows!"

He sent a flinty glare back. "We've burned through one ward already, and it took all your focus to do even that. *Don't* brush me off," he snapped as I opened my mouth to protest. "I saw how much effort that took. How many of those things do you even have? How do you expect to fight a whole *mass* of shadows on the roads?"

"I can at least track them down, find out where they're coming from—"

"How? How are you going to track them down? Wander aimlessly all over the roads until you find something? Because I'm no genius, but that doesn't exactly sound like the greatest plan."

"Fine! What do you suggest we do, then? Give up?"

He stared levelly at me. "No. Gather more information. Hasn't it ever occurred to you to wonder why the unicorn wards work, for instance? If it's unicorn power that affects them, what if Aphros could do something that would get rid of the shadows for good?"

"You think we should go talk to Aphros?"

His jaw worked as he chewed on his inner lip. "As a start, yes. Remember… Remember that book you told me about? The one about road mastery?"

My pulse skipped. Of course I remembered the book Quoise had found in the fairy library that explained how road mastery worked. I'd been kicking myself ever since for not taking it with me so I could read it cover to cover. "What about it?"

"I think we should go get it."

"But it's right in the middle of the fairies' Lodge, we can't just walk on in and ask for it."

He grinned impishly, and I remembered that despite everything that had happened to both of us, we were really just thirteen-year-old kids.

"I didn't say we were going to ask."

I stared at him a moment longer, mulling it over. I really, really hated to admit it, but he was right: heading back to the roads wasn't guaranteed to give us any more information, and it would definitely put us into danger with the shadows. On the other hand, sneaking into the fairy Lodge was also risky—Viri had tried to kill us before, and I pretty much had to assume at this point that she'd do it again, maybe even that she'd given the other fairies orders to kill us on sight—but really, I'd take fairies over shadows any day of the week.

And I really, really did want that book.

I sighed heavily and rubbed my hands up my face. "Fine! You win. Let's go break and enter." I fished out another of the unicorn wards from my pocket and handed it to him.

Scott grinned again as he wrapped the ward around his wrist, fixing it with a simple over-under knot. "I always knew you weren't as prissy as you seemed."

"Shut up." Go in, get the book, get out. This was totally going to be fine.

14

WE CROSSED THE invisible boundary between the Valley and Sanctuary warily, peering in all directions for any sign of fairies.

I'd had a brief conversation with Aphros while we'd walked, via our soulprint-connection, in which I'd learned that she basically had no idea about anything: no idea why she could cross between Sanctuary and the Valley while others couldn't, no idea why the unicorn-hair wards worked.

That was one thing she did agree with, though: it seemed very likely that 'Valley' did not equal 'shadows', and that, given what Helios had shown me, the shadows were a latecomer that needed to be vanquished before they could corrupt Sanctuary as well.

On the whole, the conversation had not been much use at all, and that, together with the sweltering humidity of the Valley and the rotting stench had combined to leave me in a fantastically grumpy mood.

But now, as Scott and I stepped into the dim coolness of Sanctuary, dripping sweat from our forty-minute trek through the Valley, we both inhaled deeply. Scott jumped a little as the unicorn hair ward around his wrist sizzled and imploded into ash; I'd forgotten to warn him about that.

Usually, the border between Sanctuary and the Valley was impenetrable; the unicorn hair ward enabled us to cross without a blood sacrifice, and it could survive a trip *into* the Valley, but for whatever reason, returning the unicorn hair to Sanctuary always made it fizzle and die. I handed him a new one, and this time he wrapped it around his ankle and covered it with his sock like the first one had been.

As I glanced around, eyes peeled for the slightest glimpse of fairy wings through the trees, the distinction between the Sanctuary and the Valley couldn't have been more obvious.

The border itself may have been invisible, but it was still clear: behind us, twisted, stunted trees almost like alpine gums, with yellowing leaves and sap stains down their trunks; ahead, cluster-leafed, soft things that stood tall and graceful, leaves vibrant and healthy, trunks smooth and grey-brown. (I had no idea what kind of trees they actually were, but they looked something like how I'd always imagined ash trees, so in my head that's what they were.)

"Come on," I muttered, grabbing Scott's arm and steering him over to the right where the trees were thicker. "We don't want to be seen."

Immediately ahead, the tall trees thinned, and after about ten or fifteen metres ordered themselves into a long promenade carpeted with thick, crisp grass that led to the fairies' Lodge, a white-stone single-storey building that sprawled higgledy-piggledy in every direction like a maze.

Its walls glowed faintly in the dim light of Sanctuary, making it look almost like a moon in Sanctuary's grey-blue sky. Vines crawled all over it, glossy, waxy leaves twinkling in the dusk, tiny, white star-flowers pulsing gently as they emitted their own silvery light.

Pretty, but right now, it was pretty in the same way a tiger was: one wrong movement, and it would eat us alive.

"Do you know another way in?" Scott murmured.

I nodded and kept moving, watching where I stepped, avoiding fallen twigs and dry leaves, detouring around low-hanging branches that looked like they might swish. Thankfully, there was basically no undergrowth; we made it around the first point of the Lodge in only a couple of minutes.

I glanced around. Still clear. "In here." I skipped the six or seven paces from the treeline to the wall, pulse in my throat. Scott followed and copied me as I spidered my fingers through the vines over the wall, hunting for the hidden door.

"What am I looking for?" he whispered.

"Edges," I said.

"There are more than one of you?"

I shot him a Look. "So. Funny. Shut up and search, will you?"

He smirked, but resumed shuffling through the vines, picking them aside and feeling his way over the seamless wall of the Lodge.

My fingers snagged on something. I pulled a pale, new tendril of vine aside and squinted. "Over here."

Scott moved to my side.

"Help me clear the vines from the door," I said, tugging at a strand as thick as my finger, woody and tough. "Try not to break things," I added when he started snapping vines. "We don't actually want the fairies to know this is where we got in."

He rolled his eyes in response, but did as I asked, bending and shifting the vines instead of breaking them.

"What are you doing?"

We both jumped at the high-pitched voice behind us and whirled around, backs pressing into the wall, my hands convulsing around the vines at the small of my back.

The fairy hovering at head height a few steps away crossed her arms and frowned at us, turquoise-blue wings fluttering.

I slumped forward and clutched at my chest, remembering how to breathe. "Quoise. Frogging elephants, you terrified me."

"Good," she said. "Imagine what would have happened if someone else had come to investigate."

I straightened, gaze sharpening. "Is anyone else coming?"

"Not yet. I sensed your soulprint here, though."

The most dangerous aspect of trying to sneak into Sanctuary: all fairies were—well, not Road Masters, exactly, they couldn't *do* things with their road mastery like I could, but they had the basic ability of sensing people's soulprints, and they could sense the print of any and all visitors in Sanctuary at any given moment, across all of Sanctuary's multiple dimensions.

"I assume you got in from the Valley?" Quoise said, eyebrows raising. "Given we've *apparently* stopped all visitors through the portals?"

I nodded. "Aphros gave me some wards."

"Good." She nodded once and folded her arms. "Don't use—"

She was gone.

"What just happened?" Scott said, still staring at the spot where she'd been.

I sighed, puffing air out over a fat lower lip. "Time skip."

"Time skip?"

"The big fissure that opened up through the meadow, yes?"

He nodded.

"There's some sort of pearly steam or something coming out of it, and every time a new puff is released, time skips weirdly and the fairies—and Aphros—all zip to wherever it is they were, or wherever they will be, or... something." I raised my eyebrows, forefinger pressing against my temple.

"But why is this affecting time?"

"I don't know!" I closed my eyes and forced myself to continue calmly. "If I knew," I said, voice still tight, "don't you think I'd have explained?"

"Is this what happened the other day at school?"

I glanced at him. "Which one? The first time, no. I mean, I guess it could have: everything went all grey and foggy, I could smell Sanctuary, and everyone else seemed frozen although I could still move, so I guess I could have moved and it would have looked like a time skip to you guys when the fog lifted. That's what happened the second time."

He frowned, gave his head a shake, and went back to shifting vines. "But that's not what happened here."

Irritation flared in my chest. "How do you—"

131

"For one we're already *in* Sanctuary," he said over top of me, hands moving on autopilot. "So it's not like some sort of fog is coming over us or anything."

"But the steam—"

"And for *two*," he continued, "what you're talking about is essentially a skip forward in time. You moved, we didn't, and when we woke up—or whatever—you'd gone ahead without us. Ish. Right?"

Despite myself, I nodded.

"But here," he nodded to where Quoise had been, "they're moving *back* in time. Not the same."

Frog it all, he was right. "Well, so what?"

"So, different mechanisms," he said. "Probably. Just something to keep in mind," he added as he pulled a final strand of vine away and stepped back. "It that enough?" he asked, nodding at the wall.

I glanced over it. "Yeah. Should be." I stepped close to it, and felt around the edges of the hidden door for the latch. Nope, nope, nope... Ah ha. I picked at the little catch, and the heavy white stone door swung inward. "Welcome to the Lodge," I said, gesturing Scott in.

He glanced at me with slightly widened eyes, then ducked into the hallway, long and straight as far as the eye could see, walls made of the same stone as the outer wall of the Lodge, except mid-grey, and the floor glowing with golden light.

I followed him in, adjusted some of the vines so they wouldn't get jammed, and closed the door. It latched with a satisfying *thunk*. "Come on," I said, taking the lead. "It's not as long as it looks."

Frog it all. Scott was right about the different time skips; on Earth, it was like everyone there was freezing except me, and I could continue forward without them.

Here, it was like everyone was reverting backwards, and I was staying still—well, and Scott too, and Helios, so probably everyone who hadn't actually—what, been born? Come from? What was the proper term here? Whatever. Here, the time skips were affecting everyone who wasn't a native. On Earth, it was affecting everyone but me, and the only thing special about me was my road mastery.

One set of skips affecting everyone from Sanctuary, not visitors; the other affecting everyone from Earth, but not Road Masters.

I shook the idea away and concentrated on navigating us safely to the library. I could have an existential crisis later. Like, age thirty or something. Right now, I had more important things to do.

15

WE ENTERED THE library and Scott paused, drinking in the room.

I had to admit, it *was* pretty grand: I swept a glance over the towering stacks, easily seven or eight meters tall, every one stuffed to overflowing with books in all sorts of sizes and colours and bindings. That could have been any super large library back on Earth, though; what made this one really special was that instead of floor space, the fairies used the void above the shelves to congregate.

Raw-hewn tables and stools hung from the roof, draped in ferns bursting forth from gilded pots, the whole aesthetic like something out of a home style magazine for rich minimalists—a style only emphasised by the huge expanse of white ceiling, splashed with gold and intersected with twining vines and intricate floral motifs. One day, I'd have a bedroom exactly like this.

My lips quirked into a tiny smile and I grabbed Scott's wrist. "Come on," I said, and dragged him down the row in front of us.

Since the fairies used the void space to read, relax and socialise, the ground area was entirely filled with shelves and rows, each row about twenty or thirty metres long, spliced by an aisle down the middle that was easily a hundred meters end to end. Every third or fourth row ended in a door like the one we'd come in—a handy feature, no doubt, but one which made it im-frogging-possible to figure out where I was now in relation to where we needed to be.

The road mastery book had been off to one side, tucked against a wall, but where that bit of wall was exactly... We reached the aisle in the middle of the row and I paused, bottom lip to one side between my teeth.

"You do remember where it is, don't you?"

The doubt in Scott's voice grated against my nerves and I clenched my fists. "Of course I do." Randomly, I turned left. "Okay. Bright yellow-green book about yay big." I held my hands up to indicate something about the size of a small paperback. "Cloth bound, lots of gold all over it, title is Through Roads Between."

Scott nodded once and picked a shelf at eye level. "I'll take this side, you take the other."

"Sure."

Scott and I skimmed shelves back to back, fingers racing over the spines, lips moving as we processed the words at top speed, trying to find something useful before the fairies found us.

"Edge?"

"Mm?"

"Where did the unicorn babies come from?"

I shot him a quizzical look. "You're seriously thinking about that now?"

He shrugged—"Care and Feeding of Unicorns"—and tapped the spine of a bright red book at his eye level.

I sighed with an exaggerated shoulder-heave and let my hands rest on the books in front of me. "Well, Scott, when a mummy unicorn and a daddy unicorn love each other very much…"

He smirked, eyes crinkling. "That's just it, though, isn't it." He leaned towards me. "Where's the daddy unicorn?"

My mouth opened as though it had an answer, and then when it realised it didn't, my tongue curled around my front molars and my lower jaw jutted out.

"Good point, isn't it."

Frog him, his eyes practically gleamed in the dim light. I rolled my own in response and resumed my search. "Sure. It's a fantastic question. But it's so not relevant to what we're supposed to be doing right now. You know?"

He shrugged and shoved his hands deep into his pockets, still grinning. "Hey, I don't ask for inspiration, it just arrives."

"Yeah," I muttered, scanning the spines in front of me with both my eyes and my fingertips. "Sure. Can you put in an order for something relevant next time, though, please? We have a world to save, remember."

He sagged like a puppet with its strings cut. "You're no fun."

"As advertised. Come on, I'm done with this shelf."

I ducked around into the next row. It had to be around here somewhere—unless the fairies had moved it, of course, or *removed* it.

I bit the inside of my lip. If they'd removed it...

Scott kept trying. "Oh hey, here's a book about dragons! I knew they had to be real somewhere!" he'd say, or else, "Whoa, why would you want to read about that?"—clearly fishing for my attention.

But it wasn't until he made an exaggerated, full-body shudder and said, "Ew, come on. I used shadow magic on a regular basis and even I think that's gross. I know everyone thinks the fairies are supposed to be nice and all, but why isn't this kind of thing in a restricted section or something?" that I snapped upright, left hand gripping the soft bit at the top of the spine on the hardcover I'd been scanning. "Restricted section!"

Scott glanced at me. "You really want to check out the restricted section *now*?"

I shook my head a little. "That's where the road mastery book will be. Come on."

I led the way back down our current row, heart tripping in my chest. Restricted, restricted... I supposed all the signs for the stacks would be up high, where the fairies could see them. If I was designing a library like this, where would I put the restricted section?

We reached the aisle—and my heart stopped as a red-winged fairy appeared at eye-level from around the corner.

I froze, forgetting how to breathe, and Scott stumbled lightly against my back before he too saw the fairy and tensed.

The dark, lithe fairy simply stared at us, her red dress some sort of fabric that shifted colours in the light, sometimes the colour of bright, healthy blood, sometimes the colour of the dark sap on the trees of the Valley.

My spine crawled.

But something about her seemed familiar, and she still hadn't said or done anything; I risked a breath, remembered to blink.

"Ruby?" I whispered.

Months ago, on my very first visit to Sanctuary, another fairy had drawn Quoise aside to talk about the shadows. Her presence had led to the discovery that I was a Road Master. I'd never spoken to her, or seen her since, but I'd gotten the impression she was Quoise's friend.

She blinked, a slow, exaggerated movement like time had slowed right down. "Run," she whispered, eye contact never wavering.

Time skipped.

Ruby vanished.

I frowned, opened my mouth.

Scott frowned back. "Well that was—"

A gentle chime rang out through the room, as though someone had tapped a triangle.

The note hovered in the air for a moment, swelling instead of softening.

Our frowns deepened. I opened my mouth again.

A rushing sound: quiet, louder, loud.

I swivelled, looked down the aisle to my left.

My eyes went wide.

A huge wave, tall as the shelves, roared toward us, sloshing and angry, tearing books from shelves and tossing them into the air.

I snatched at Scott's wrist. "Run!"

We pelted down the aisle, and I fought Scott as he twisted to look behind us.

"Wait!" he said.

I ignored him and dragged him onward.

My shoulder nearly broke out of its socket as Scott stopped suddenly.

"Wait!" He braced against my tugging.

Closer, closer.

"Scott!"

"The ward," he said, turning slightly to clench my arm.

"What?"

"Use the unicorn ward."

"I know what you meant!" I snapped. "Why am I using a ward"—I dug furiously in my pocket—"instead of running like a *sane human being*?"

He lifted his chin at the wave, staring it down, the roar of it so loud we had to shout to be heard. "It's not real!"

I looked between him and the wave, eyes wide. "You're kidding me, right?"

His jaw twitched. He let one hand drop from my arm so he could face the tidal wave square on.

I guessed not. Pulse hammering at my chest, body bursting with adrenalin, I clenched the ward in my hand in front of us, gripping the braid part, loose, bristly hair sticking out the top and bottom.

"What exactly do you want me to do?" I shouted, angling my head toward Scott without taking my eyes off the ward.

"Just activate it!" he shouted back, grip still firm on my upper arm.

I could feel the spray as the wave roared closer, twenty paces away, fifteen, ten. The smell of salt water, spray spitting on my face...

I closed my eyes, gasping for air, and forced my road mastery toward the unicorn hair.

Please let this work. Whatever Scott's seen, whatever he's thinking… please let it work.

The pre-surge hit us; my legs were soaked.

More road mastery, more power…

"Edge, hurry!"

The bright flash of silver and the smell of old roses; the smell of mint.

The darkness behind my eyelids turned gold, like I was staring at the sun through closed lids, the veins of my eyelids visible.

Nausea gripped my stomach in its fists.

Scott grabbed me by the shoulders, spun me to him, held me tight.

The wave crashed over us, roaring like a freight train on loose tracks at high speed.

I cringed, waiting for the blow…

But it never came.

"Come on," Scott shouted in my ear. He felt around for my wrist, laced his fingers through mine, and by the time I'd opened my eyes was dragging me along the aisle in the direction the wave had come from.

I stared in wonder at the back of the wave, still crashing its way through the library, wreaking chaos on the books—only, I realised as we ran, the books were perfectly fine. Once the wave had passed, the library had returned to normal, although the roar still echoed through the high-roofed room and the smell of salt water still overpowered the smell of old books.

"Where are we going?" I asked, a stitch starting in my side.

"Elsewhere!" Scott said. "I don't know about you, but I feel like that was one heck of an intruder alarm."

I glanced back over my shoulder just as the wave hit the far wall and vanished with a final, impressive splash.

Non-water sprayed from one side of the room to the other in the wake of the impact, settling, sloshing to the floor, a foot-deep ocean that slowly began to drain away.

"Come on," Scott said, tugging me gently to a stop in front of a tall, brown door, like all the doors that led out of the library, this one at the end of the aisle. He pushed the brass handle down and slipped through the doorway.

"Shouldn't we try to find the book now that the defence systems are down?" I whispered as I followed.

He shook his head. "What if they just set it off again? How many wards do you have left?"

"Two." I ran my fingers over the bumps of the braids in my pocket.

Scott shook his head a second time and set off down the dim hallway, thick green carpet muffling his footsteps, strip lights in a lip around the roof barely bright enough for me to read his face. "Not enough. We'll have to try again another day."

My chest ached—and not just from the frantic run. I skipped a couple of steps to catch up, and bumped his shoulder with mine as I fell into step.

"Thanks for coming with," I said. Who knew what the wave would have done if I hadn't used the ward.

He flicked me a half-smile, glanced around, and ducked left as the hallway widened briefly into a square landing.

"Wait," I said, jerking around to follow. "Where are you going?"

"Trust me," he said. "I have a feeling about something."

I halted, leaning over my knees, trying to get the stitch in my side to let go.

Trust him?

I watched as he snuck further down the hallway in the gloom, practically bouncing on light feet. If the whole high school thing didn't work out for him, he could definitely consider a career in cat burglary.

That sparked an uncomfortable twinge in my guts, but I shoved aside images of Georgia on a white-tiled floor in a bathroom in Melbourne, forced the kernel of worry over mob bosses closing in on my family back into the closets of my mind.

Trust Scott? Well, first of all, he'd trusted me when no one else did, and although we hadn't gone to investigate the roads (yet), he'd come here to help me look for my book.

I straightened and took a deep breath. Secondly, he'd pretty much just saved our butts.

I guessed I could trust him for a little while longer.

16

"YES!" SCOTT HISSED a few minutes later. "I knew it!"

I glanced around under sceptical eyebrows, working my mouth. This landing looked pretty much identical to the last two we'd crossed: dim, boxy, and moody with all the dark wood and mossy carpet. Except this time, the left-hand option ended in a door. "What did you know?"

He turned to me, eyes alight, and bounced once on his toes. "That defence system in the library. That was one heck of a magic trick, don't you think?"

"Uh, sure?"

"Lot of power behind that. Big magic."

I wrinkled my brow. "Yes? And?"

He grinned, although it looked like he was trying hard not to. "Magic that big needs a source, right?

It's not like there were dozens of fairies hovering around conjuring it up. It seemed more like an automated thing, an in-built defence."

I shook my head as though dislodging a fly. "Scott, I know you're enjoying this, but will you just get to the point already?"

"Permanent defence system," he said, holding up an index finger. "Really big power source to run it." He held up the other. "If they are way apart"—he stretched out his arms—"the power drains before it gets where it needs to go. They need to be close." He lined his fingers up side by side.

"So," I said, still frowning, "you think there's a big power source nearby. This helps us how?"

Now he really did cut loose with the grinning, teeth gleaming in the light reflecting off the roof. "What's the biggest magical power source you've seen?"

My eyebrows drew even tighter. "The big ball of Sanctuary-Valley magic."

Scott huffed, eyes rolling. "Second biggest, then."

My lips twitched as I finally glimpsed where he was going with all this. "Tie between the heart of Sanctuary and the heart of the Valley," I said deliberately to annoy him.

He narrowed his eyes at me like he knew. "Well *obviously* the fairies aren't drawing on the Valley to power their little death-wave, are they."

"Obviously."

He stepped aside, pointing at the door behind him, the one blocking the way to the left. His head dipped, eyes gleaming and wide. "Look!"

He was pointing at a door that at first glance looked like yet another clone of the ones we'd seen so far: tall, brown, and wooden.

Which—I tilted my head, frowning—why *were* all the doors here so tall? Surely a building designed for fairies should have fairy-sized doors, not these towering over-sized human ones?

Though granted, I realised, looking more closely, this one did have a fairy-sized door cut into it in the middle at the very top.

Something tickled at my subconscious, and I squinted.

Oh, road mastery. Right.

I shut my eyes and focused my road mastery—and sure enough, the door flared to life in the darkness behind my eyes as though it was a living thing. "That's weird."

Limey leaf green swirled through a golden haze, the smell of something fresh and sharp filling the air—almost like mint, but not quite, less sweet, more *green*-smelling.

"What can you see?"

"A soulprint," I said, looking at him again. "What can *you* see?"

His eyebrows twitched upwards and he pointed higher up the door.

This time, I saw the tiny line of gold script on the fairy door at the top. I stepped closer.

My breath caught. The Forbidden Chamber.

I glanced back at Scott. "You think...?" It made sense. He was right: *something* had to be powering that wave, and a direct connection to the heart of Sanctuary would definitely do the trick.

The million-watt smile was back, and he nodded, bouncing on his toes again. "Let's have a look."

Immediately, I frowned. "Scott, it's forbidden. Like, it's literally there in the name. And just because the current Keeper is a nasty piece of work, that doesn't mean that there isn't a good reason for the chamber to be forbidden."

"Quoise went in."

"Quoise is a fairy."

He tugged on my sleeve and tilted his head toward the door, eyes wide, chin tucked so he peered through his lashes at me. "Please?"

If the fairies caught us there, we could kiss our freedom goodbye—and maybe our lives. On the other hand, it did seem like a good place to start getting some answers. I sighed. "I hope I live to regret this," I whispered furiously.

Scott beamed. "Oh, don't worry," he said. "You will." He gestured for my hand, flicking his fingers impatiently when I took my time. The instant he had a firm grip on me, he grasped the door handle. "Ready?"

"No." But my pulse quickened, and despite my best efforts, my own eyes were probably just as alight as Scott's.

"Three-two-one," he said quickly, and pushed down on the handle.

It didn't budge.

"Well, it is forbidden," I pointed out. "You couldn't exactly expect them to keep it unlocked so anyone could waltz in."

"There's got to be a way," he muttered, releasing my hand and skating his fingers over the wood.

I inhaled to speak, thought better of it, and bit my lip to one side again. The door had a soulprint. As far as I knew, only people—fairies, humans, unicorns— had soulprints. People, and the magics of Sanctuary and the Valley. Why would a door have a soulprint? How? Tentatively, I let my road mastery brush against it.

The soulprint twisted to life, twining around me in the same way Veve wound through my legs when she was after a pat.

Instinctively, I scritched at the door.

It arched against me like a cat.

"What are you doing?" Scott asked, and I felt him pause next to me, curious.

"It's alive," I said softly, eyes still closed, fingertips skimming in circles over the polished wood.

"The door or the chamber?"

"The door."

"You don't... You don't think it's another alarm, do you?"

My hands stilled. Scott, being the cautious one. Had the world ended without me noticing? "It might be," I said. "I don't know."

More than that: I had negative five-billion clues. Since when did doors have soulprints? Either the wood had been alive somehow to begin with—alive differently to a tree, because I'd seen plenty of those, and even the zombie trees that had attacked me hadn't had soulprints—or someone had put the soulprint there somehow. Which was impossible, at least as far as I knew. You couldn't just make something and stick a soulprint in it.

Almost instinctively, my fingers resumed skimming over the surface, the soulprint of the door arching with delight where my road mastery met its soulprint.

The connection between us strengthened, and I could feel the pulse of power feeding back through my fingers, like the door was purring.

My fingertips began to sting. I tried to let my hands drop to my sides—but I couldn't tear away from the connection with the door. Like a strong magnet, it held me tight.

My breath caught in my throat and my eyes flew open as I sought out Scott's face.

"Are you okay?"

"It's holding me," I said, voice breathy, adrenalin like ice through my chest. "I can't let go."

Scott took half a step back, staring wide-eyed at the door. "It's a trap."

"Please don't leave me," I whispered. *Look at me. Look back at me. Please don't leave me here.* My heart trilled.

He glanced at me, unease vanishing in an instant as he straightened, shoulders square, chin high, eyes soft. "Of course not."

The sting intensified until it overtook both hands, skin burning like a thousand tiny cuts rubbed with lemon juice, tendons and ligaments aching at every joint like they strained to keep my hand bones together.

I gasped.

Immediately, Scott put a hand on my shoulder, warm and firm. "Hey, I'm not going anywhere," he said.

"It hurts," I bit off, jerking my chin at my hands, stuck to the door at shoulder height.

He grabbed my forearm and tugged.

"Hey, hey! Ow!"

"Sorry," he said, releasing me. "I had to try."

"Yeah, well it *hurt*."

"I said sorry."

I closed my eyes and reminded myself not to breathe so fast. I took a long, slow breath, trying to force my pulse to slow down too. It didn't work.

The pain crept up to my wrists.

Why? I thought at the door. *Why are you doing this?*

The power thrummed like purring again—*ow*—and the door's soulprint arched against me.

I didn't understand. Not just that the door had a soulprint, but that it seemed genuinely friendly. *You're hurting me*, I told it. *Please stop.*

The door's soulprint stilled, the restless shift of green and gold pausing in its movements.

My breath hitched. *You… You didn't know you were hurting me?*

Slowly, the pressure on my wrists began to ease.

Thank you, I breathed. *It still hurts,* I prompted when nothing happened.

The door didn't speak, as such, but I got a clear sense of conflict: it was supposed to hold me here for its masters, but no one had ever talked to it before, petted it before; no one had paid it attention in a very, very long time.

If you let me go now, I told it, hoping desperately I wasn't falling into old habits and promising things I had no intention of keeping, *I'll come back and play with you. I… I promise.*

"What's going on?" Scott whispered.

"Shh!" I snapped as the door's soulprint tensed. *It's okay,* I told it. *He's a friend.*

Frustration, a darkness like total blindness. The door couldn't sense him.

No, I agreed. *He's not... like me. Or the fairies. Do...* Froggity frogging frogs. This was either about to be genius, or the dumbest thing I'd ever done—and that was saying something. *Do you want to meet him?*

It leapt back to life at once, stirring and twirling and twining, impatient, restless, excited.

"Scott," I murmured. "You know how you said you trust me?"

"Yeeeees..."

"Touch the door."

Suddenly, raised voices sounded down the hallway behind us. Fairies. My pulse raced again.

"You sure that's a good idea right now?"

"Please trust me," I said. "Please." The pain had reduced to that first initial sting in my fingertips. Just a little bit more, and I'd be able to rip my fingers away—and even if Scott was stuck, I could probably do something with my road mastery to get him free.

He stepped shoulder to shoulder with me as the voices behind us grew louder; no one was shouting yet, just talking urgently between themselves. Holding my gaze, he reached out slowly and let his hand rest next to mine against the door.

The door's soulprint sharpened its focus, homing in on him.

Frustration. Still blind.

Let this hand go, I said, tugging on the hand closest to Scott. *I can help.*

My hand dropped away. My eyes rolled up and my shoulders sagged a little. Halfway there. I laid my hand gently over Scott's, partly covering it, partly touching the door.

"What are you doing?" he whispered.

I kept my eyes closed. "The door wants to see you." Slowly—but not too slowly, because those voices were getting loud now—I reached for Scott's soulprint, letting it take up all the space behind my eyes until all I could see with my road mastery was the bare hilltop under early morning stars, the dawn just kissing the horizon.

The door hissed.

I didn't realise it was audible until Scott reacted. "What was that?"

I gave a mute shake of my head. *What is it?* I asked urgently.

The door's response was pure, golden light—the same colour as Sanctuary's power, the same colour as the dawn.

Yes, I said quietly. *Yes, he is connected to Sanctuary's heart.*

"Two of them!"

I glanced left, back down the hallway, and fear prickled through my whole body. Three fairies, silver, copper and green—but not Viri, I realised, and remembered to breathe again. *They're coming*, I told the door. *Please. If you don't let us go right now, if they capture us, I'll never be able to come back and play with you.*

"Please tell me you're doing something," Scott murmured from my right.

My jaw twitched as the fairies came closer.

"Oh ho!" said the copper-winged one. "It's none other than Emma the Breaker herself. Viri *will* be pleased."

Please. He is tied to the heart of Sanctuary. Please help us.

Pain burned through my hands again—and Scott's, I assumed as he hissed.

"What do you think Keeper Viri is going to do with them?" the green-winged fairy asked the others casually. "The lightning?"

"Maybe to start," silver-wing said, grin like a wolf showing all her teeth in her pale face.

Please. He practically is Sanctuary. At least help him.

A gentle click echoed through the landing. The door to the Forbidden Chamber swung open.

Scott and I stumbled forward, dragged with the movement—then, suddenly, we were sprawling on the floor as the door disconnected us.

"No!" screamed a fairy. "You can't be in there!"

"Get them, hurry!"

The door swung shut with a thump.

In complete darkness, I felt for Scott, finding his leg, his knee—then his hand as he reached for me and wrapped his fingers tightly through mine. I could hear his breathing, could hear my own—and my pulse.

Scott shifted. "Edge?" he whispered.

"What?"

He lifted my arm up, stretching forward until my fingers met cold rock.

Stomach sinking, chest constricting, breaths coming hard and fast, I whirled around on my knees.

The Forbidden Chamber was about a metre and a half squared, walled with solid rock, and pitch dark.

"We're in a tomb," I whispered, and clenched Scott's hands.

"We'll find a way out," he said. "I promise."

17

"IT CAN'T JUST be this," I whispered in the dark that smelled of stone.

"Where's the book, for a start?" Scott replied.

I felt him shift against my right arm. After the first few moments of panic when we discovered the Forbidden Chamber was little more than a five-foot box of stone and darkness and that the door wouldn't—or couldn't—speak to me from this side, we'd ended up sitting against the wall shoulder to shoulder so we could at least feel that someone else was there with us in the dark.

I had my knees up and splayed against my elbows, hands clasped in front. "Or the connection to Sanctuary's heart," I said dully, letting my head tip forward to my chest. I didn't know what I'd expected of a 'forbidden chamber', but it had definitely been something more impressive than this.

Scott gripped my arm. "Did you see that?"

My head snapped up. "See what?"

"Look up."

I did. Darkness yawned above us, a storey, two, three—there was no way to know; the darkness was absolute. "I don't see anything."

"Keep watching."

Seconds ticked by, but the tense anticipation between my shoulder blades slowly dissipated. There was nothing but breathing in the dark, Scott's warm skin against my left arm, and the mineral smell of stone.

Plus, it was starting to feel cold in here. I rubbed my arms briskly. "I still see nothing."

"It will come again, just wait."

I sighed, and decided to ignore the desperation in his voice.

I tipped my head back again, letting it fall sideways onto Scott's shoulder as I stared up at the infinite black. I was too tired to care about the way he tensed for a moment before letting out a careful breath. It had been, what, four thirty when we'd left home? We'd walked all the way through the Valley, crept through Sanctuary to the library, spent some time searching, had come looking for the Forbidden Chamber... It had to be at least six thirty according to my body, maybe close to seven.

And I hadn't eaten a thing. No wonder my energy was fading.

"There, did you see it?"

I jerked upright, blinking rapidly; I didn't even remember closing my eyes. "Where? Where?"

"There!" he said, pointing—not that I could see it, but I felt his arm lift.

But regardless, I didn't need his gesture: this time, I'd seen it myself, a flash of gold high, high up above us. "Of course!" I stood up, running my hands over the walls as I traced out our tiny space.

"Of course what?" Scott said. "Where are you? What are you doing?"

"Feeling the walls," I said. "Get up and help."

The scrape and shuffle of him standing sounded, then, "Okay, what are we looking for?"

"Handholds. I mean, I can't guarantee there will be any, the fairies can all fly, but if they have human-sized doors, why not a way for humans to get up there?"

Scott was silent for a second. "Oh, right. Flying."

I nodded, remembered he couldn't see me, and paused with my hand resting in a cupped hole in the rock at about shoulder height. "Right. Of course the entrance here is nothing much. They can just fly straight on up to wherever it is, and it's an extra barrier for people who shouldn't be here."

"Like us."

I grinned. "Like us. Here, give me a hand will you?"

Shuffling footsteps, then Scott's hands patted my back and shoulders an instant before he walked into me. "What?" he said.

"I've found a handhold." I grabbed one of his hands and directed it to the handhold in the wall. "Hold onto that for me for a sec." I crouched and searched the wall below, and sure enough, there was another one around knee height. "Got it. You going first, or am I?"

"Feel free, by all means."

I rolled my eyes and began to climb, one dark handhold after the next. For a moment I was suspicious of Scott's motives, but the concentration it took to climb, feeling out each handhold, slowly shifting my weight up, reaching for the right spot with my feet, soon drove everything else from my mind.

It felt like forever, my limbs getting shakier and shakier as the golden light flashed intermittently above us. Realistically, it was probably only about ten minutes until we reached the top and clambered out into a circular chamber, like Sanctuary's heart but smaller.

This chamber also glowed gold, but whereas in the heart the light seemed to come from everywhere at once, here it was a twisting, twining pillar of light on the opposite side of the room that lit the circular, brown stone walls—and where the heart of Sanctuary was blinding in its brilliance, this room was barely brighter than a cave with a fireplace.

I crossed the room in ten easy steps to the foot-high semi-circular dais jutting out of the far wall, which the pillar of light stood on. A waist-high lectern stood between me and the pillar, a heavy, ornate book resting on it, looking like a relic out of the sixteen hundreds.

The pillar flickered, light flaring.

"That's the light we saw," Scott said.

I glanced back over my shoulder at him, still standing by the chute. "Yeah," I said. *Obviously*, I didn't say. "Here, come look at this." I leaned over the book and squinted, trying to make out the lettering. The lectern tilted away from the light, leaving the book's cover in shadow, and part of the gilt letters had peeled away, making them even harder to read than they'd been originally, in their heavy, gothic font.

Book... My heart skipped. *Book of Laws.* "Scott," I whispered urgently, fingers hovering over the cover without quite touching. "This is it."

Scott reached around me and lifted the cover. It brushed against my fingertips, soft and firm, little dints where the letters had been pressed in for the embossing.

I shifted aside, and Scott flipped a couple of the marble-edged pages gently.

"Wait," I said. "Flip back. What was that?"

He flicked back a bit until I put a finger down to stop him.

"There. World Creators," I read from the heading on the page. I didn't know what it was talking about, or what had snagged my attention, but something about it seemed vaguely familiar.

Scott skimmed the page with his finger. "Here," he said, stopping about two thirds of the way down and tapping the page. "This is what Gemma did."

I read the paragraph he was pointing at, then looked up at him, wide-eyed. The first time we'd been on the roads all together, when we'd been trying to take Gemma to the heart of Sanctuary to link her to it and save her life, the guardians of the roads had attacked us. Or, well, they'd appeared menacingly, anyway; I still didn't know exactly how dangerous the guardians actually were, and if they *would* actually attack. But either way, they were pretty darn terrifying, and I'd tried to distract them with my road mastery, which had worked for a little while. But in the end, it had been Gem who'd saved our butts: we'd fallen off the roads into a strange, grey world, completely empty of anything except ourselves. It had only been a few paces square, and the sky, or roof, or whatever, had been low enough that I could brush it with my fingers.

A whole new world, one that Gem had created in a hurry and had transported us all to without a seed, without blood, fuzzy and small because that was all she'd had time to imagine.

It was exactly what the book was describing.

I drew my eyebrows down, thinking. The fissure in Sanctuary was definitely a problem, but shadows getting into the heart seemed like the most pressing issue we were dealing with right now. "So could we, like, create a new world to shove the shadows into?"

Scott bounced on his toes. "I don't know. Let's go try!"

"What, now?" I cut a glance at him. "I thought you didn't want to go on the roads with the shadows there."

"Yes," he said, bouncing again, "but this is new information. This is something we could actually try to fight them with. We have to at least figure out how to make the new worlds, and we can't do that without going on the roads." He tilted his face up and fluttered his eyelashes. "Come on. Please?"

I rolled my eyes and worked my mouth. On the one hand, I was tempted. On the other, it was getting late back home, and I really didn't want to stress my parents out any further than necessary. "I'd really better not," I said. "I need to get home."

Scott sighed, but didn't say anything, which was pretty decent of him.

"Come on." I turned to the entry chute, leaving the book open behind me.

Scott strode ahead. I watched as he walked to the chute and turned to face me so he could begin the climb down. "What?"

I hadn't moved from by the dais.

"What is it?"

"Quoise said she wanted the book," I said, looking back at it for a moment. I met his eye again. "That if she had it, it would make things much easier."

Scott raised his eyebrows. "You think we should take it?"

"I don't know." Rules were rules. Viri wasn't the one who'd invented these rules, who'd created the Forbidden Chamber... But what was it Quoise had said weeks ago when she'd decided to help us save Gemma, going against Viri's wishes? Neither of us broke rules until we met each other; maybe we'd never met rules that needed breaking until then.

"Well, I do," Scott said with a curt nod. "Anything that will help Quoise get rid of that cow Viri is alright by me." He grabbed the book off the stand. His grip fumbled, and it slipped.

I cringed as the page we'd been looking at tore.

"Sorry," he said, guilt flashing over his face. He smoothed the page out and closed the book carefully. "Come on. Let's go."

Green light flashed through the chamber, and when it died away, Viri fluttered over the dais, silver and gold lightning crackling around the ball-shaped head of her golden sceptre, tiny gold tiara glittering in its light, viridian-green dress dancing and snapping in a wind generated by her magic. "Emma, Scott," she said, dangerous smile glinting behind the lightning. "I'm so glad you've come."

Lightning crackled toward us.

We dove to the side, Scott grabbing my sleeve, the seam tearing as we tumbled to the ground, me hugging the book to my chest.

"Get that book!" Viri pointed at us as three other fairies—oh look, it was our friends silver, copper and green again—appeared behind her.

They separated and flew toward us from the left, the right, from above.

I curled my body around the book; it probably wasn't worth my life, but I definitely wasn't giving it up without a fight.

"Edge!" Scott grabbed my arm and hauled me off the ground. "Get up, we have to get out of here!"

"How?" I shouted back over the crackling of the lightning; the acoustics in here amplified it until it took on a life of its own, stabbing my eardrums, disorienting me.

"Come on!"

I got my feet under me and ducked as Viri sent another bolt of lightning our way. "Where are we going?"

"The only way out!" He leapt, dragging me with him toward the dais.

Lightning sizzled past us again as Viri screeched. Behind her, the connection to the heart pulsed.

The heart. Scott was going to jump straight into the heart.

"You're not a Road Master!" I screamed at him as he dove to the right to avoid being caught between a bolt of Viri's lightning and the copper-winged fairy.

"You are!"

Urgh! I dodged left, leapt over another lightning bolt, and flung myself behind Viri toward Scott.

"Get that book!" Viri screeched.

Something jerked my arm.

The silver-winged fairy had the back cover of the book in her hands, and somehow her magic was strong enough that I couldn't pull her through the air. She dug her heels in like the air was solid, wings buzzing, jaw set, and yanked white-knuckled on the cover of the book.

"Edge!"

In the corner of my eye, Scott dove toward the heart. "You'll die!" I screamed.

Book, Scott; book, Scott.

Pulse thundering, limbs burning with adrenalin, skin tingling from the magic-thick air, I gave the book one last solid yank, and launched into a sprint.

With an angry growl, the book tore in two, suddenly lighter in my hand. The abrupt release gave me an extra burst of speed that sent me stumbling.

I tripped.

Scott reached for the glowing pillar of light.

"No!" I scrabbled across the ground.

His hand stretched closer.

To my right, Viri flung the sceptre toward us.

"Look out!"

Scott dodged to one side as the lightning sizzled into the heart.

The heart's next pulse boomed through the chamber like an explosion of light.

I collapsed to the floor as it passed over me, my free hand clapped over my head, light blinding even through tightly shut eyes.

"Quick, now!" Scott fumbled at my arm.

I raised my head. Viri and the other fairies had been blown backward by the force.

I got to my feet, doubled over, and grabbed Scott's hand.

We ran for the heart, leapt—for a moment it felt like jumping into a window, too solid to let us through.

I flung out my road mastery. *Let us through!*

Light shattered around us. I screamed as it sliced my skin—face, arms, legs.

Scott shouted too, grip on my hand tightening.

Thud.

We hit the ground.

Instantly, the light and sound died away, and all I could hear was the two of us panting and gasping.

I tensed, fingers gripping at the floor, my hip bone aching, waiting for Viri to follow us.

Nothing.

My cheek was wet.

I touched it, and my fingers came away bloodied. They matched the scores of tiny cuts up and down my arms, each one releasing a couple of pinpricks of blood—and the ones on my legs, and on Scott's face and arms.

I closed my eyes, shoulders sagging, tension draining, and collapsed back against the floor. We made it. We only had half the book, but we'd made it.

Scott shook my shoulder. "Uh, Edge?"

"Mm?" I contemplated exactly how long I could get away with lying here. If I slept for a few hours... I sighed. Quoise could only get us back at the right point in our personal timeline, and it was already probably late enough that my parents were going to freak out. Guilt twanged through my gut.

"Edge, you'd better take a look at this."

I took a long, slow breath and hauled myself upward so I was sitting.

Scott stared at the wall of the chamber to the left of us, tense, rigid.

I followed his gaze—and froze. The walls of the heart usually glowed gold, filling the room with light and warmth.

The wall to the left of us was black, the chamber partially dim.

As we watched, the darkness crept along, spreading in both directions. In the centre, the wall had cracked, and shadowy tendrils wafted toward us.

"I think," said Scott, licking his lips, "we'd better go."

I glanced down at the Book of Laws—or the half I had left. It felt like sacrilege, what I was contemplating, but on the other hand, it was pretty much desecrated now anyway, torn clean down the spine. I set my jaw, gripped the pages in one hand and the hard front cover in the other, and tore.

The cover came away surprisingly easily. I tossed it on the ground, rolled the rest into a tight cylinder, and shoved it into my back pocket. I had a feeling I was going to need both my hands free.

18

WE CREPT OUT of the heart on the opposite side to the shadows, where the heart was still golden and glowing. I halted as we exited onto the roads, overwhelmed as ever by the mass of sensations: sweet roses and honey, musty carpet, stiff bristles, the sound of pages flicking, the long scrape of a pen over thick paper, soft fur, a warm hug, the feel of a toenail on the tips of my fingers, flashes of emerald, magenta, fire-engine red.

Scott tugged at my hand.

Right. Moving. I blinked away the disorientation and took a few steps. But what was I supposed to be following? Where were we going?

This was no good.

Sighing, I tugged Scott back the few paces to the wall of Sanctuary's heart. With a quick flick, I pulled the scab off my shoulder, and walked through the wall, the golden light melting over me as I did.

"What are you *doing*?" Scott dropped my hand like it had gone red hot and stared at me.

I eyed the shadows on the opposite wall. "Listen. There's no point going on the roads without a plan. It's not like we're following them to Sanctuary or anything; we're already here! So where are we going? And since we're here..." I inhaled. "Since we're here we should try the world creation thing."

His jaw worked for a second as he considered it, darting glances at the shadowy tendrils snaking their way into the heart on the other wall.

They didn't seem to have sensed us, or to care about us if they had.

"Fine. You're right. Something needs to be done, and soon by the look of it. Do you want to try first, or do you want me to?"

I took a depth breath, a little tension releasing with the knowledge that he'd agreed. "Okay, here's what we'll do. We'll head back onto the roads, go about fifty or sixty paces away so we're not so close to the shadows, and then you have a go. Remember, Gem said it was just like travelling, but she imagined a blank world instead."

"I know."

I nodded. "Good. You have a try, and if that doesn't work, then I will." While it would be super cool to be able to just create my own worlds from the roads, if only one of us could do it, I actually hoped it was Scott. I already had road mastery, and that was enough to be solely responsible for.

"How will you know I've tried?"

"I don't know, six squeezes," I said impatiently.

"Six?"

"One through five are taken."

"I thought we only—"

"Do we really need to talk about this now?" I said, nodding pointedly at the drifting tendrils of shadow.

Scott's mouth became a line. "You're right. Let's go."

The second entry to the roads was no less overwhelming, but Scott got me moving quickly again, and kept me going for a good minute until he tugged me to a stop.

Then, nothing.

Well, nothing from Scott. From the roads, I caught the sound of a boat motor, a baby crying, the smell of oranges, the feel of shopping bags heavy in my hands, a soft cheek against the back of my hand, sunlight off steel, magenta light, tangerine, the smell of new leather shoes.

Six squeezes. He must have failed.

I inhaled deeply and blew out through my lips like I could blow the nerves away. *Okay. Just like travelling. Just like travelling.*

A sharp tug on my hand; pressure on my shoulder.

I turned—and my chest clenched. Shadows, closing in fast—inasmuch as it was possible to tell distance in a place with no fixed landmarks, anyway.

Okay Edge, this is it. Travelling time.

I closed my eyes—not that it made any difference—and tried to clear my mind—an impossible feat on the roads at any time, let alone with shadows bearing down.

Scott's grip tightened.

I know. I know!

Think of nothing. Greyness, that's where Gemma took us. Just think of grey.

The sound of clinking china. The colour red. An upbeat, pulsing drum. The smell of coffee.

The shadows, whispering: *"Sweet, so sweet your blood. Want your blood, your life."*

Scott's grip on my hand.

Nothing. Think of nothing!

For an instant I was able to blank everything out and make it grey. I twisted almost instinctively, as though it might help the travelling.

"So sweet your blood."

I yelled as the shadows swarmed around us, tendrils darting in close, jerking away before I had time to do anything.

Travel, frog it all! Think of nothing!

Emerald, crimson, the smell of wet dog, corn chips crunching in my teeth.

Nothing! Nothing!

There! Grey nothingness!

I grabbed onto the sensation, twisted, gripping Scott's hand like death.

A shadow darted forward, latched onto my thigh. I screamed as ice-cold pain shot up it, trying to push the shadow away.

But it was too late. We were falling sideways—travelling! We were travelling!—and the shadow gripped my leg like jellyfish tentacles, hooking into my skin, dragging along with us. Wind roared around us in darkness.

Light flashed around us again and spat us out into my new world—not nothing at all, but something, somewhere, some sort of room. Something about it seemed vaguely familiar—but there was no time. No time to concentrate on anything but the shadow, rearing behind me, drawing on my leg, the wind still roaring and snapping around.

My thigh. The ward. In my pocket, right near the shadow.

Frantically, I shot my road mastery into it, faster, faster, harder, until—

Flash!

The world burst into silver bells and roses for an instant, and the shadow shrank back, shrieking.

"Get it out, get it out!" Scott shouted.

I whipped the final unicorn ward from my pocket and brandished it at the shadow. "Get back!"

"Eat your soul, your blood, drink your life."

The strange wind roared.

"Get back!"

I poured power into the ward—more, more, more—and it too exploded in a flash of light and roses, crumbling to ash in my hand.

I blinked frantically, trying to clear the afterimages from my sight. The shadow. Where was the shadow?

But the hall was bright and clear. The shadow had gone.

I slumped against a nearby wall, head nearly falling off my shoulders.

"What in the..."

The voice sounded familiar. I mean, it made sense that if I was going to create a world of my own, it would be similar to what I knew—but Anna? Could I create *people* for my new world too?

"Edge, was that a shadow in our hall?"

I looked up, chest still heaving as I fought for breath. Strange. This new world looked exactly... like... our front hall. With Anna, emerging from her bedroom, and Scott standing by the front door.

"Princess?" Scott said though equally gaspy breaths, one hand knuckling his side. "I don't think this is a whole new world."

19

A STRANGE, PEARLY shimmer flickered over the hall around me, obscuring the apricot tiles and warm-toned walls. I frowned, blinking rapidly as the momentary shimmer disappeared. New... world? What was he *talking* about? "What?"

Scott opened his mouth, then frowned down at it as though it had decided to speak without him. He looked back up at me. "What what?"

"Edge?" Anna was still watching us from around the doorframe. "Was that seriously a shadow in our front hall just now?"

I stared at her, brow wrinkled. "Why would there be shadows in the hall?"

She rolled her eyes, then inclined her head at Scott. "Who's he?"

I turned from her back to Scott, still frowning. So was he. "Scott."

Anna's fingers appeared around the doorframe, followed by the rest of her. "Is he your boyfriend?"

"No, Anna." Something about the familiarity of Anna's teasing melted away the strange confusion. I pretended I hadn't noticed the way Scott had gone rigid where he stood, not two paces from the front door. "He's a friend. He's..." Urgh. This whole talking-to-Anna-about-magic thing was really weird. "He's here to help with the roads."

Anna's gaze sharpened. "You're going on the roads again?"

I nodded, brow furrowed, lips slightly pursed. "I have to." *Please, Anna. I have to do this. Please understand. Please.*

She sighed explosively. "I suppose there's no point telling you to take your phone."

I shook my head. "It doesn't work over there, you know that."

"Or telling you to be careful." She folded her arms and leaned against her doorframe.

"Of course I'll be careful."

She sniffed. "Yeah. Right." She rubbed her chin with one shoulder. "Going anywhere near those shadows isn't being careful, Edge, it's verging on suicidal."

I stared at her, hands fisting by my sides. "It's not. You know I have wards." I stuck my hand in my pocket to feel for the bundle of unicorn-hair wards Aphros had given me.

My stomach jolted.

My pocket was empty, except for something silty that felt suspiciously like ash.

Scott moved to my shoulder. "Ward? Is this something I should know about?"

"Never mind," I muttered.

Anna had shifted as Scott had stepped to my shoulder, her chin jutting up, arms tighter. "She gets hurt, you pay," she said, staring Scott down.

He nodded. "We'll be careful."

"Pssh." Anna rolled her eyes. "Sure you will. You're using your own blood to cross over to a weird world that stinks so you can travel roads that screw up your brain so you can fight shadows that want to suck your soul. Super careful."

I opened my mouth to protest, but Anna cut me off with a wave. "Why are you still here? Don't you have, like, a world to save or something?" She tilted her head meaningfully to the family room.

"Right." I exchanged glances with Scott. "Yeah. Let's do that."

I led him through the family room and out the sliding door to the yard. Veve greeted us both ecstatically, licking and slurping and pushing through Scott's legs so he'd scritch her back. He staggered, arms flung wide, and I grabbed his forearm to steady him. He laughed quietly, shook me off, and bent over to snuggle Veve's face in between his hands, running his thumbs over her ears.

Touching, but we had more pressing matters to deal with. The warm sun of late afternoon beat down on us. I glanced at it, trying to judge the time as I steered Scott by the forearm around the corner of the house. I checked the windows. No Anna. Good.

"So where's the crossing?" Scott said.

"Doesn't matter, we're not going." I halted abruptly against the side of the house, just under the cool shade of the eave on the edge of the footpath, facing the prickly bushes across the grass.

Veve tried to weave through my legs, but I pushed her away.

"What?"

"We're not going." I took a depth breath and turned to him, ignoring Veve as she nudged my hand. "Scott, there was a time skip."

"What? What are you talking about?" He shook his own hands free of Veve's slobbery attentions; she finally gave up and flopped on the grass at our feet, panting like a train coming into station.

"You know how I told you time kept skipping in Sanctuary?"

He narrowed his eyes. "Yeah…?"

"We've just been through a time skip. We went to the Valley, we did stuff, and then we got skipped back here."

He blinked, as stunned as if I'd just punched him. "How do you know?"

Chewing the inside of my lip, I pulled a tight roll of paper out of my back pocket. "My unicorn wards are gone," I said. "And..." I held the roll of paper out to him. "I didn't have this in my pocket when we walked in my front door."

"What is it?" He took it and began flicking through the pages of what seemed to be a pretty mangled book. A few pages in, he gasped, and locked gazes with me. "Edge, we didn't just visit the Valley. This is Quoise's Book of Laws."

My eyes transformed instantly into saucers. "The Book of Laws?" I said, voice hushed as I huddled shoulder-to-shoulder and elbow-to-elbow with him so I could read it too. "No way! How the frogging elephants did we get away with the Book of Laws?"

"Half the Book of Laws," Scott corrected, flipping to the end of the section we had.

I glanced at him, eyebrows way up. "So who has the other half?"

Scott exhaled heavily and leaned against the bricks. "We don't remember a thing. All that"—he flapped the book—"and we have no idea what we did."

"No, Veve. Down." I shooed her away from the temptingly-flapping book with my knee, then shoved my hands into my pockets and joined Scott back against the bricks, one foot up against the wall to keep my balance. "I don't know," I said as my fingers traced out the empty space of my pocket again. "But it wasn't a fun trip."

"How do you know that?"

I let my head fall back against the bricks and stared past the eave at the endless depth of the vivid blue sky. "I had six unicorn wards in my pocket when we got here."

I turned my head, met his yellow-flecked brown eyes, pulled out the linty lining of my pocket. Black dust drifted to the ground, dusting my shoe on the way. "Now I have none, and this?" I flicked at the top of my right sleeve, where the fabric had torn away from the body of the shirt. "My shirt was perfectly fine when we walked in the door of the house. I know that a hundred percent for certain."

He glanced down at the blue-and-black-stained cotton of my pocket lining before meeting my eyes again. "I don't get it. What are the wards?"

"Unicorn wards," I said, stuffing my pocket back where it belonged. "Aphros's hair. They let you cross from Sanctuary to the Valley without a blood sacrifice, and I can activate them with my road mastery as protection against the shadows."

"That's pretty cool."

"We burned through six of them, Scott. Six. That means that, on average, each of us just risked our lives *three* times." I turned to him again, searching in his eyes for some glimmer of understanding. "We just nearly *died, three times each,* and we have exactly zero memory of how, or why, or where."

His mouth twitched like he might be biting his inner lip. "Okay, yeah, that's not so cool."

"Not so much, no." I bumped the back of my head gently against the bricks a couple of times. We had the Book of Laws, or at least part of it. We'd burned through six unicorn wards. And Anna had asked me if there had been a shadow in the hall.

Frogging elephants, we were in so much trouble right now. I exhaled with a huff.

"Wait," Scott said. "Thick, itchy unicorn hair?"

I wrinkled my eyebrows at him. "Yes?"

Lifting his foot up, Scott peeled his sock back to reveal a braid of Aphros's creamy hair. "I guess we only went through five."

Good, but hardly enlightening. "I guess so."

Adrenalin drained from my chest, dragging uncertainty in its wake. I let my head fall back against the bricks. Of all the frustrating things in the whole wide world...

"What do we do now?" Scott said quietly.

I shrugged, a half-hearted twitch of my shoulders.

Veve, who'd been resting on her belly on the grass, grunted and flopped sideways, legs and tail fully extended. I've never taught her to play dead, but if I had, it would have looked just like that.

I sniffed. Even Veve agreed the situation was hopeless.

"Why unicorn?" Scott said after he'd finished fixing his sock.

"Why unicorn what?" I didn't exactly snap at him, but honestly, I just wanted him to leave and let me be miserable in peace—miserable about something I didn't even know the size or shape of, about lost memories and whatever it had cost us to get the book.

"Why unicorn wards?" he said, shifting his hips against the wall and propping one foot up, mimicking my posture. "Why not, like, fairy wards, or, I don't know, shadow wards?"

I stabbed a quick glance at him. "You really want to wear bits of shadow tied around your ankle?"

He shook his head, not a no, but a dismissal. "Why *unicorn*? Why Aphros? Why can she cross the border but no one else can?"

I bounced the inside of my cheek between my molars; this conversation tickled something in the depths of those locked up memories. I danced around the edges, trying not to force the memory... but it slipped away regardless, water through sand. I sighed.

"I don't know," I said. "And she doesn't know. Her soulprint," I added, realising I hadn't told him yet, "looks like the combined magics of Sanctuary and the Valley before the shadows arrived, though."

Aphros had seemed genuinely surprised and intrigued when I'd told her that her soulprint matched that of the Sanctuary-Valley magics before the Valley had been corrupted, presumably by the shadows, so there'd been no help to find there, either.

He drew his eyebrows down.

I watched for a second, but when no revelation was forthcoming, I switched to watching Veve instead, her sides huffing, ear twitching as a fly landed briefly. No point crossing to the Valley now anyway. We had no more wards. I'd have to sneak over at some point and ask Aphros to make some more, but that would take her an hour or so, and there was no point Scott hanging around that long. "We'll have to try again tomorrow," I said, right as he said: "I know that that's important, but I have no idea how." We exchanged glances and half-smiles, and he pushed off from the wall. "Tomorrow, then?"

I nodded. "Come over whenever. I'm not going anywhere," I added with wide-eyed, head-waggling irony as I remembered the reason Scott had to be here in the first place. Urgh.

"Sure," he said. "See you then."

I should have walked him to the gate in the front fence; instead, I stood motionless and watched him unlatch it, shift Veve to one side with his knee, and slip through, latching it closed again behind him. He looked up at me once, but he didn't speak, so neither did I, and then he'd disappeared off toward the neighbour's house, toward the end of the cul-de-sac, toward the path that led down to the creek, and the crossing to Sanctuary.

I rubbed the centre of my forehead with three fingers. I'd thought we were making progress, with our plan to check out the shadows this afternoon. Now, it felt like I'd slammed into a brick wall instead, and at high speed.

Well. Not quite. Scott had left me the Book.

I stared at the curling font of the title page for a moment—Book of Laws. *Book* of Laws. Book *of* Laws. Book of *Laws.*—and exhaled. I couldn't check out the shadows, but—apparently—I had some reading to do.

20

"EMMA?" MUM'S VOICE cut through a half-formed dream of feathery wings and shadows. "You might want to get up, your friends are here."

I rolled over blearily in the dimness of my bedroom just in time to see Mum withdraw. As the door clicked closed, I let my eyes do the same; holding them open felt too much like scouring them with sand. I must have only been asleep, what? Four, five hours? Urgh. Carefully, I unpeeled my tongue from the roof of my mouth and swallowed a couple of times. Really should have cleaned my teeth before bed.

Now that I was semi-awake, the room felt oddly warm around me, given how early it was. I exhaled and snugged my doona up around my chin. Way too early.

I cracked an eyelid open. Oops. I'd fallen asleep with my lamp on last night. I stretched up to the low bookcase by my bed and felt around for the switch.

Wait, I'd been reading. If I hadn't turned the light out before I'd fallen asleep, I probably hadn't put the book—the Book—somewhere sensible either.

I flailed for a second in the sheet, untangled myself, and sat up. Book. Where was the book? I hunted through my covers. I hoped I hadn't slept on it and wrecked it.

But the book wasn't on my bed.

I peered over the edge, but it wasn't on the floor either.

Urgh, fine. I flumped down onto the floor, dragging half the doona down with me, and felt around under the bed. My bed had one of those heavy bases that were practically another mattress, only solid, so there wasn't much room between it and the floor; the book wasn't there.

I shoved away the anxiety knocking at my chest. It had to be in the room somewhere. I sat for a second, staring around the room. Not on the white bookcase next to the bed. Not on the bed, now definitely the most dishevelled part of the room. Not at the foot of my bed near the laundry hamper, or peeking out from the gap in the wardrobe's sliding doors. And the rest of the floor was clear. Urgh.

Something tugged at my consciousness and I glanced out the window. The sky was bright and blue. I frowned at it. Why was it so blue this early in the morning?

I crawled my way back onto the bed and leaned on the sill. Ah. Right. Despite what my body was telling me, it was *not* early in my room; it was late. Quite possibly after-midday late. Whoops.

Someone tapped at the door. "Edge? You in there?"

Gemma! Right, Mum had said friends. "Just a second!"

Ah ha, and there was the book, wedged down between the wall and the bed. I scooped it up, stumbled my way across to the wardrobe, shoved the left door open (it flew aside with a zzzzzzh, landing against the wall with a satisfying *thunk*), and snatched some clothes out of my drawers.

Dressed and semi-presentable, I went to the door opposite my bed and yanked it open. "Hey," I said, trying to look like I'd been studying or reading or something.

Gem's lips twitched. She reached out and smoothed the frizz of my bed-hair down. "Big night?"

"Funny," I said, still blocking the doorway with my body, door handle firmly in my left hand. "What are you doing here?" It was strange, the way my heart was still pounding in my chest. It wasn't like it was unusual for Gemma to be here. But after this week, I didn't know.

She gave a half smile and wry eye contact that suggested she was feeling a little awkward too. "Scott said you guys found something important."

My eyebrows lifted, then lifted further as she stepped aside a little to reveal none other than Scott himself behind her. "Okay…" I let my door swing all the way open. "Come in then, I guess." I stepped aside while they did, Gemma making herself comfy on the bed with the messy doona, Scott sitting on the floor right by the door, leaning against the wall, knees up and encircled by his arms as though he was trying to take up as little space as possible.

"It's okay," I said to him, sitting against the window on the bed, next to Gem but a little way apart.

He flicked me a quick glance then resumed staring intently at the carpet by my bed.

I didn't *actually* roll my eyes, but I imagined doing it.

"So what's going on?" Gemma said.

I rotated my left wrist slowly in my right hand and inhaled slowly. "See that book on the bookcase by the lamp?"

Gem raised an eyebrow at it. "You mean the one that looks like Veve's been mangling it?"

I nodded. "Take it."

She did. I caught the exact moment she realised what it was by the widening of her eyes and the little intake of breath—and the way her fingers suddenly became gentle as they traced the title on the first page. "No way," she murmured.

"Yeah," I said, stretching back against the window. "There's only one little problem. We have no idea how we got it."

"What?" Gem's eyebrows knitted together. She looked at Scott, and when he only shrugged a little, looked back at me. "What do you mean you have no idea how you got it?"

"Time skip," I said, then remembered I'd never actually explained properly to her what they were. I did, and she rocked back a little, blinking.

"So let me get this straight," she said. "You two went into the Valley, planning to get on the roads to investigate why the shadows are there—which, can I just say, is monumentally stupid, even if you did have unicorn wards—and sometime during the trip you just *happened* to take a detour, where you just *happened* to find the Book of Laws, which you just *happened* to be able to steal... Then time skipped and you ended up back here with a shadow?"

Scott shifted on the floor, loosening up a little, but didn't say anything.

"Yeah," I said. "Pretty much. Only," I reached over and took the book from her, holding the spine in my left hand and running my right fingers down the edge of the pages, feeling for the rough spot I'd found, "there's more. I think I know why we took the book."

My fingers snagged on the tear that made one of the bible-thin pages stick out just a fraction, and I flipped open to it. "I read the whole thing last night," I said as Scott scooted closer until he was kneeling by the bed.

I lay the book down on the bed between the three of us. "The book's pretty roughed up—I'm guessing it's torn in half because the fairies tried to stop us taking it, either that or the shadows, but why would the shadows want the book?" I shook my head. "There's stuff in here that will definitely help Quoise's bid for Keeper, I can see why she wanted it. But anyway, this section here," I said, tapping the page, "is the only part with a torn page. I think this might be what we were reading when we were interrupted."

"World Creators?" Gemma said, reading the title aloud as she and Scott bent over the page to read.

I closed my eyes and leaned back against the window, arms wound around my legs, fingers knotted.

She'd see it. Of course she'd see it. How could she not? And then, maybe then...

I worried at the inside of my lip.

Even with my eyes closed, I could still see them both: two visions of the night sky, one diamond stars studding the velvet darkness, the other the silhouette of a dark, treeless hilltop high above rolling hills in the dimness just before dawn.

"Scott," I said without really meaning to.

"Mm?"

"Why has your soulprint changed?"

Silence. The kind of silence that was utterly without pages scuffling, or people shifting, or even the sound of breathing. My pulse quickened and I tried to ignore the burning sensation of being scrutinised.

"When... When did it change?" His voice was low and husky, and he had to clear his throat.

"Right after you connected with Sanctuary."

"Has mine changed?" That was Gemma.

I hesitated. It wasn't a big change, not like Scott's, not something that changed the whole feel and character of her print. Still. "A little," I said softly. "Around the same time."

I'd always thought of soulprints as kind of a shortcut for someone's personality; Scott had been filled with emptiness and darkness when I'd first met him, a lingering sense of disquiet and vast, open spaces. But it was true: since he'd connected with Sanctuary, some of that metaphorical darkness had begun to fall away. He even seemed actually happy sometimes.

Gemma's soulprint I'd always taken to mean that she was bright and sparkly and a little annoying at first (that was the high-pitched sound on the edge of hearing and the feeling of being about to remember something important), but with hidden, comforting depths. And it was true that she'd been a little less sparkly of late, a little more cautious.

But surely that couldn't be everything. That felt too... small. The roads were full of the kinds of sensations that made up a soulprint, sights and sounds and smells and tastes and feels; there were so many possibilities, so many combinations.

That someone's soulprint could just... change, that it wasn't a fixed piece of something that uniquely identified them...

Could people really just change like that?

Gemma gasped, derailing my thought train. "No *way*."

"You said that," I said automatically.

"You really think Gemma's a world creator?" Scott said, and I didn't even have to open my eyes to know the exact tilt his head would have, part curiosity, part contemplation.

I opened them anyway. "Yeah." I rubbed the back of my neck. "And... The unicorn wards. We burned through five of them. I figure I must have used one back here to get rid of the shadow Anna said we brought, but... If we'd been on the roads just to check out the shadows, and they'd come, we wouldn't have hung around. We'd have used a ward each to get free if we had to, and we'd have left. I think..."

I swallowed and closed my eyes again. It was easier if I could pretend they weren't both staring at me hungrily, like I'd received a special revelation that they needed or something. "I think we went to the roads *after* reading this, to see if either one of us could make a world. Like Gem did."

"And could you?" Gem asked, and I felt the shift of her weight as she leaned forward.

"We don't know," Scott said levelly. "The time skip."

I heard him inhale, and when he didn't speak, opened my eyes to see him chewing consideringly on the inside of his cheek.

"What?" I said. "Just say it."

He lowered his brows. "You told us about the time skips the other day at school."

I frowned back at him. "Yeah?"

"They didn't affect you. You were in Sanctuary, you saw the time skips, and they didn't affect you."

My chest lifted and my frown cleared as I saw where he was going. "We *must* have been on the roads," I said, "because time skips in Sanctuary and the Valley didn't affect me."

He nodded, while Gemma glanced back and forth between us as though we were a particularly riveting tennis match. "So we were on the roads. We were probably trying to create a new world, but the shadows interfered. Has..." He paused to breath in, gaze flicking from one of my eyes to the other and back again. "Has it ever seemed to you like we could take the shadows with us when we travel?"

My eyebrows twitched down. "I don't think so. Gem?"

She shook her head.

Scott exhaled loudly. "I think we were trying to create a new world to put the shadows into, but either we couldn't make new worlds at all, or something went wrong and we shoved the shadow back here, instead."

My eyebrows lifted. "Actually, that makes perfect sense. Which means…"

I turned to Gem, adrenalin squirting into my stomach once more; if she said no, I wasn't sure I could bear it. I wasn't sure our *friendship* could bear it. "Gem," I said softly, searching out her eyes. "I know you don't want to go into Sanctuary while it's dangerous, and I'm not going to lie and say the roads are safer, because they definitely aren't. But the shadows are breaking into Sanctuary's heart, and Quoise has seen them in the Valley again. We can stop this," I said, leaning toward her. *Please. Please say you'll help.* "But we need your help." I glanced from eye to eye. *Please.*

She took in a deep breath and exhaled slowly through her lips. "Yeah," she said. "Yeah of course." She shook her head gently, blinking. "This is bizarre, you know. You're supposed to be the one with fancy powers," she said, nudging my knee with hers.

I was so relieved I could only give her half a smile; a full one would have blinded her. "Funny." Ah, what the heck. I launched myself at her and tackled her backwards, squeezing her tight.

She shrieked, but hugged me back.

"Thanks," I mumbled into her shoulder.

"Duh," she said softly.

"When you two are finished rolling around on the bed," Scott said pointedly, standing up and striding to the door.

I laughed and sat up, pushing Gemma off the bed with my legs.

She squeaked, flailing, but clung to the doona and managed to avoid thumping onto the ground. She got her feet under her and joined Scott at the door.

I bum-shuffled to the edge of the bed. "There's one other thing," I said, breathing deeply, filling my lungs right up, stomach tingly.

Anticipation washed over me, and I felt my eyes light up as Scott and Gem paused, looking at me curiously. "You guys," I said breathily, "the roads are *alive*. Like, sentient-alive. The roads can think. They can *communicate*."

I pressed my fingers to my cheeks. Sentient roads. Roads we could communicate with. The whole concept was so magical, my chest was going to explode.

"Alive?" Scott leaned forward, two tiny vertical lines marking the inner edges of his eyebrows.

Frogs. I'd forgotten about the roads stealing some of his memories. A lot of his memories. Glow thoroughly diminished, I nodded. "The book says so, anyway."

He nodded, just once, tightly. "So let's go talk to them." He vanished out into the hall.

"Yeah," I said softly as Gem exchanged glances with me. "Let's."

21

"AND WHERE ARE you three going?"

My heart sank as I paused halfway out the sliding door to the yard and turned back to Mum, who was in the hallway on the other side of the family room, a couple of steps away from my bedroom door. "Just outside," I said. "We'll stay in the yard. I promise." Scott and Gem busied themselves greeting Veve, trying hard to feign innocence.

Mum narrowed her eyes at me, lips pursed. "Is this the kind of 'staying in the yard' you did with Anna the other day?" she asked, sketching out the air quotes with two fingers.

Be cool, I told myself. *Don't lie,* my conscience told me. As a compromise, I just kind of stood there, heart hammering, forcing myself not to chew on my lip.

Mum snorted softly, closed her eyes with a wobble of her head, and pressed two fingers in between her eyebrows. "I am going to regret this," she muttered, before letting her hand drop and looking at me again. "Fine. I don't want to know, but fine. Stay in the yard. I am going down the road to pick up some groceries with your father, and if you are not physically, bodily present in that yard when I get home, I swear, you won't leave this house for a week apart from school. Okay?"

I nodded, little tiny bobs of my head.

Mum stared at me a moment longer, like she was wondering what exactly had possessed her to say what she had. Just as I was wondering if I should maybe go, or maybe say something, she deflated, shoulders rounding, and headed off down the hall toward the front door, her bedroom, and Dad.

I slipped out the sliding door, breathing out through rounded lips. "We're good," I said as Scott and Gem shot me questioning looks. "We have an hour, an hour and a half tops though."

Scott nodded briskly. "Let's get this show on the road then." He led the way around the corner of the house, striding purposefully.

I hung back for a second so I didn't have to walk right next to Gemma. I wasn't quite ready to forgive her for not believing me sooner.

We congregated by the prickly bushes in an odd triangle-circle-thing, and Veve tried to push her way into the centre. "I'm sorry," I told her as I shooed her away. "The roads aren't a good place for a dog."

Gemma snorted. "They aren't a good place for a person, either."

I ignored her. "You'll be safer here," I told Veve as I made her lie down on her mat on the edge of the paving. "And I'll take you for a nice big walk when we get back."

I rejoined Scott and Gem and lifted the sleeve of my shirt.

"I can do that," Scott cut in quickly.

I rolled my eyes. "Don't be ridiculous. I have a scab here ready to go."

"So do I," he said, and showed the back of his left wrist.

I would have placed real money on the fact that that scab hadn't been there when we'd got back from our little excursion yesterday. But before I could protest, Gem grabbed his elbow and he grabbed mine.

"We don't know how dangerous it is," he said. "We should share the load around." Without waiting for my reply, he flicked the scab away and closed his eyes.

I barely had time to close mine before we were in the Valley—and I had to admit, although it wasn't like I *needed* Scott to do the crossing for me, it *was* nice to arrive in the Valley without the usual swamp of nausea and dizziness. The decomposing smell was bad enough without adding the need to vomit to the mix.

I watched as Scott bent over with his hands on his knees, drew in one long breath, and straightened, shoulders square.

If I hadn't spent the last few months watching him closely, I wouldn't have seen the tightness around his eyes. I knew exactly what he was feeling, and how long it lasted—and he was doing a frogging good job of hiding it.

"Come on," Gem said, totally oblivious, having never done the crossing herself. "Time's a-wasting."

"Oh, so now you're in a hurry," I muttered, falling into line behind her as she set off through the trees, footsteps swishing in the yellowed tussock grass.

"Hmm?"

It wasn't worth a fight. "Never mind."

The muggy heat of the Valley seeped into our clothes, our hair, our shoes as we walked; before long we were all wringing wet and gleaming with sweat.

The still air was stifling, a thick pillow over my face, and yet again I cursed my lack of forethought: when all this was over, I was going to convince Mum to buy me one of those big, twenty-litre containers of water from the supermarket, the ones with the built-in tap, and I was going to stash it here near the entry point from my yard. I flicked a few strands of hair off my face and sighed.

"Never gets any comfier, does it," Scott said, glancing sideways at me.

I shrugged, staring mindlessly at Gemma's back, the way her shoulder blades moved as she walked, the shape of the sweat patch forming on her shirt. *It is what it is,* I would have said, if I could have been bothered moving my mouth.

The real problem, as I saw it, was how we were going to make sure we were back in the yard when Mum got home. Gem's mum, Mrs Caro, was a Time Master, like I was a Road Master: for most of us, travelling back to Earth meant a random time skip that might get us back on time, or late, or even earlier than we'd left (although that was far less common). In Sanctuary, if we got a fairy to manage the crossing for us, they could guarantee getting us back 'at the right point in our personal timeline', as they called it: if we'd spent half an hour in Sanctuary, they could ensure we got back to Earth half an hour after we left.

Mrs Caro, though, being a Time Master, could control the timing of the crossing perfectly, up to about five hours either side of travelling into Sanctuary (or the Valley, I assumed, though she'd never been there to help us travel back out of the Valley again). Mastery powers seemed to be at least a little genetic: Gemma was a Time Master too, although not as strong as her mother; despite several years of practice, she could only control the timing of the crossing within about two hours.

Which meant our clock was now ticking: we had two hours, max, before Gemma would lose control of crossing back home, and we'd be subject to the totally random whims of travelling. We might arrive back before Mum got home—or we might not.

I frowned.

"What?"

I glanced over at Scott, who was looking curiously at me. "Just thinking," I said. "You know how when we travel back home, the timing can go off?"

He shrugged, pouting out his bottom lip. "Sure."

"Time skips," I said, twirling a finger around in the air to indicate the general vicinity.

He also frowned. "Maybe?"

Gemma halted abruptly, causing both Scott and I to crash into her. "*Probably*," she said. She glanced back at me as I rubbed the hollow of my shoulder. "Sorry. But it's a pretty big coincidence, don't you think?"

"Yes," I said, a littler snappier than I'd intended. "That's why I said it."

"Hmm." She set off again and, rolling my eyes, avoiding Scott's pointed looks in my peripheral vision, I followed.

Fifteen minutes later we were at the entry to the roads, and only a handful of seconds later, the muddled, glorious chaos surrounded me. I blinked slowly, even though I saw the same things with my eyes closed as open: flashes of tangerine in darkness;

the bright light of early sunrise; a gleaming silver reflection.

As ever, other sensations bombarded me too: the sound of a car pulling away; the gentle, inconsistent knocking of someone rummaging around a floor above your head; a flock of screechy birds heard from far away.

The taste of a perfectly ripe mandarin; the cloying feel of rancid oil on my tongue; the way cold, winter air tasted as you breathed it in.

Rough wool tugged past my fingertips; the warmth of a fire; the chill of a shadow.

That chill slithered down my spine and I shivered, gripping Gem and Scott's hands tightly. I steeled myself with a breath. "Hello?"

I'd never spoken on the roads before; there'd never been anyone to speak to. Talking into the middle of the chaos of sensation felt about as useful as calling down an empty corridor at night—with the same prickly, not-quite-real feeling of being watched. I shrugged my shoulders back in circles, trying to get rid of the prickling.

Through the overwhelming sensations, a breath of air brushed against my cheek, so real I lifted my hand to touch it—only to be pulled back by Gem, gripping firmly.

The air smelled fresh, minty—like Aphros.

Hello? I sent.

Nothing.

"Hello?"

The breath of air again, amid the smell of sausages barbecuing, the feel of soft, freshly moisturised skin, the exact colour of the roses we'd had outside our house in Melbourne.

Well. It was as good a direction as any, so I set. off, following the breath of air, Scott and Gemma clutched tightly at my sides.

It was as impossible as ever to keep track of passing time on the roads, but with Scott and Gemma prompting me every minute or so to keep moving, before too long—twenty minutes, maybe?— we reached a place where the sensations of the roads seemed to dim a little, as though being filtered through fog that grew denser and denser as we walked.

The path we were following began to climb steeply; although you tried hard not to think too much about 'up' and 'down' in this place, it was impossible to ignore the sharp angle when your knees and thighs protested with every step.

It dawned on me that I could see a little of Scott and Gemma on either side of me: not just their soulprints, but their actual, physical shapes. "Hello?" I said, pressing one hand against the stitch in my side, a little breathless. "Can you guys hear me?"

They turned toward me, Gemma beaming and throwing her arms around my neck, Scott half-smiling and running a hand through his hair.

"But what does this mean?" Gem said when she'd finished impersonating my collar. "Why can we see you? How?"

"I don't know," I said softly, staring around. I detached Gemma's hands from my arm and took a few steps forward. The strange, grey fog had gathered thicker around us, muffling the overwhelming sensations of the roads, creating a kind of curtain around us. "Hello?" I ventured again.

Hello.

The answer was soft, barely there, and, I suspected, mostly in my head. "Did you guys hear that?" I murmured.

They shook their heads.

An overwhelming sense of shyness flooded over me, and it took a second before I thought to question it. Why was I shy all of a sudden? What was I shy *of*?

Oh. It wasn't me feeling shy; it was me sensing shyness with my road mastery.

Carefully, I separated the feeling from my own thoughts, reminding myself that I was feeling perfectly okay, that it wasn't me that was worried or nervous, drawing in a long breath and slowly letting it out through pursed lips. My heart still knocked at my chest regardless. "It's okay," I said, for the benefit of whoever it was that was feeling nervous. "We won't hurt you."

The sense of something peering at me from around a corner, or up from under a table, or out from under a blanket, or possibly all three sensations at once.

I rubbed my temple with two fingers.

"What is it?" Gemma said softly.

"I don't know," I murmured back. "Might be the roads."

Yes, came the reply. *Yes, we are the roads.* A bundle of sensations accompanied the thought, a dim, scaled-down version of the experience of actually being on the roads. *Why are you here?*

I took a deep breath. "To help." I hadn't meant to say that, but it was the answer, truth at its most simple.

The roads recoiled a little. *With what are you here to help?*

"The shadows," I said. "The shadows are taking over again, and we think there might be a way to stop them."

"This is really weird," Gemma muttered behind me.

"Shh," said Scott.

The shadows, said the roads. It shivered, grimacing, horrified. *Please. Please get rid of them.*

"We want to," I said. "But we're not sure how. Do you think we could create a new world to put them in? Would that contain them?"

Yes! the roads said, leaping forward hungrily. *Yes, the other, the one with you, she is a World Dreamer, she is stronger than the ones before, she can do it!*

"Roads confirm you're a World Dreamer, Gem," I murmured. "And they think you're strong enough to dream up a new world to stuff the shadows into."

Her grip on my hand tightened. "I'm afraid."

I squeezed her hand back. "Me too." Because sure, okay, Gemma could create a new little world just for the shadows; but how would we get the shadows *in* there? I had a sinking feeling it would involve me, and my road mastery, and using myself as bait.

We were going to need a *lot* more unicorn wards.

The roads shuffled nervously—or at least, my road mastery received the sensation of nervous shuffling, again with that sense of having multiple images of a similar-but-not-identical concept thrown at me at once. *The shadows…*

More nervous shuffling.

"What about them?" I said, trying to keep my voice kind without slipping into 'older person talking to a small child' voice.

They're… they're breaking into Sanctuary.

"I know," I said, and even though I did, adrenalin still stabbed my chest. "We saw."

You have to hurry, the roads whispered. *Please?*

Maybe a small child wasn't such a bad comparison after all. I rubbed my temple again as the roads' multiple layers of imagery squished my brain into a pretzel. "We need to get home first," I said. "Prepare properly. I need more unicorn wards."

No!

I cringed as sensations drowned me, anger and pain, terror, desperation, dark shapes looming over me, branches threatening to hit me.

No, the roads repeated, gentler this time, a loving touch on my cheeks, a tight, sweaty grip on my hands. *Please. You must do it now. Otherwise it will be too late, and Sanctuary will be gone.*

"We have no wards," I said. "No protection." But my chest ached at the desperation the roads were projecting, and tears born of a frustration that wasn't mine threatened to fall.

Please. We'll help you. We can keep the shadows from eating you. We can. But please. Please help us now. Please.

The tears fell.

Wordlessly, Gem wrapped her arm around my shoulder.

"Are you okay?" Scott asked in a low voice.

I nodded, fighting back the heavy misery of the roads that weighed down my chest like a rock. "We have to try," I said. "Now."

"Now!" Gemma squeaked. "But—"

"Please," I said, and I didn't know if the word was mine or if it came straight from the roads through my mouth. I sagged. "Please."

That one was mine. I took a deep breath. "The roads say they can prevent the shadows from eating us." Eating us. Great terminology, thanks for that image there, roads. I sighed. "Let's just do this and get it over with." I gave Scott and Gem the best smile

I could manage, a thin-lipped thing that never reached my eyes. "Please."

Gem stared at me a moment longer, her own eyes tight, afraid. She swallowed; she nodded. "Okay." Her voice was hoarse.

"I'm with you," Scott said, lacing his fingers through my free hand.

I squeezed it gently. "Thanks."

22

MY PULSE FLUTTERED in my chest like a bird, so fast I might as well have sprinted the whole way here from Sanctuary. But the roads had said that it was nearly too late for Sanctuary—and we'd seen that for ourselves. I exhaled slowly and shot Gem a tight smile. "You ready?"

She nodded, thin-lipped and serious.

"Do you even remember what you did last time?" Scott said quietly.

I nearly snapped at him—the last thing we needed right now was buzzkill negativity—but seeing the concern in his eyes, I realised he hadn't meant it like that.

And anyway, Gemma nodded. "Yeah," she said, hands fisting at her sides. "I think so."

I exhaled firmly this time. "Okay. So here's the plan: a few steps away from here, I'm going to lose sight of you guys. Scott, you're on communications. Gemma's going to be too busy to keep me moving if we do need to move—or, you know, run, if it doesn't work. Whatever you do, don't let us get separated."

I waited until he nodded, then turned to Gemma. "Gem. I don't think it's going to take long for me to attract the shadows' attention, so maybe get started right away. How long is it going to take you to create a new world for me to throw them into?"

She frowned, then scrunched her eyes closed, mouth bunching side to side as she thought. "Less than five seconds."

I nodded. "Good. Okay. So maybe wait for my signal then, because there's no point you being ready too early."

"But Edge," Gemma said, eyes round. "From what I remember of last time, there's no real difference between imagining the place and travelling to it. How are we going to draw all the shadows with us at once?"

I bit the side of my lip. "We can't, I guess. We'll have to do it in waves. I'll grab as much of the shadows as I can to drag through with us, and we'll just have to keep doing it till it works. I'll... I'll squeeze once when I see the shadows, and then a good, hard squeeze when it's time to go."

Gemma nodded, though her eyes were still too round.

Scott shook his head. "I don't like this. We should go see Aphros first, get more wards—"

"We don't have time," I said, cutting him off with a sharp look. He'd given the last one we had to Gemma; I had my road mastery, and Scott had insisted that he was disposable, whereas if Gemma was taken by the shadows, we'd have no hope at all. I didn't like it, but I had to admit his reasoning was sound. "The roads said Sanctuary could fall at any moment," I continued. "We have to do this now." I inhaled deeply and held it.

Scott nodded.

I breathed normally again. "Okay," I said. "Let's go." I Scott's hand, and together the three of us stepped forward.

Within three paces, Scott and Gemma were misty outlines at my sides, and the sensory stimulus of the roads began knocking against my senses.

Cold wind. The sound of traffic. Horse's hooves clopping on a stone path. The smell and taste of dust. Baking sunshine as insects chirped and whirred.

I squeezed my eyes shut. Another step, two more, three. I couldn't see the others now, but their soulprints were there: twinkling stars in a velvet night, the high-pitched whirring noise overlaying it; dawn over rolling hilltops, grassy silhouettes all the way to the end of night.

I turned my attention forward. Somewhere out there were the shadows.

A hot orange sunset; rippling emerald satin; a waterfall, pattering into a limestone pool; the sweet taste of purified water; the smell of bitter coffee grounds.

Scott squeezed my hand.

Shadows. I needed the shadows.

Once before, I'd sent my road mastery out away from me on the roads; maybe that would attract the shadows, if I could make it noisy enough.

Slowly, carefully, breath light and shallow, I eased my awareness forward and away from my body. The world spun for a moment. I pushed forward as the dizziness subsided, something silvery and transparent crinkling and crackling around me, like pushing through cellophane.

Yes. This was what it had felt like last time, and that had been noisy enough to distract the guardians of the roads. Hopefully... I pushed further forward, my body somewhere behind me reeling and swaying.

There: a patch of darkness, the sense of being stared at.

I pushed toward it.

Somewhere, bile rose in my throat.

Come on, shadows. Come and get me.

The darkness mounted in front of my road mastery, like slow clouds boiling. A tendril of shadow broke away and waved toward me.

I darted back before it could touch me—touch my road mastery.

The shadowy tendril hesitated for a moment, then followed, bolder, more confident.

I eased backward further, closer to my body one hair's breadth at a time.

The tendril stretched and lengthened, keeping pace with me—but the rest of the shadows stayed away, and I had the sense that they weren't too interested.

I had to *make* them interested.

But how?

If only I had a ward on me. Even though the shadows didn't like the wards, they definitely *reacted* to them.

But then, it wasn't the ward so much as me activating it; could I mimic that, somehow, with just my road mastery?

I braced myself and *flowed*, the same way I did when I was flowing my power into a ward—only this time, I just flowed *out*.

Silver light surrounded me and nausea gripped my stomach in a vice like I was vomiting out my insides—but I had the shadows' attention, for sure.

Their susurrus began: *"Eat your life, so sweet, so sweet your life, want to drink your life."*

I hauled my road mastery toward me as they closed in. The smell of roses and the tinkling, otherworldly melody filled my senses.

Shadows leapt toward me.

My road mastery collided back into my body with the force of a two-storey drop. I gasped, then gasped again as I saw with my eyes rather than my road mastery the shadows leaping over and over each other, a pack racing toward me.

I swallowed hard, and tugged on Scott's hand.

Five.

My heart pounded.

Closer, closer.

Four.

Sweat trickled down my temple. Scott's hand was slippery against my palms.

Three.

I swallowed, trying to wet my mouth. Just one. I only had to grab one shadow.

Two.

That one, the one at the front.

How the frogging elephants had I grabbed onto it last time? And why the froggity frog-frog couldn't I remember?

One.

The shadow touched my outstretched hand.

I closed my fingers, and my road mastery, hanging on with all my might.

The world spun.

There was a brief flicker of a grey-fog world like the one Gemma had made last time.

The world lurched.

My stomach emptied, burning my throat and sinuses with acid. We were back on the roads, the shadows a little way from us but closing the gap again fast.

Three.

Two.

One.

I grabbed the lead shadow again and clamped down with my road mastery, forcing a connection between us.

The world spun.

Grey.

A lurch.

More vomit.

Back on the roads, the shadows ahead once more.

Time skips. Somehow, instead of staying in Gemma's created world, we were bouncing back onto the roads, and it was causing a brief time skip.

Thank goodness, I added, swallowing down stomach acid again as the nearest shadow made contact and the cycle began again. Because if it wasn't for the skip, the shadows would have us.

Grey.

Lurch.

Retching this time, my stomach too empty to bring up anything else.

I wiped my mouth with the back of my free hand, panting as the roads appeared again, shadows a little way ahead and gaining.

We were alive, but for how much longer? I only had to slip once, miss a shadow…

Gemma only had to miss the timing once, and the shadows would be on us for good.

My heart was going to break my ribs in a second.

Shadow contact.

Squeeze Scott's hand.

World spinning.

Grey.

Lurch.

Retch.

Breathe for five seconds until it starts again.

I couldn't keep this up much longer.

The lead shadow reached me. I reached for it. We connected—and something slipped, like I'd overbalanced, lost my footing.

The shadow leapt up my arm, triumphant. *"Your life, so sweet your life!"*

That's it, I thought, exhausted, detached. *We're done for.*

Stop! A voice shouted through the chaos, piercing my eardrums. *Stop!*

The voice was in my head, even though my ears hurt. Was it me? Was I screaming?

This is how they died! the voice screeched. *This is how they died! We can't let you die too!*

Ah, I thought, watching the shadow envelope my elbow. Not me. The roads.

Trust me, I sent back. *I'd stop it if I could.* But all I could do was keep watching, chest aching, throat burning, as the shadow gulped at my shoulder.

Vaguely, I realised it was cold.

23

FIRE BURNED OVER us, so hot in comparison to the shadow my skin felt immediately crisped. I shrieked, ducking, arms shielding my head. Scott and Gem did the same.

But the fire was only warm, not blistering hot, and as I peered out through slitted eyelids, I realised I had my arm back. The shadows screamed, fleeing as fast as they could, leaping over each other and away.

When they were gone at last, the fire vanished. Grey fog thickened around us.

The air felt suddenly cool.

I stood up, heart still pounding as the adrenalin worked its way through my system. I opened my mouth, but it was dry; my tongue wouldn't work. So I swallowed, worked my mouth, swallowed some more, and when I could finally speak through cracked, split lips, I said, "What do you mean, you can't let us die *too*? Who else has died trying to do this?" *And why didn't you tell us before?*

The fog thinned and sensations from the roads out there began to leak through: chocolate sponge cake on my tongue, teal green plastic, air-conditioning humming, a shout.

"Go keep watch," I muttered to Scott and Gem. "Let me know if anything comes."

They nodded and headed off behind me, one left, one right.

"Roads?" I said.

Still nothing.

I tossed my head, straightened to full height. "Answer me!" My hands clenched at my sides.

The firsts, came the hesitant reply. *The firsts died trying to save me.*

"The first what?"

A deep breath, like a rush of air before storm, or the tide sweeping in through narrow rocks. *Many people have stumbled upon us,* the roads said, and visions of hundreds of thousands of people of all ages and heights and ethnicities and builds swept over me, leaving me reeling like I'd been plunged into the middle of a bottomless crowd. *But only for a short slice of time. They come, they vanish, and while they are here, for only an instant, we see what is in their head, what is in their minds.*

"And you take it," I said. "You steal people's memories."

The roads gave simultaneous images of cringing and shaking heads. *No! No, we do not steal! We borrow! Only borrow.*

"But they don't get them back again," I said, thinking of Scott's diary, with all his missing information recorded in it. "Once you take the sensation from them, they don't have it any more, and they never get it back."

They can regain it, the roads pleaded. *They can experience these things anew. How can they, who have so many of these experiences, who are always gathering new ones, constantly, forever… How can they begrudge us one or two, when we have nothing, when we go nowhere, when we experience nothing that is not brought to us by others?*

I scrunched my eyes tightly. "They can't get all of them back," I said. "Not the important ones." First kisses, parents or friends now dead, or even just moved away, favourite childhood memories… There were plenty of things you couldn't repeat again.

I swallowed. "Who died? Who were the firsts?"

Nodding, eagerness. The roads continued: *Many people visit, but only fleetingly. From all lands they come. But then came the one, the first one, and we could not draw memories from him. And then he brought another, like him, and together they travelled our lengths until finally they found us here, and met us, and talked with us, and from them we learned many things.*

But then the third one came, and although we could draw memories from him, he was different. We didn't know how until one day, they stepped from us to return home, and landed... somewhere else.

"Sanctuary?" I asked, imagining it as clearly as I could in case the roads were sensing what I was thinking.

Agreement, longing, sorrow. *Yes. The place you now call Sanctuary. The... the place where they took the shadows, and hid them.*

"But someone broke the rules," I said, recalling conversations with Quoise, with Viri—and the Book of Laws. "And the shadows were set free."

Yes. Pregnant silence; a blank wall. The roads were hiding something—presumably the identity of whoever had broken the rules.

"The firsts," I said instead, heading back toward something it seemed like the roads might actually discuss. "How did they die?"

Because... because they locked away the shadows, and when the containment broke, the shadows took them first. Because they were angry, the shadows, for being contained.

So, two road masters and a world dreamer had travelled the roads that first time, whenever that had been, and had dreamed up Sanctuary, then trapped the shadows there.

Plausible, I supposed, but it felt like a key piece of the puzzle was still missing. I frowned. "So where did the shadows come from?"

The fog around me froze; I stood in a grey cocoon, sightless, soundless, alone.

"Roads?" My heart hammered in my chest, as though it knew the answer. "Where did the shadows come from?"

The fire flashed around me again, burning bright. Anger lashed at me, hot and terrible.

My heart pounded, my nails bit my palms, adrenalin shook me and tears leaked down my cheeks—but I stood steady, chin raised, waiting for the roads to calm.

At last, the maelstrom subsided.

Us, the roads sent, tiny, forlorn, hopeless, abandoned. *The shadows are ours.*

"Yours?" I said, wide-eyed, hands hanging loose as I tried to process what the roads were suggesting. "But how can they be *yours*?"

In the beginning, the roads said, *we were not careful. We did not know to be careful. We took any sensations, all of them, anything we could find. We were…*

Hunger filled me, the kind of deep-seated ache and longing that came from living half-starved your entire life. I nodded. "I understand," I said quietly. "And then?"

A battery of sensations assaulted me: bad experiences, pulled from the heads of the people who walked the roads: grief, regret, longing; prickling of the spine, someone watching from behind, echoes in an empty hallway, a presence in the dark, creaking floorboards, a bloody face, a body more meat than human—

"Stop, stop!" I hugged my head, covering my ears and eyes. "Please! Stop!" I had enough images like this of my own; I didn't need to add any more.

The bombardment stopped, a tentative apologetic feeling drifting toward me.

"It's fine," I said, still breathing heavily through my nose, letting an imaginary river wash away the thoughts of blood and death, just like the police psychologist had taught me. The river turned red in my thoughts; I made it deeper, stronger.

I exhaled slowly. "You stole bad thoughts from the others," I said, eyes still firmly closed, hands pressed against my cheeks. "And they overwhelmed you." Dots connected in my head, understanding lighting me up. "The shadows are the bad thoughts?"

Affirmation.

"And you tried to lock them all away in Sanctuary, or the Valley I guess, but they... got out?"

Yes, was the barely-audible reply.

I sighed. I knew a thing or two about those kind of thoughts, and it wasn't too hard to imagine them taking over and becoming just like the shadows. Thank goodness I'd had the psychologist to train me. I rubbed the centre of my forehead. I was *pretty* sure I remembered how she'd taught me, but I hadn't memorised it or anything; it wasn't like I'd expected to one day have to teach someone else.

You… you have to get rid of us, the roads said, but the images that accompanied the thought read more 'murder and destroy' than the bland 'get rid of'.

"No," I said. "No. I can help you. We can find a way to deal with this. I can teach you how to deal with the shadows. If you want me to," I added belatedly.

It is too late. The shadows have nearly pierced the heart of Sanctuary. We can hold them off a little while longer, and the heart is strong… But you are running out of time. We are running out of time. You must destroy us.

"But what about putting the shadows into a new world?"

It will not hold them, not forever, and when they break out again they will be stronger than before. The roads' echoing voice was heavy with despair. *The rules will be broken. They always are.*

"I can help you," I said, throat tight. "Please, just let me help you."

You cannot. You cannot help us.

Someone tapped my shoulder. I jumped. "It's been nearly two hours," Gemma said in a small voice.

Frogging frog it all. Frogging elephants. Elephanting frogs, too, for good measure. Urgh. I clenched my fists. "I can help you."

Darkness flashed over us, thick and absolute—but just as suddenly, it was gone.

"What was that?" Gem asked.

Well? I asked the roads.

The heart, it replied, with golden light and warmth. *The heart has fallen.* The golden light dimmed to shadow-black.

I inhaled sharply. "Sanctuary?"

A chorus of heads shaking. *Not yet. But soon.*

"How soon?"

"Edge, I don't know what they're saying, but that darkness wasn't good," Gem said.

"What's going on?" Scott had rejoined us, peering intently around.

I exhaled in exasperation. "I know it wasn't good!" I said, holding up my hands. "The shadows have reached the heart of Sanctuary!"

"What?"

"Oh no! Are they in Sanctuary yet? Can we stop them? Edge, we don't have long until they take over entirely," Gem said.

"I know!" I said. "Just shoosh for a second, will you?"

They subsided and I turned away from them, back to the roads.

"How long do we have? Until the shadows take over completely?"

A storm building on the horizon; the whistle of a kettle growing louder and louder; a pin, drifting in slow, inexorable motion into the skin of a balloon.

"I *know,*" I said. "How *long*?"

Confusion; uncertainty; the sense of time as an infinite, unravellable loop.

Hesitant fingers on my shoulder. "A few hours, at most," said Gem quietly.

I turned to her. "How do you—" My road mastery took her in. "Oh." The dark cord that threaded away from her soulprint, her permanent connection with the power of the Valley, was steady—but, I realised, with a jolt of panic, the glowing gold cable that signified her connection with Sanctuary was dimming.

I swallowed. "Okay," I said hoarsely. "Okay." There was no way I'd be able to convince the roads to listen to me in only a few, short hours, no way I could try to teach it everything the psych had taught me—and it had taken me weeks of practice for the techniques she'd offered to start working. It was too late. *We* were too late.

I should have come three weeks ago.

How do we destroy the shadows? I sent to the roads.

The only way you can. A pause, a sense of vast horizons, time unravelling. *You must destroy us.* A sense of floating, flying, freedom. *Please,* the roads said. *Please promise you will help.*

I set my jaw. *Yes,* I sent. *Yes, I will help.*

So. A few hours to figure out how to completely destroy the roads, in order to destroy the shadows, in order to save Sanctuary—and the Valley—and, assuming the shadows would try to leak out and corrupt the Earth as well, the world.

Three hours to save the world.

It had been nearly two hours since home; regardless of anything else, we had to head back first so Gemma could control the timing of the crossing.

Home, then three more hours. I just loved deadlines involving actual death.

24

MY BACKYARD FADED into view and I searched the sky frantically for signs of the time.

But there were no shrieks from the house, no one waiting to pounce on us and cling to us and tell us desperately that they'd been looking for us; the sun was still midway up the sky, and it looked like we'd beat Mum home after all. Gemma had done it. I sagged with relief.

"So what now?" Scott asked, running a hand through his hair with a wide grip.

I frowned, though not at him. There was still someone who should have noticed our return. "I don't know," I said. "Wait here a sec, I just need to check something."

I left him and Gemma at the prickly bushes, and ducked around to the back of the house. "Veve?" I called. "Puppy?"

Nothing. I slid the door to the family room open and stuck my head inside. "Veve?"

Anna strolled out of the bathroom, hair wrapped up in a towel, heading toward her bedroom. "Not in here," she said, frowning. "I thought she was out with you."

"Yeah," I said. "Of course." I closed the slider, heart hammering at my chest. "Come on, Veve," I muttered. "Where are you?"

But she wasn't around the far side of the house near the laundry, or in her kennel, or anywhere else in the yard, and by the time I got back to Scott and Gem, my chest was tight, icy adrenalin zipping through my veins.

"Veve's gone," I said before Gem could speak.

"She might just have got out the gate, though," Scott said, eyebrows drawn.

I closed my eyes and nodded, swallowing hard against the lump in my throat.

"I'm sorry, Edge," he said, stepping closer and squeezing my shoulder awkwardly. "But we have to stay focused. You know what the roads said: we only have a couple of hours to fix this, or we lose Sanctuary for good."

"I told you we had to hurry," I said blindly. I swallowed again until I was sure the tears wouldn't fall, then glanced at Gem. "We should have been working on this weeks ago."

Gem shrank. "I know. I'm sorry. I was afraid." She straightened and lifted her chin. "And with good reason, look what's happened to Veve. I suppose you're just sad it wasn't me this time."

"Don't be ridiculous," I snapped, right as Scott said, "We don't even know the shadows have got her."

"Of course we do," I said, glaring at him. "The gates are shut, Anna thought she was in the yard." I tensed as our car pulled into the driveway. We were back on time, but what would Mum say when she found out Veve was missing again?

"That doesn't prove anything," Scott said, while Gemma cut in: "It doesn't matter. We have to save Sanctuary."

"I know!" I shouted, stepping back with my hands fisted. "I told you that! I tried and I tried to tell you that, but you wouldn't listen to me, and now we only have a couple of hours left and Veve is gone, and I'm not sad it wasn't you, I'm just sad that you wouldn't *believe* me! But if you still don't want to help, then fine! Go! Just go!" And despite my best intentions, I burst into tears.

"Um, Edge?" said Gem. She pointed at the prickly bushes.

Veve's dark red leather collar, snagged, still buckled, in their thorns.

Scott stiffened—but not at the collar, he was facing the house still.

I turned toward him and realised why: Mum was emerging from around the corner, pale and tense. "They're coming," she said before I could speak. "We have three hours at most before we have to be packed and gone."

"Who's coming?" I said stupidly, dazed. Veve. I had to find Veve.

Scott stepped forward, shoulder to shoulder with me, as Gem gripped my other arm painfully tight. "No," she said. "No, you can't go."

"I'm sorry, Gem," Mum said. "But you know we have no choice. I'm so sorry." She stared at the three of us for half a second before shaking her head. "You two need to get home. The police will come to see you soon to talk you through things."

Scott's jaw twitched.

"We can't go," I said, stomach clenched, chest tight.

"Emma, don't do this," Mum said, voice steady, but nostrils quivering. Her bottom lip trembled as she stopped, then twisted as she jutted out her chin and worked her mouth. "You know we have no choice. Your friends—" She drew in a breath. "Scott and Gemma need to go. And you need to come in to pack."

Dizzy.

The edges of my vision blacked, but I clenched my hands and stared at Mum. "Veve's gone," I said. "The shadows have her. I have to find her."

Mum's breath hissed inward. She shook her head, face crumbling. "Edge," she whispered. "We don't have time. I'm sorry. We have to go."

Was I doused in ice, or burning in fire? Both at once, it seemed. *"I am not going without my dog."*

Mum swiped the corner of her eye, jaw twitching as she fought for control. "Gemma," she said, and I turned to Gem in surprise.

"Yes?" she breathed.

"Is it true? That you can get Emma back before she leaves? When you cross to Sanctuary, I mean."

Gemma knit her brow, lips stretched and thin. "No," she said. "That's my mum. I can get us back an instant after we left, though, if I'm concentrating hard and everything goes right."

Mum focused Gemma in a laser-beam stare. "Then make sure it all goes right."

I inhaled sharply. "You mean…?"

"Go," she said, turning on her heel and stalking back to the house. "Be safe," she threw back over her shoulder. "Find Veve."

I exchanged glances with the others.

"Two hours," Gem said. "I can only control the crossing within two hours."

"We only have two hours anyway," Scott said. "Or the shadows will have won."

I whirled to face the bushes, grabbing my friends by their shoulders. "Two hours," I said grimly, "is enough. Let's go destroy some roads."

25

APHROS, I CALLED as we hiked through the Valley toward Sanctuary's Lodge. *Veve's missing. I think the shadows took her from my yard. Have you seen anything?*

Silence for a moment, except for the swish-crackle-thud of our footsteps through the yellowed, brittle grass clumps, then, *You are right. The shadows have her. She is alive, but they have her trapped. I am sorry, Edge, but the only way to save her is to vanquish the shadows, and I am not certain that can be done again this time. Already they have taken over the heart of Sanctuary.* She sighed. *We will fall. I can hold them at bay for a little while, but unless a more permanent solution can be found, Sanctuary will fall for good, and Veve with it.*

I bit my lip. No. Veve was not going to die. Not here, not today. And neither was Sanctuary.

Everything rested, really, on figuring out a way to get rid of the shadows. The roads had told me that the only way to destroy the shadows was to destroy the roads themselves, but honestly, I wasn't sure that was even possible.

And even if we did get rid of the shadows, what about the Valley's glowy heart? The pillar of light might not have caused the shadows, but it certainly didn't hesitate to use them, and it killed Scott's mum and nearly killed him, and it had tried to suck the life right out of Gemma.

That didn't match with the sense I'd got of what the Valley had been like back when it was green, and not black.

I tugged on the tips of my hair in frustration. I was missing something, some jigsaw piece of information that would snap the picture into focus for me—and I had two hours to figure it out. Maybe less, if Veve was in physical danger right now, though from what Aphros had said, I didn't think she was.

My frustrated reverie was interrupted by Scott and Gem stopping abruptly in front of me.

"Shhh," Gem said to me, even though I'd stopped and hadn't made a sound. "Look."

Through the trees right at the border of the Valley, right where the leaves that tickled my ear began deepening to fresh green, we peered through to the grassy avenue that led up to the Lodge. My heart pounded in my chest: thick swirls like sooty smoke spiralled up from the roof of the Lodge, and the usually white walls were greyed and dim. Instead of Sanctuary's usual smell of jasmine and salt water, everything smelled of ash.

"Is it burning?" Gem whispered near my ear.

I shifted, trying to get a clearer view. "I don't think so," I said, wiping a bead of sweat from my temple as my body cooled from the trek through the Valley. I tried my road mastery—and recoiled. Yup, definitely not smoke. "It's shadows," I said softly. "They're here."

Gem inhaled sharply, and Scott tensed. "Look," he said, indicating upward with his eyebrows.

I gasped. A ring of fairies had exploded out of the Lodge's roof, right where the spiral of shadows was most concentrated. The fairies circled the thickest branch of the shadows, wings flashing emerald and ruby and sapphire and magenta in the twilight of Sanctuary—even darker than usual because of the shadows.

One fairy cried out, and at her signal the others raised their arms, and I caught the flash and sparkle of the silver sceptres they'd wielded against us last month.

Another cry. Silver lightning shot from the sceptres.

The shadows shrieked, twisting upward, sucking inward, pinched at the waist where the fairies attacked them.

"I don't think we can help here," Gem said, then bit her lip.

Much as I hated to admit it, she was right. It was unlikely that Veve was in there, given she'd been taken through the portal to the Valley from the backyard, and there was little we could do to attack the shadows like the fairies were.

My stomach flipped. We couldn't attack them, yet somehow we had to get rid of them entirely. What in the world were we thinking?

The world shifted, a pearly sheen rolling over everything for the barest of instants, and the fairies disappeared, the shadows winding back to mere exploratory tendrils. A time skip.

I chewed the inside of my lip. If we could find a way to predict the time skips, or even cause one, it could be a serious advantage in our fight against the shadows—because although the roads had said that the only way to get rid of the shadows was to destroy the roads themselves, I was still pretty sceptical that a) we could even do that, and b) that it was really the only way.

I mean sure, the roads might have caused the shadows—sort of, without meaning to—but that didn't mean we had to kill the roads to destroy the shadows, did it?

Bad memories.

You didn't have to kill yourself to erase bad memories.

A shiver slid down my spine as I saw Georgia again, face bruised and battered, lying in her own blood.

I'd give quite a lot to be able to time skip back past that one. Which... The time skip just now had rewound the shadows' take-over of Sanctuary a little. Could we skip back far enough to erase it entirely?

Tempting, and probably full of complications. But regardless, even a small time skip could make a difference.

I exhaled through pursed lips. "The fissure," I said. Gem and Scott glanced at me. "If we can figure out how it's causing the time skips..."

Scott nodded grimly as Gemma inhaled. "Yeah," she said. "And I'm positive there's a link between them and the fact that time skips randomly when we travel between home and here." She nodded emphatically. "We need to know what's going on. Let's go."

I didn't smile, because the shadows had still taken over Sanctuary, and my dog was missing, and somewhere back at home literal, actual bad guys were hunting my family down... But my chest did lighten, because Gemma was with me, in every sense of the phrase—and it felt good to know my best friend had my back again.

2 6

THE FISSURE THAT cleaved the meadow in two had widened even further since I'd seen it a week ago, now easily six good, long paces across, its edges crumbling to reveal dark dirt and large rocks with veins of silver.

Well, probably not *actual* silver, but something that glimmered silver in Sanctuary's twilight. I tiptoed cautiously to the edge and peered in.

"Please be careful," Gemma said fretfully behind me.

"I am," I said. It was hard to tell in the dim lighting, but as I leaned over the crack in the ground, it looked like it was maybe—six, seven, eight—I tried to measure it out—maybe ten feet deep, narrowing toward the bottom in a V that meant it didn't really have a floor.

Possibly, I decided, the crack ran much, much deeper, and only as it widened would we see how deep it really went.

Hissing filled the air, and I leapt back, Scott grabbing my shoulder, Gemma snatching at my arm as pearly white fog issued from the crack like steam from a train funnel and a sweet, sharp smell enveloped us.

Around us, the world shifted a little, and even though there was no one nearby to measure it against, I was sure Sanctuary had just experienced another time skip.

"That was close," Gem said.

"Yeah," I said, shaking her off and stepping back to the edge of the fissure as the fog drifted away.

Time skips. Sanctuary had only started experiencing them since we'd returned from the roads with Helios, since the fissure had opened in the meadow—or maybe since Scott had used death magic—blood magic—there, clashing it against seed magic.

Before, we'd assumed that because the clash between blood and seed magic had caused big, booming earthquakes, it had caused the fissure too. But the fissure was clearly connected to the time skips, and maybe so was travelling, and…

Something niggled at my mind. The roads. The roads had seemed confused when I'd asked them how much longer we had until Sanctuary fell completely; they'd given me that sense of time as something cyclic, something looping, rather than something linear.

And.

Before Gem or Scott could protest or stop me, I sat down on the edge of the fissure, my feet hanging into the crack, my fingers digging deep into the thick, moist dirt of Sanctuary to make sure I didn't fall. But I had to get closer, because it was almost like I could hear something, or feel something, deep in the heart of the fissure.

"What are you doing?" Gem squeaked, but Scott shushed her gently.

"Trust her," he said, and I glowed just a little.

I closed my eyes and let my road mastery spool out around me, becoming gradually more aware of my surroundings, like tuning into background noises you hadn't realised were there until you stopped and made yourself listen.

Sure enough, the faint tug of sensations grew stronger—and it was coming from the bottom of the fissure.

I bounced my inner lip between my teeth. Did I dare? What if I was wrong?

"Gem," I said carefully. "You know how you said before that travelling was probably related to the time skips?"

"Yes," she said, matching my slow, careful tone as she sat down to my right, far enough back from the

242

edge that I couldn't see her in the corner of my vision as I stared into the fissure.

"Elaborate," I said.

A waft of fog rose from the fissure, deep below my feet, pearly white and rising in a puff. It swept over me in an instant, cool and dewy and sweet-smelling, while the tug of sensations down in the fissure grew stronger.

I leaned forward a little, raising my chin as the fog lifted, as though a little of my stress and fear had gone with it.

Gemma released her painful grip on my shoulder and exhaled. "Are you okay?"

"Perfect," I said without turning to her, letting the corners of my mouth soften upwards. "Travelling?" I peered back down into the crack and watched as fog played down below. "Time skips?" I was so sure I was right.

Dirt bounced off the wall of the fissure as Scott sat beside me, peeling my the fingers of my left hand up out of the dirt and lacing them one at a time through his.

Gem cleared her throat. "Um. Yeah." She took a noisy, steadying breath. "Right. Well, obviously, every time this fissure does its... thing, Sanctuary skips back in time, maybe randomly, maybe in proportion to the amount of steamy stuff released, I don't know. And when we travel from Earth to Sanctuary—"

"Or the Valley," Scott added, and out of the corner of my eye I could feel him staring at our hands.

"Or the Valley," Gemma repeated. "When we travel from Earth to *here*, time is, I don't know, fluid. It's like the trip doesn't have a fixed length of time it should take, like the, the path we're taking to get from there to here changes length, or like there are multiple options for a path, different ways to get here." She shuffled forward to sit beside me, legs tucked firmly up underneath her as she risked a quick peek into the fissure and then straightened. "When I use my time mastery, it's like I can sense different paths in front of us, all going to the same place, and I can choose the shortest one. But the longer it's been, the fainter they become. And the stronger *I* get, the more paths I can sense."

I nodded. "Thanks," I said, using my free hand to unlace my fingers from Scott's. "That's what I hoped you'd say." I braced my hands against the dirt, tensed, and jumped into the fissure.

27

AS I FELL, I closed my eyes and twisted, the way I'd done in the heart of the Valley when I'd been twisting through dimensions looking for Gem. Only this time, I was twisting toward the roads.

I thudded to my feet—and sure enough, the roads whispered around me, my vision lighting up with tea-tree green, chocolate brown, autumn-leaf red, umber orange; my ears full of the sound of distant, rolling thunder, the faint drone of a TV, the keening, haunting cry of a black cockatoo; my skin prickling with ice-cold dread, a frost-laden breeze across my cheeks, the blast of an opening oven; my mouth full of the feel of melted butter, thick with the cloying sweetness of store-bought pastry cream, burning with the heat of a dry curry.

A smile spread slowly across my mouth, and then, before I could forget myself, I threw myself sideways, twisting again just as I'd done when I'd moved between dimensions—and, I suspected, exactly how I'd twisted when I'd fallen off the roads back into the front entryway of my house.

The cool twilight of Sanctuary washed over me, salty air breathing in from the ocean across the meadow, the calming nature of its atmosphere flooding my senses.

My smile widened.

Fifteen paces ahead of me, Gemma and Scott leaned over the edge of the fissure, Gemma sobbing so her shoulders shook, Scott gripping her arm, eyes tight, body rigid.

"Hey," I called. "Looking for something?"

They whirled, surged toward me, and as Gemma crashed into me, holding me tight, and Scott hovered for a split second before giving up and wrapping his arms around the both of us, regret surged through me.

"Hey," I said, wiping tears from Gemma's face. "Hey, it's okay. I'm fine."

Gemma flung herself away. "Why would you *do* that?" She scrubbed at her face, then glared. "We thought you were dead!"

Scott folded his arms around his chest, jaw set. "It was a pretty dumb thing to do."

"I'm sorry," I said in a tiny voice. "I didn't mean to scare you."

He nodded once, a jerky, upward movement. "I hope you found something worth risking yourself for."

I did a quick inhale-exhale and gave myself a mental shakedown. "Yeah," I said. "Yeah, I did. The fissure connects to the roads."

Gem's forehead wrinkled. "The roads? But then how did you get back here?"

I couldn't help it: I grinned, because this was our secret weapon, our trump card, the one thing that meant we actually stood a chance against the shadows. "Time skip." And it was now under our control, and we'd find Veve and find a way to beat the shadows, because we had all the time in the world.

"What do you mean, time skip?" said Scott, brow furrowing to match Gemma's.

"It's like Gemma said," I said, pacing back to the fissure. The others waited a second, then followed. "When we travel, we're not just skipping straight from Earth to here. We're using the roads. All of us, even if you're not a Road Master. That's probably why we have to use a sacrifice to travel, in order for it to work properly for non-Road Masters. Or maybe everyone who can travel is a Road Master," I added as the thought came to me. "Only their abilities are too weak to get on the roads properly, so instead they can just do a sort of slide, where they cross in and out again in an instant, getting onto the roads in one place," I said, gesturing to my left, "and getting off in another." I waved to the right.

Gemma nodded. "But what about the time skips?"

"Right." I grinned again. "So we know that when we travel, time can slip randomly. While I was talking to the roads, they showed me something. I asked them how long we had, until Sanctuary was lost, and they were confused, like they didn't understand what I meant by 'how long'. They showed me a bunch of images of time as a circle, or a loop. You know how the fairies say that you can get anywhere from Sanctuary?"

Gemma nodded, little enthusiastic bobs, while Scott continued his serious eyebrows.

"In all your years of coming here, have either of you ever met someone from another world? Have the fairies mentioned specifically other worlds? Like, individual, identifiable ones?"

My grin broadened further as they both shook their heads.

"The roads don't connect all *places*, you guys. They connect all *times*."

Gemma's eyes went saucer-wide, and even Scott looked a little awed. "No way," said Gemma. She pressed her fingers over her mouth. "But that makes so much sense, though. What you said." She shook her head. "It fits."

"Can we prove it?" Scott said.

I raised my eyebrows. "Do we need to? Isn't it enough that it works?"

"If we're going to use this to fight the shadows, no, it's not enough. We need to know what the limits of this are. How…" He stopped, clearing his throat. "How far back we can go, what we can change, what… impact it will have."

Oh. My chest constricted and tears prickled my eyes. I dug my pinky nail into the tip of my thumb to stop them spilling over.

I very much doubted that we'd be able to go back and save his mum, just like I doubted we really could rewind Sanctuary to a time before the shadows—and he probably did too. But I knew he needed to know if we could try.

Impulsively, I hugged him tight, pinning his arms against his body as he stood rigid.

He flashed me half a smile, though, as I let him go. "Yeah."

I nodded, screwed up my face to make sure nothing was going to leak, blinked a few times, and inhale-exhaled. "Right. What we are going to do is this. Someone is going to go fetch Mrs C so she knows what's going on, and in case we need backup. You guys can flip a coin. The other two of us will go back on the roads and try to figure out how we can force the time slips; I can't create a new world off the roads like Gemma can, but I can slip us off them back into the real world, and I need to see how much I can control that."

Gemma tossed her hair. "Well I'm not going back, you need me to handle the timing of the crossing."

Scott turned to her. "That's exactly why you need to go. What if I try to go back and get your mum and I end up hours late? That's not going to help anyone."

"But that's not fair! I—"

"Wait." I held my hands up at them. "There's another option here." I closed my eyes so I could concentrate and called. *Aphros? Are you there, can you hear me?*

Cool fog shushed out of the fissure again, lifting a stray hair off my face. Sweetness, like walking into the kitchen while Mum was making something with lots of icing sugar, with a hint of something sharp and sneezy underneath.

Aphros? I sent again, in case the time skip had erased my call to her.

Edge? Why are you here? It is not safe! You must leave Sanctuary, leave at once!

Aphros, we think we have a way to fix this, I sent, focusing on her mint-and-gold soulprint. *The fissure in the meadow is causing the time skips, and it's linked to the roads. We've found a way to control the time skips. Sort of. Aphros, we can do this. We can beat the shadows.*

Somehow. Without stuffing them into an alternate world, or destroying the roads. A somehow that would likely involve hunting down the shadows and destroying them one by one—for as long as it took.

Silence, my pulse thrumming in my ears.

What do you need from me?

We need someone to fetch Mrs Caro while we try to figure out how exactly this all works.

A snort. *I cannot fetch her.*

No, but could you find Quoise, and send her? And… I set my shoulders. *And we're going to need a lot of wards. As many as you can make. And fast.*

Gemma clutching at my arm tore my concentration away from my conversation with Aphros, and I opened my eyes. "We need to hurry," Gemma said in a low voice.

I followed her gaze up the slope to the Lodge—and my heart skipped. Dark shadows oozed out through every crevice, through every door and crack and window, the vines and blossoms that covered the Lodge withering, crackling to dust. The shadows drifted out of the Lodge, inexorable, unstoppable—and heading for the stables.

28

THE LODGE. DID that mean all the fairies were…
That the shadows had them all? My jaw twitched.
Aphros, where's Quoise?

She is well, Aphros replied. *I have her. She will get
Maria. Please, hurry.*

"It might be time to try your escape route,
Emma," Scott said from just behind me.

I glanced back at him, his mouth tight and eyes
strained as he watched the shadows drifting slowly
toward us down the slope. "Yeah." I said. "Let's go."

"Wait!" Gem clutched at my arm again, pointing
away with her other hand. "The stables! Lily and
Filibere!"

Adrenalin pumped through my stomach. "What
are we going to do?"

"We can't do anything!" Scott said, trying to haul
Gem and I back—but he was too late, and we were

already sprinting toward the stables where the baby unicorns lived.

"Aphros says she and Quoise are in there with them," Gemma gasped out.

I flicked her a glance; I'd forgotten for a moment that she was connected to Aphros too. "Quoise is supposed to be going to get your mum."

"Fine," Gem panted. "She'll be safer back on Earth for now. Aphros reckons she can hold the shadows off them, but they trapped her last time. What do we do?"

I really did not remember this slope being so long. A stitch was burning in my side, and my throat hurt as I tried to gulp down air. "I don't know." I'd seen Aphros hold the shadows at bay before—heck, we used her hair as a ward against them. But I also remembered clearly the very first time I'd seen Aphros, before I'd even known who she was, the time she'd dragged me over the border to the Valley and I'd cut her soulprint free from the shadows. She'd been trapped, and scared, and helpless. And yes, afterward, once her soulprint was detangled, she'd saved our butts—but while her soulprint was trapped, she'd been entirely at the shadows' mercy.

And Lily and Filibere were only babies.

We stumbled up to the darkened doorway of the stables, and I pressed my hand against the rough, wooden doorframe, leaning down as I fought for breath.

Gem pushed past me, brushing aside the grey cloth that functioned as a door.

I straightened so I could follow her—and Scott stopped me, gently pressing the back of his hand against my upper arm.

"We have to save Sanctuary," he said, eyes round and serious.

My gaze flickered between his eyes, left, right, left, right, noting again the flecks of yellow in the deep, woodsy brown.

"I know," I said. "But we have to save Aphros, too." And Veve, frog it all, but Scott was right, there: my best chance of saving Veve now was to save Sanctuary. Aphros, though, was right here. Her I could save right *now*. I turned and entered the stables.

Warm air full of the green sweetness of hay greeted me, soothing and comforting.

A large stall lay to either side of me, and at the end of the aisle, fifteen or so steps away, was the biggest stall of all, partially lit where the light drifted in through a gap in the corner of the roof.

Gem was already down there, palm pressed against Aphros's nose, face buried in Aphros's neck, while Quoise fluttered nearby, arms folded, blue wings flashing in the dim light.

The twins, Lily and Filibere, were curled up in the far corner, golden limbs entangled with each other, one foal's nose over the other foal's flank—asleep, I thought, until I drew close enough to see their wide, brown eyes staring up at us.

With my road mastery, I caught the flash of blue that was Lily, and the streak of copper that was Filibere. Otherwise, the two golden foals with their nubby, fuzzy horns looked identical.

"We have about five minutes," Scott said from just inside the door, arms crossed firmly over his chest. "The shadows are heading this way, but not too fast. Yet."

I drew in a deep breath, full of equines and hay and straw and dust. "Quoise is going back to Earth to get Mrs Caro," I said firmly. "You'll be safe there," I said directly to her. "Obviously come back if you can, but if you can't, we'll meet you in the glade."

I stepped up to Aphros, leaning my head against her neck on the opposite side to Gem. "Aphros," I murmured. "I know you can hold the shadows back for a while, but what if they trap you, like last time? What if they trap your babies?"

She trembled. "We will be fine."

But I caught the hesitancy underlying her words, and Gemma must have too, because she reached under Aphros's chin, searching for my hand.

I clung onto her fingers, my other hand twining through the roots of Aphros's mane. I took a breath and held it, scrunching up my face, searching for some alternative. But the plan I'd come up with was the best I could think of, and I couldn't see any other options. "Aphros," I said carefully. "You can stay here and try to fight them off. Or you can run somewhere else in Sanctuary, or the Valley." She could run fast, that was true. But would it be fast enough? And could she stay away for long enough?

Gemma's fingers tightened around mine.

"Or," I breathed into the soft, white hair of her neck, "you could come with us on the roads."

I'd been whispering, but the tension in the stall was so high that everyone had been quiet as a pin-drop anyway—and everyone tensed as they heard my suggestion.

"I know the shadows can get there too," I said, "but if we stick together, our chances are better. And Gemma and I can both twist us on and off the roads. We can get away. I need you," I added, and my fingers tightened in her mane. "I need you to help me figure out how to use these time skips to end the shadows once and for all."

Because I couldn't destroy the roads, and I meant that in two senses: one, I had zero clue how to even accomplish that, and two, how could I? How could I destroy them now, knowing that they were the only thing that enabled us to get to Sanctuary in the first place? If I destroyed the roads, we'd never see Sanctuary again.

And Sanctuary was a dreamed world anyway; it seemed at least possible that destroying the roads would mean Sanctuary would be destroyed forever as well. I was trying to *save* my second home, not endanger it further.

Which meant destroying the shadows somehow, which meant figuring out how to leverage the time skips to our advantage.

Scott was right: we had to figure out how far back we could go, and what we could fix.

I needed to get to the heart of the Valley, and I needed to get to it before the shadows did—the *first* time. "Please, Aphros," I whispered. "Come with us. Help us."

She snorted and shook her mane, brushing Gem and me aside. "Fine," she said. "I do not even know if it is possible, but for you, for them"—she pointed her horn at her foals—"I will try."

29

WHEN THE GREAT heart of the Valley appeared before us as we trekked along the roads, I thought at first that I'd done it, that I'd taken us all the way back in time before the shadows had appeared—but as we drew closer and the foals began to prop and start, nostrils trembling, tails and ears flicking uncertainly, I realised I was wrong.

The shadows weren't here, for sure, but that was because they weren't here *anymore*, not because they weren't here *yet*; the heart was black and silent, with no trace of green at all.

"I will wait outside," Aphros said as we reached the outer barrier of the chamber, curved round like that of Sanctuary, but grimy and charcoal grey instead of glowing gold. "With Lily and Filibere."

It had turned out that getting the unicorns on the road was no more or less complex than getting ourselves on the road—with the added bonus that I could actually see them as we walked. It was strange to have someone else visible, and not just as a soulprint, and we'd made excellent time with Aphros able to keep me moving. The whole thing was practically social, since Aphros could see not only me, but also Scott and Gemma, and so relay conversation back and forth between us.

But as we'd drawn nearer and nearer to the heart of the Valley, conversation had lulled, and even Scott and Gem reported feeling uncomfortable and grim.

"Okay," I said to Aphros, ignoring the way my heart pattered at my ribcage. There were no shadows here, nothing to be frightened of.

Memories of the glowing pillar of light swirled in my mind, the way it had sucked at my thoughts, my willpower.

But Gemma said the Valley's heart was quiet, and the connection she had to it through her soulprint didn't look any stronger than before to my road mastery.

I gripped Gemma's hand (and presumably she gripped Scott's), peeled the scab on my shoulder free, and stepped through the barrier into the heart of the Valley.

Thick, acrid smog covered me for an instant as I passed through, burning my sinuses, my throat. I emerged, coughing, into a round chamber about the same size as the heart of Sanctuary—about twenty or so metres across. Gem and Scott, also covering their faces and coughing, were right behind me.

"Cozy," Gem noted.

I took a few steps around the chamber, running my fingers over the wall next to me, watching as black smoke or paint or something flaked away. Odd. Sanctuary's walls had always seemed to be made entirely of light.

"It's dead," Gemma said. "Empty."

Scott pushed past us and strode to the centre of the room, stepping up onto the dais that took up about a quarter of the floor space. He closed his eyes, face tense, hands fisted.

But after a moment, he sighed and opened his eyes again. "She's right," he said simply. "There's nothing here."

My back crawled. This was weird. Way too weird. "Are you still connected, Gemma?"

She shifted her shoulders experimentally. "I'm connected to *some*thing."

"But there's nothing here. No shadows, no light," I said striding around the perimeter. "And no power." I glanced at Scott. "How is the Valley still there?"

He frowned. "The power source must be hidden. There's something here, Gem says she's connected to it, and as you said, the Valley exists. So there has to be something here still. Something we're missing." He stared around at the walls, all in similar condition to the one I'd touched, with flaking, fading paint, or whatever it was like paint that was flaking off the smoky barrier.

Aphros, I sent. *There's nothing here. It's empty. What are we missing?*

"I'm going to tell Aphros to come in," Gem said.

I nodded, half smiling that we'd both had the same idea.

A second later, her gleaming golden horn appeared through the grimy wall, followed by her white nose, brighter than ever in this gloomy room.

She entered fully, flicked her tail once, and stopped dead, the foals on either side of her peering around wide-eyed, noses still trembling, tails still twitching.

I gasped. Around Aphros, the floor was turning green.

Mint green.

The colour of Aphros's soulprint—and the Valley, before the black had corrupted it.

Gem clutched my arm and even Scott inhaled sharply as the minty green spread, black flaking off the walls faster and faster and faster and faster until the black flecks spiralled upwards in a kind of reverse tornado, up into the roof of the chamber, through it, away, beyond—leaving behind walls of pristine minty green.

I breathed deeply, and the room smelled of mint. "Aphros," I said, a hundred speculations colliding in my head. "Why does your soulprint look like the Valley before it was corrupted? Why do unicorn hair wards repel shadows? Why are you the only one who can cross into the Valley without a sacrifice?"

"And Aphros," Scott said softly, stepping up to my side. "Where do unicorn babies come from?"

That jagged something in my memory; he must have mentioned it before, once, in passing.

It was Gemma who broke ranks first, running to Aphros, laughing, arms wrapping around Aphros's neck.

The babies shied away, snorting at this sudden outburst.

"It's you," Gemma said, running her hand down Aphros's nose. "It's you!"

Scott shook his head, and despite the happy adrenalin thrilling through my stomach, I had to agree. "But how?" I said. "How could Aphros be connected to the Valley? Her soulprint has the same green, yes, but Aphros, you told me yourself that you're made of both Valley magic *and* Sanctuary magic. And what about the glowing light?"

"And if you're the avatar of the Valley," Scott said in a strange voice—I glanced over: his eyes were oddly tight, too—"why didn't you stop the light when it took my mother? Or me? Or Gem?"

Point. No wonder his voice sounded strange.

I realised Aphros hadn't moved, even though the twins had drifted away to sniff at the floor, the walls, the dais. "Aphros? Are you okay?"

She began to shiver.

Slowly, one hoof at a time, she backed away—then the shivers became shakes, and she was swinging her head, her horn scribing a glimmering arc in the air. "No," she said. "No, no, it is not I. No!"

"Aphros, wait!" Gemma flung herself around Aphros's neck, hugging her tight. "It's okay. It's all going to be okay." She burst into tears—which at least stopped Aphros.

Aphros tucked her nose over Gemma's shoulder, hugging her back. "Oh, Gemma," she said. "Oh, Gemma."

Lily and Filibere crept back to Aphros's side, nuzzling at her in concern, tiny gold ears trembling.

Scott's jaw twitched. "I need an answer, Aphros," he said quietly. "Why didn't you help us?"

Aphros raised her gaze to meet his, liquid brown eyes wide. "I did not know," she said, just as soft. "I still do not."

I sighed explosively and swung my arms. "Right, well, there's only one way to figure this out, isn't there. Scott, get down."

I motioned him off the dais, and he glared at me, but obeyed. "Aphros, over here. Gemma, hold the twins back, please."

"Help me out," she said to Scott, and they took a foal each, hugging them firmly but gently around their shoulders.

Aphros hesitated with her front hoof suspended over the dais, the step a mere half-foot high but with the heady significance of a skyscraper.

I crossed to her and placed a hand on her neck. "Come on," I said. "It's going to be okay."

She snorted and gave her mane a little toss, but put her foot down—then the next one, and the next, and the next.

Nothing.

I let out my breath. Fine. We'd do this the hard way.

I reached toward her again, road mastery at the ready—

Green fire swept up through the room, blinding, glittering, and I raised my arms over my head as the wave of light flashed from floor to waist to ceiling.

I stood for a long moment, head tipped back, staring at the place where the light had vanished into the ceiling.

"Whoa," Gemma breathed—and the spell was broken.

I giggled. "Well, I think it's safe to say you're *some*thing, that's for sure." I glanced back at Aphros. "You sure you don't know anything about this?" I asked curiously.

She shook her head, one hind foot stomping.

A pop echoed through the chamber, and a puff of darkness dissipated over the middle of the plinth. My heart leapt to my throat—shadows, what were we going to do?

But as the smoke cleared, my eyes went round: it was Viri, green wings glittering, her face just as surprised as mine.

30

"YOU!" VIRI CURSED, face narrowing to hatred.

But unusually, it wasn't directed at me; she was glaring at Aphros.

"You cannot be here!" she snapped, practically crackling with anger. "It is not allowed!"

"Well why not?" Scott snapped back, arms still firmly wrapped around Lily's shoulders. "It's clear she belongs here, definitely more than you do. Why *shouldn't* she be here?"

"Yeah, what else have you been hiding?" Gemma added.

"That is not for you to understand!" Viri tossed her hair, eyes spitting metaphorical fire at us all.

Aphros stamped a hind foot. "I disagree, Viri," she said carefully. "I think it is exactly for us to understand. For me, in particular. You cannot be unaware of how this chamber has reacted to me. Perhaps that is even what called you here." Her ears lay back flat against her head and she stamped again. "In point of fact," she said, voice still level, "I demand an explanation."

"Oh, you demand, you demand," Viri sneered. "Well I hate to break it to you, *horse*, but it's none of your business. The fundamental rules being broken were bad enough. I won't tolerate them being flouted again." She raised a hand, and lightning crackled over her fingertips. "It's for your own safety, you know."

The lightning zapped from Viri's fingers, straight toward Aphros.

I didn't consciously think about it—I just sort of twisted sideways, and immediately back the other way again, and all of a sudden I was standing right behind Viri as she raised her arm—and I simply reached out and stopped her.

Her eyes widened so much they practically swallowed her face.

I smiled, a small, terrifying little thing. "I don't think so."

She remembered to breathe again. "No," she said, shaking her head in tiny, frantic movements. "No, you haven't."

"Haven't what?" I said, the smile still curled on my face like a waking lion.

"You can't have." She fluttered backward a little— and bumped into my other hand.

It had never really hit me before just how much *bigger* I was than the fairies—and Viri, it seemed, was having that same realisation, eyes darting this way and that as she realised I had her trapped.

"You were about to say," I told her, "that this is for Aphros's own safety. Something to do with the rules. I *think*," I added gravely, "that it's just about time you told us the truth. For once."

"Or what?" Viri sneered.

I shrugged. "Or nothing. We'll figure it out whether you tell us or not. Look at how much we already know. How much we can already *do*." I paused, holding her gaze for just long enough that I'd be able to make a point.

I twisted sideways and back again, landing on the other side of Viri just as she finished hearing the word 'do'.

Viri squeaked.

I smiled without my teeth. "What do you think?"

She held my gaze for a moment. Abruptly, she sank to the floor.

I moved with her, ready to slip back and catch her at the slightest hint she was up to something—but instead, shoulders slumping, head bowed, she stroked the minty-green floor of the dais. "I am sorry," she whispered. "I have failed you."

She vanished in a tongue of green flame and a quiet 'puff'. I jumped back as greenish-grey ash rained to the floor, forming a small pile—just small enough to have maybe weighed the same amount as Viri.

"Did she just...?" said Gem from the side of the chamber.

"I think so," Scott said back in a hushed voice.

Frantically, I skipped back.

But although I could see her, I couldn't touch her, couldn't interact with her—couldn't stop her from dying, even though I skipped, and skipped, and skipped.

I stopped, shoulders heavy with defeat, and tears prickled my eyes. Yes, fine, she'd tried to probably-kill us all last month when we'd been saving Gem, but this... This was too sudden, too unexpected.

I couldn't help it. I crumpled to the floor, face crumbling too, shoulders shaking as I cried. It wasn't fair. The whole thing just wasn't fair. If the stupid roads had just guarded themselves in the first place, not taken the awful memories from people... If they hadn't been so *selfish*, then none of this would have happened.

Aphros's soft nose touched the back of my bowed head, and she snorted gently, ruffling my hair.

I sat up, wiped my arm across my face with a great, sniffly inhale, and sighed. "I know," I said. "I know. We have to keep moving."

I stared at the pile of ash that, only a minute or so ago, had been Viri—alive, and annoying, and bright and sparkling. And alive, had I mentioned that?

I clenched my jaw against thoughts of Georgia. At least this death was clean. No blood, no bruises. I stared at the pile again. Just a little heap of ash, green and grey and—

I tilted my head. Green and grey and something shining metallically. Holding my breath, I reached for it with a single finger.

"What are you doing?" Gemma gasped, right as Scott said, "Ew, Emma, no."

But they couldn't see what I did. Gently, I brushed the ash aside—soft as butter, light as air—and underneath was a shining, metallic, greeny-gold stylised acorn, fat and round like a walnut shell, but definitely, from the little cap on top, supposed to be an acorn. I pick it up; it fit perfectly in my hand, and it reminded me of something, something I'd seen.

I inhaled sharply; the acorn was growing warm.

Hurriedly, I set it back down—and the cap popped open, and a tiny seedling made of nothing but green-gold light began to unfurl.

And that reminded me of where I'd seen it before: as the seedling became a sapling became a small tree, I remembered the first vision Helios had given me, of the kernel I'd discovered floating adrift in his power, and how when I'd touched it it had sprouted into a tree, showing that the Valley and Sanctuary had indeed once been whole.

The tree reached the ceiling and stopped growing up, instead putting out more branches and widening its trunk, until the whole chamber felt less like a room and more like the natural circular space created under the canopy of a tree.

The trunk widened and twisted until two people could have easily fitted inside—three people, four.

An arch began to glow in the trunk, and while the rest of us stood transfixed, it was Aphros who dared approach, one careful footstep at a time.

The arch widened to a doorway.

Aphros drew closer.

"Be careful," Scott said, and the trance jarred loose, and we all blinked and looked around to see how everyone else was reacting to this magic tree. He flushed, staring at the floor, one arm still draped around Lily. "Sorry. But it is the Valley."

"My babies," Aphros murmured, looking back at them, then at the tree again, then back to her babies. She tilted her head, ears flickering wildly. "I see them here, and yet I hear them within the tree." She stepped toward it again, nose outstretched, trembling.

Be okay, I thought, hands knotted at my sides. *Please let this be okay.*

Aphros stepped into the light of the tree.

The tree rustled, shivered—and in a flash of gold edged with sooty black, the whole tree sucked inward, shrinking in an instantaneous whirl, zipping back down to nothing—inside Aphros.

Aphros swayed.

"No!" Gem cried, reaching for her. But before she could make it, Aphros swayed again and fell to her knees.

Lily and Filibere whinnied and raced for their mother. They only barely beat the rest of us.

I sat, scooping Aphros's head into my lap while Gemma clung to her shoulder, sobbing.

"Aphros," Gem sobbed. "Aphros, get up."

I looked up as Scott knelt next to me, his eyes wide and serious and fearful.

"I should have stopped her," he said.

For the second time, my face crumbled. I swallowed and shook my head. "You warned her. We didn't know. You tried."

But as he reached for her face, his hands shaking, Aphros inhaled dramatically.

I dodged as her horn waved wildly, nearly skewering me, then Gemma, then Scott as she thrashed her head back and forth.

She stood, oblivious to us, and we scrambled aside as she shook violently, mane and tail flying, horn scribing a figure eight in the air.

Her eyes flew open; she stilled, statue-like.

Another great inhale—but this time she exhaled normally, and peered around. "Gemma? Scott? Edge? My babies!"

They flocked to her, nuzzling against her side and making little crooning noises, and she sniffed them over nose to tail, assessing them in a blink before tossing her head high and exhaling again. "I remember," she said, voice full of wonder. "I am made whole, and *I remember*."

31

APHROS STOOD. THERE was an almighty *floomp*, and two great, white wings suddenly unfurled from Aphros's sides, the wind of them knocking the three of us backward, though the babies stayed nuzzled against their mother's side.

I stared, wide-eyed, lips parted.

Aphros snorted and shook her head, her mane, stamped her front feet, danced on the spot—and flapped her massive, feathered wings, each one easily as tall as I was.

Lily whinnied.

Aphros swung around to nuzzle her, folding her wings neatly at her sides.

"What... What's happening?" Gem said, hesitantly. "Why... I mean... *How*? What's going *on*?"

Aphros snorted again. "That, Gemma, is an excellent question. But the real question is, what are we going to do about it?"

Scott hissed through his teeth impatiently. "Aphros, we're on a deadline to try to save the place. Riddles aren't going to help anyone."

I stepped toward her. "You're... You're the Valley's avatar, aren't you," I said. "Like Helios is for Sanctuary."

Gemma clapped a hand over her mouth. "The twins!" she mumbled.

Scott glanced at her curiously. "What about them?"

Gemma pointed. "They're gold. Like Helios. I always wondered why they were gold!"

Scott raised an eyebrow at Aphros. "But the twins were around before Helios, right? Unless they've been around forever, since Aphros"—he waved vaguely at her—"you know. Forgot. I mean, babies don't just actually spontaneously appear, right?"

"They appeared to me," Aphros said with a hint of amusement. "One day, I went home to the stables, and there they were, and I knew that they were mine, but I did not know how or why they came to be there."

I sniffed. "Mum'd *love* that."

"But I see now: they have come to me through the roads, through time." She nuzzled them again, first Filibere, then Lily. The two foals shook their heads and danced. "They have not yet been born," Aphros added. "And yet, on the roads, time is fluid. And so, here they are."

"Fascinating," Scott said with a strange expression, "but what does this mean? Edge is jumping back and forth in time on the roads, you're apparently the Valley's avatar... What happened to the glowy light? What happened," his hands fisted at his sides, "to the people it devoured?"

Oh. Right.

"I'm sorry," I murmured. "I don't think I can go back far enough." It was sort of like Gemma had said: I could sense the options stretching around me, and could feel where they stretched into the distance, beyond my reach.

And even if I could go back that far, the skips hadn't let me save Viri.

He shrugged me off. "I wasn't talking to you. I'm talking to Aphros, and I'm wondering why, if she's the literal embodiment of the Valley's power, she didn't do something to prevent all this happening in the first place!"

Lily and Filibere hid from the shouting under their mother's wings, peering out through the feathers and looking adorable, and tiny, and vulnerable.

I stepped to Lily's side and placed a reassuring hand against her flank.

"The rules were broken," Aphros said sadly.

"Yes, so we've heard. But are you going to tell us what those rules *were*, and why this *matters*, or are you going to just keep hiding things, like the fairies?"

"Scott," Gemma said reproachfully.

But personally, I thought he had a point. "What rules, Aphros? What happened? Helios showed me that the Valley used to be one with Sanctuary, and then they were two places but they were healthy, and then... then the black. Was that the shadows? Did they break the rules?"

Aphros was trembling. *Edge*, she sent softly. *Edge, I am sorry. I was not there, I could not help. I am sorry. I am sorry.* She hung her head, and I lay my free hand on her shoulder, and Gemma came to her other side.

"Hey," I soothed. "Hey, it's okay."

A gentle pop sounded behind me.

I jumped.

Quoise fluttered over the middle of the plinth, her arms clutching a spring-green book to her chest. "Aphros?" she said, peering around. "I couldn't get out of Sanctuary to find Maria. What's going on?" She saw Aphros and her new wings, and her mouth dropped open. "Oh my goodness," she said, her hand covering her mouth. "But, the rules!"

"Yes," said Aphros gravely. "But I rather think we are past that now, do you not think?"

Scott stamped his foot and flung his hands up in the air, whirling to pace a few steps away and then back again. "Will someone tell us what is going on?"

It wasn't like him to lose his cool like that, but I was glad he had, because it saved me from doing it.

"You haven't told them?" Quoise said, wide-eyed.

"Obviously," I snapped.

There was a moment of intense eye contact between Aphros and Quoise, and it struck me that perhaps Gemma and I weren't the only ones who could talk to Aphros without speaking.

Quoise sighed and fluttered over to perch on Aphros's head, trying to find somewhere to balance the book before giving up and hugging it to her.

Aphros twitched her ears as Quoise landed, but stayed still.

"I'll tell you," Quoise said.

"Thank goodness," Gemma murmured. "One of us was going to pop any second now."

My lips twitched, and I let myself down to sit cross-legged on the floor. Gemma came around to join me, and after a moment, Scott did too.

"A long time ago," Quoise began from up between Aphros's ears, "Aphros was the Valley's avatar. All the fairies know this, but until this happened just now"—she waved a hand around at the green room, the same colour as sunlight filtering through a soft-leafed forest—"Aphros didn't remember."

Aphros stamped her foot at that, and I realised that it wasn't just the humans here who were upset—with good reason. I'd been upset at the thought of the roads taking *one* of my memories; how would I feel if they'd taken all of them, and I'd had to start over again?

"We didn't remember as far back as the Valley and Sanctuary being one," Quoise clarified. "That was in the Book of Laws, which only Viri was allowed to read. Until, you know. Last month. But we knew about Aphros."

Last month Quoise had entered the Forbidden Chamber for the first time in order to save us from the Keeper, Viri—all while we tried to save Gemma from the power of the Valley.

"Wait a minute," I said. "If Aphros is the avatar of the Valley, the"—I waved my hands vaguely—"you know, it's body, then why did it have the weird glowy light thing that kept trying to take over people?"

"I'm getting to that," Quoise said. "So. A long time ago, Aphros was the Valley's avatar. But then— well, I told you the rumours about Sanctuary and the Valley being created, didn't I?"

We nodded, Gemma and I more agreeably than Scott.

"It's true," she said. "It's in the second part of the Book. The very first people to use the roads created Sanctuary and the Valley, and somehow set the land up with its own power source so it would continue to run after the creators died. Created worlds usually die with their creator," she added.

"I read that bit," I said. "About being able to create worlds. Gemma can do it."

Quoise nodded. "That may come in handy," she said, but instead of elaborating, she continued with her story. "Unfortunately, the roads became corrupted with the shadows. The only thing the creators of Sanctuary could think to do was to seal them within the Valley, sacrificing one half of their land in order to protect the other, and the roads."

"Bad memories," I said.

Quoise looked puzzled.

"The shadows came from the bad memories the roads skimmed from the people who travelled them."

"Ah," she said, brightening in understanding. "That makes a certain kind of sense."

She rubbed Aphros's ear, which had been twitching rapidly in front of her.

"Shhhh," she soothed. "It will be okay."

She looked back at us. "So. They tried to trap the shadows in the Valley, but the shadows were too strong. The hearts of both Sanctuary and the Valley are weak spots, thin places where it's easier to reach the roads than anywhere else. And the shadows broke through into the Valley's heart. The creators were there, but the best they could do was use the power of Sanctuary to cut Aphros free from the Valley in order to save her, and pen the shadows back into the Valley's heart." She bit her lip. "They…"

I nodded jerkily. "They died doing it," I said. "We know."

Quoise sighed heavily. "Aphros was connected to Sanctuary as a source of life for her, the shadows were trapped in the Valley. It lasted a good, long time. But then your mother arrived," Quoise said, nodding at Scott, "and she was a stronger Road Master than we'd had in centuries. She found the roads, and the Valley's heart, and..." She bit her lip again, eyes round.

Scott twitched his shoulders uncomfortably. "Yeah," he said. "They used her to get out."

Quoise nodded. "They did. They sucked her dry creating their own avatar, the glowing pillar of light, and when they'd used up all her power and still didn't have a proper body, they... came after you. And then Gemma."

Gemma shivered and pressed her knee close against mine, leaning her head on my shoulder.

I tipped my head over and hugged her with my cheek.

Scott's fingers twitched, and although he was fighting it, tears welled in his eyes.

I took his fingers and squeezed them so they'd stop, and he shot me a grateful look.

"There's one thing missing, though," I said, looking back up at Quoise. "What were the rules that were broken in all of this?"

Quoise hung her head. "That," she said, "is the greatest failure of the fairies, for it is we who broke the rules and failed Sanctuary." She took a deep, steadying breath. "The fairies were also created," she said. "Imagined as a later addition to Sanctuary by the world creator, and given life by the Road Masters, who took sensations from the roads to give us soulprints—and life."

My eyes grew round as saucers.

Scott edged his fingers out from where I was crushing them.

"It was our duty to protect the hearts," Quoise said. "Especially from the shadows. When it became clear that Aphros wouldn't be able to hold the shadows back alone, we were created to help her, to push back against the shadows from Sanctuary. But we failed.

"Viri… One of us listened to the shadows' pleas, felt sorry for them, trapped and penned. They convinced that fairy to let them out, and she agreed—only for a moment before she realised what she'd done and changed her mind, but it was long enough to break Aphros's hold on them."

She hung her head. "We failed, and the shadows escaped, and the creators of Sanctuary died to buy us time, and Aphros was sealed away from everything she was ever supposed to be in order to save her life."

32

I INHALED DEEPLY, the smell of mint filling my lungs, the taste of it sharp on my tongue. It felt good: fresh, and clean, and energising.

"Okay," I said, and everyone looked at me from where they'd drifted around the chamber, Quoise and Aphros in deep conversation just off the edge of the dais, the twins curled up asleep at Aphros's feet, Scott examining the wall where we'd entered in minute detail, and Gemma lying sprawled on the dais next to me.

I shifted slightly so I could see everyone. "We need to do something. While we've been sitting here, the shadows have probably taken over the heart of Sanctuary entirely, and I know we have the advantage of using time skips now"—probably, assuming I could always get them to work reliably—"but I really think it's time to move."

Scott raised an eyebrow. "And you have a plan for said movement, which you're going to share?"

I grinned. "Of course. Here's what we're going to do. Everyone?" I paused until I was sure I had their complete attention. "We're going to re-imagine Sanctuary."

Gemma sat up next to me. "Edge, I can barely imagine a twenty-foot grey box. How am I supposed to re-imagine the whole of Sanctuary?"

My grin didn't waver. "With help." I pointed around the room. "We have here the avatar of the Valley. We can get the avatar of Sanctuary no problems. You have a Road Master to help"—I pointed at myself—"and someone who knows how it was done before." I pointed at Quoise.

Gemma's gaze slid toward Scott, who I was studiously avoiding looking at.

"It's fine." He shrugged. "I'm sure I'll come in handy somewhere. Or not."

I chewed at the inside of my lip. I felt sorry for him, sure, but not enough to jeopardise my plan to save Sanctuary. Like he said. Priorities, right? "I'll need to figure out exactly how the time skips will work—"

"Oh," Quoise interrupted. "Here. This should help with that." She held out the green book she'd arrived with.

I took it, blinked—and a smile blossomed over my face. "The road mastery book!" I waved it at Scott. "This is the one I was looking for in the library!"

"There's a section in there on using the roads to time travel," Quoise said. "I tracked the book down the other day when you two disappeared from the library without a trace."

Scott and I exchanged glances. "Uh, yeah, we may or may not have, um, found the Forbidden Chamber that day," I said.

"You *what*?"

"Um," I said, "is this a bad time to tell you that the first half of the Book of Laws is currently on my bedside table at home?"

"First... *half*... Table? At *home*?" Quoise said faintly. She fanned herself and closed her eyes dramatically. "Well," she said. "I hope you at least had the good sense to *read* it, though you must actually have less than half if you didn't get to the bit about Aphros and the creators and the shadows."

I nodded. "Probably. I do have the bit that proves that Viri's been overstepping her role as Keeper, though." I tried hard not to grin, I really did. "I'd say our shiny new re-imagined Sanctuary might be just the cue everybody needs for a new person to take on that role."

Quoise giggled behind her hand. "Oh, Edge."

Gemma shook her head. "Edge. You know this is madness, right? You get how impossible this all is?

285

Create a whole new world out of nothing? But one which is exactly like another world that already exists?" She shook her head. "Impossible." But her tone was one of wonder, not defeat. Still, she added, "Couldn't we just try locking the shadows away again?"

I shook my own head at that, and emphatically. "Gem, the original creators of Sanctuary, the firsts, they died trying to make that work, and Scott's mum died because it didn't."

"It worked for a little while," she said, sighing.

"Do you really want to be responsible for any future deaths the shadows might cause?"

"No," she said, and sighed again. "You're right, of course. You always are. I..." She darted a glance at me. "I'm sorry I didn't listen to you. Earlier. When you said we had to come do something."

I shrugged. "If we had, we might not have uncovered all of this." I gestured broadly at the room. "After all, we definitely wouldn't have brought Aphros here unless we were desperate."

"I'm going to need help," Gemma said, firmly this time. "I believe that what you're suggesting is possible, but it's too big for me to manage on my own. I can't keep the whole of Sanctuary in my head at once, and you have to do that to build the world—it's like travelling, only you have to keep the *whole thing* in your mind, not just the entrance alcove."

"Aphros," I said. "And Helios. You're connected to both of them. You can talk to Helios long range, too, like you can with Aphros, right?"

She nodded.

Aphros tossed her head. "We can help you with this," she said. "Helios is made of Sanctuary, and I of the Valley. If you stay connected to us, we can hold the vision of them in your mind for you."

"See?" I nodded firmly. "Great. So that's that part organised. Quoise," I said. "What did the Road Masters have to do to help?"

She pointed at the book in my lap. "The last chapter in there suggests you'll need to work with Gemma to infuse a soulprint into her imagined world, in order for it to function effectively without either of you around. The creators made the hearts, remember, so that Sanctuary and the Valley wouldn't die with them."

My heart pounded at my chest. "So... You're saying Gemma needs to re-imagine Sanctuary, and I need to re-imagine the hearts?"

No wonder they'd needed two of them to do it. Oy.

Quoise nodded. "Not quite, though. You only need to connect the hearts that already exist; you won't need to make entirely new ones."

"And the fairies? They were created too, right, so..." I trailed off. "How do we do this without erasing you all?"

She smiled gently. "You'll need to re-imagine us, too. Just like the first Road Masters did."

"But I don't know how to do this," I said too quickly. "What if I get it wrong? What if one of you comes back different, or doesn't come back, or—"

Quoise waved dismissively, grinning. "The last chapter." She nodded toward the road mastery book. "All you need is our soulprints."

"Well, sure," I said, "but how many of you are there? A hundred? More?" I shook my head. "I don't have time to learn all your soulprints, and even if I did, I couldn't guarantee I'd be able to remember them accurately to bring you back."

Quoise tilted her head. "Oh, my. If only there were some permanent record we had of everyone's soulprints, something contained and small and portable that you could, I don't know, activate when you needed them."

My face lit up. "You have them saved."

When Gemma had been missing a month ago, stolen by the shadows, I'd needed a way to track her through the Valley and its layers of dimensions. Quoise had taken me to a room with two walls covered in tiny drawers, all locked behind glass that vanished when Quoise touched it with a key.

Inside each drawer had been a glass vial about as big as my pinky, each one containing the soulprint of a visitor to Sanctuary—*every* visitor, and, it appeared, every fairy.

I frowned. "But Quoise. There's still well over a hundred of you. To open and activate every single one will take at least..." I trailed off, trying to do the maths. From what I could remember, I might be able to do maybe two or three per minute.

Which meant... "Thirty minutes to an hour. We don't have that long. Gemma will have the place reimagined in under a minute once she gets going."

Quoise shook her head, grinning. "Edge, you're thinking too linearly. All you have to do is activate one, cycle back in time using a skip, activate the next one, cycle back, and so on. You don't need thirty minutes when you're on the roads and can use the same minute over thirty times."

I hugged her—gently. "Quoise, you're a genius."

"Pshaw." She flapped her hands down from the wrists.

"It's going to be rough," I said though. "That's a lot of concentration, all while I'm on the roads. What if I forget what I'm doing? What if I get distracted by the roads and lose myself?"

Scott stepped up. "That sounds like a job for me," he said. "See? I told you I'd be useful somehow." His face was mostly serious, but I caught the light in his eyes that meant he was joking around.

I bumped him with my shoulder. "You?" I said. "Useful? Pah. Never gonna happen."

I grinned though, and although he narrowed his eyes at me, his lips twitched. I inhaled, shook myself all over, and exhaled firmly. "Right. So Gemma is going to re-create Sanctuary-slash-the-Valley, with Helios and Aphros's input. I am going to connect the hearts to the land that she creates"—somehow, magically—"and then Scott is going to help me re-create the fairies."

I turned to Quoise. "Two things. One, are the portals into Sanctuary still sealed so no one can get in, and is there some way to do that for the Valley as well? The last thing we need is someone appearing as everything's changing."

Quoise nodded. "I can manage that. If I go back through here"—she waved to the centre of the dais— "I'll be well placed to lock down access to the Valley. There are one or two others who can help me."

I nodded once. "Good. And the second thing I was going to say is, Scott"—I turned to him—"I'm probably going to need to be able to see you and speak to you." This whole thing was too complicated, too important, to leave to coded hand squeezes—and I might need both my hands free. "So we're going to have to find that part of the roads again where we can talk."

He gave a tiny shrug. "No worries."

"Gem," I said, "where will you be? We need to sync up our activities somehow so I can do the soulprint thing as you're creating the actual world, so, I don't know; could you work from that place on the roads too?"

She shrugged. "Probably. Yeah, I don't see why not."

I looked around at everyone, holding my breath. Aphros, with her beautiful new wings; the gorgeous, golden twins; Quoise, looking determined and wildly excited; Gemma, just about ready to faint with nerves, I thought, but jaw also set in determination; and Scott, the very last person I'd ever have expected to be here to help us save Sanctuary.

Just look at us all, about to save the world. I snorted softly. "All right, team," I said. "Let's get Helios and get this show on the road."

33

"ARE YOU READY?" I asked Gem, trying not to let nerves waver in my voice. Around us, the grey stillness of the heart of the roads lay silent. I wasn't sure if they'd cottoned on to what we were trying to do yet—I could only assume they had, since they could pretty much pluck things from our minds—but they hadn't responded to my greetings.

Still. So long as they weren't going to interfere, that wasn't really a problem.

"No," said Gemma in response to my question. Her lips twitched briefly into half a smile. "Let's get started, this is killing me."

"And Sanctuary," Scott added.

I rolled my eyes, but he was right: we'd snuck back a little to get into the Lodge and retrieve the soulprint records before the shadows could get there, but the only way to find Helios had been to travel back to Sanctuary in the present—and it was looking pretty bleak.

Darker than ever, it was hard to see even the stables from the Lodge at the top of the slope, and instead of the usual calming atmosphere, I'd spent the whole brief excursion with the back of my neck prickling and my spine between my shoulder blades crawling.

"Okay," I said. "Gem, the timing's on you. Let me know when you're ready for me to pull in the soulprints."

She nodded, brown cheeks flushed, and gripped her hands tightly together in front of her. She shut her eyes. "Wait." She flung her arms down by her sides. "This feels stupid. Here, I'm going to sit down." She sat cross-legged and looked up at me.

I sat, one knee touching hers, the other touching Scott's as he made the third side of our triangle. "I'm not going to be able to stay here," he murmured, gesturing to the three huge backpacks behind him that contained the glass vials of the fairies' soulprints.

I nodded. "Let's just start."

Gemma closed her eyes again.

A breeze began to play over us; strands of hair tickled my cheeks. I swept them aside.

She must be talking to Aphros and Helios, getting her vision of Sanctuary straight.

Frogging elephants, I wished I could hear what was going on. I shifted restlessly.

The breeze picked up to a wind, and I glanced around. Was this Gemma's doing, or an unavoidable side effect, or something else?

Aphros, I sent. *What's going on?*

Shhh, Edge. We are dreaming the world.

I closed my eyes—and inhaled sharply. With my road mastery, I could see dark clouds swirling in a vortex around us—not dark like the shadows, but a darker version of the grey world Gemma had taken us to our first time on the roads.

And beneath it all, a sense of unease, my stomach rolling, shoulders tensing...

It took a moment for me to realise that, once again, these sensations weren't mine, but the roads'.

It's okay, I told them. *We can do this.*

Fear, dread.

Images of projects going wrong—a rocket exploding just after takeoff, someone falling from a wire.

The wind swirled, hard enough now that my hair streamed back and my t-shirt flapped.

A long, high-pitched whine built around us.

Roads, I said sternly, *you have to let us do this.*

A child hiding under a blanket; someone pulling away from a nurse holding a needle; a toddler wailing as firm hands brushed her hair.

Bass notes, pounding, thumping, deep drum beats starting slow, but getting faster, faster, faster.

I'd heard these noises before, seen the same flickering flames and darkness that I could sense out on the very edges of my road mastery: the strange and awful guardians that we'd seen on our first trip into the roads, and never again since.

Acknowledgement.

A sense of curiosity, of someone watching a small group of travellers with interest; then fear, and the creatures appearing like claws out of their sheaths.

The drums beat louder, closer.

Different travellers, in ones or twos or threes, seeing the creatures and falling away, terrified, off the roads, never to return.

Suddenly, I understood: the beasts were just the roads, a defence system, the roads' way of scaring off people it didn't want on them.

At the edges of my road mastery, I felt them draw nearer.

But you let us through, I shouted over the roar of the wind that now whipped over us. *You let us through! You liked us!*

Sadness, a tear rolling down someone's cheek—I could feel it as though it were my own—a sense of loss.

Nothing's changed! I told the roads, shouting now over the noise of the wind and the constant, frantic pounding of the drumbeats. *We're still here to help! We're* trying *to help. Please, let us try this.*

Fear. A body of a woman—one of the creators—lying still on the ground, limbs at haphazard angles, eyes staring lifelessly.

We are not going to die.

Possibilities. Options unfurling like fractals in fluorescent green and yellow and blue in the roaring darkness around us.

My hair whipped against my face, sticking to my mouth.

Drumbeats, faster, faster, until they were nearly seamless.

No, I said. *Not today. Today we are going to save Sanctuary—and you.*

The roads stilled, the thumping beat of the drums cut short, though the wind still swirled and roared.

Please, I said. *Let us try.*

The roads didn't answer—but the feeling of being watched slowly drained away, the flickers of flame faded.

I breathed out, and my shoulders dropped. *Thank you.*

"Okay," Gemma shouted over the wind. "I have the vision stable, I can see Sanctuary, and I can see the Valley, but there's something missing. They're not linking like they should!"

I forced my attention away from the roads and back to the problem at hand. With my road mastery,

I could see exactly what she meant: above us, her vision of the new Sanctuary shimmered—but it was two visions, not one, Helios's and Aphros's, with an ugly seam in the middle.

We needed something else, something extra, some tie between Aphros and Helios...

Of course. "The babies!" I shouted back. "Use the babies as a link!"

"Duh, of course!" Gem went silent for a bit, then, "It's working! They're working perfectly as a bridge between the two!"

I grinned, covering my mouth with the side of my index finger. We were really going to do this. Above us, the seam began to blur gold with little streaks of copper and blue, the light diffusing out into the Valley and into Sanctuary, erasing the gap between them.

Gemma tensed. "I've got it," she shouted, melting in relief. "It's nearly there! The babies, they did it! Go Lily! Go Filibere!"

Yes. Yes yes yes yes *yes*.

"Wait!" Gem cried.

My heart jolted as I saw what was happening: power siphoning out from the distant babies into the vision above us, the gold shimmer, the vision growing clearer and sharper—and the sense of Lily and Filibere fading.

"Wait, it's using them up!" Gem shouted. "Aphros, pull them back! No! No, stop!"

She grabbed at my hand, and I held it tightly.

"Edge, I can't stop it! They've connected Sanctuary and the Valley but the connection is draining their life force, they're going to die and I can't save them!"

"I see it!" I shouted back. Frantically, I tried tugging at their connection with my road mastery. "I can't detach them!"

It is alright, Aphros sent, voice eerily calm amid the roaring wind. *They have not yet been born. I will see them again one day soon. Let them help us now as they may.*

"They're still too young to die!" I screamed back, both aloud and internally to Aphros. "If the connection drains all their life force, you might see them again when they're younger, but this will be it for them both!"

"A time skip, Edge," Scott said urgently into my ear. "Can you reach them from here?"

I shook my head—I'd never reached something from so far away before, and I couldn't time skip now, I had to stay here. "I can't leave!"

"But they can!"

Could I send someone away without me? I had no idea—but this seemed like a mighty good time to try.

I stretched my road mastery out toward the heart of the Valley where the twins had stayed with Aphros. Further, further...

It wasn't far enough. I couldn't reach. Not like this, anyway.

The wind raged as I disconnected my road mastery from my body like I'd done twice before and pushed it onward, further.

The green. Follow the green.

I swayed.

My stomach heaved and lights flashed around me.

Further. Further. *Come on! You have to do this.*

Somewhere back near my body, Gemma was sobbing.

It hurt.

I couldn't breathe.

But the twins were *just there*, copper streak and flash of blue.

"Send... them out," I gasped, hoping I was saying it to Aphros. "Can't... quite reach."

Please. Please understand, I begged.

My heart skipped as the two soulprints began moving toward me.

That's it. Closer, closer...

I grabbed them, registered how faint and weightless they were—nearly completely gone—and *twisted*.

At the last possible instant, I let go—and the twins twisted through the roads without me. I had no idea where I'd sent them, but I'd felt a flash of gratitude from them, and a sense of calm.

They were going to be okay.

I stopped straining, and my road mastery snapped back into my body with the force of a speeding car.

Knocked flat on my back, I worked at reminding my body how to breathe.

Beside me, Gemma let out another sob, but she didn't move—I couldn't see exactly what she was doing right now, but I could tell it was taking all the concentration she had.

Scott reached for my hand, and I clung to it, hauling myself back up.

Aphros was right. We'd see them again. They weren't gone for good. I smeared the tears off my cheeks and shuffled to reform our triangle, knees pressing against Scott's and Gem's.

Gemma tensed again, leaning forward, staring intently at something no one else could see. "There's something else now," she said urgently. "I've got the vision whole, but something's preventing it from taking hold."

"Soulprints?" Scott shouted at me, eyebrows raised questioningly.

I nodded. Time to feed the soulprints into the new land, and hopefully blot out the shadows. I took a deep breath, and closed my eyes.

34

ABOVE US, SANCTUARY and the Valley unfurled, dim and ghostly and—from what I could make out—perfectly formed. Gemma had done well.

Now it was my turn, and hopefully I could do her handiwork proud.

The wind raged around us, swirling, biting. Soulprint, soulprint. Somehow, I had to get the soulprints of Sanctuary and the Valley back in there, connecting them to their hearts.

A movement caught my attention—shadows. The shadows were forcing their way through from the roads as they sensed the new world forming, travelling down the connection between Gemma and her imagined world, fading in and out as Sanctuary did. The harder Gemma worked at forming the world into reality, the stronger the shadows became; but if she slackened off and they faded away, so too did Sanctuary. She had no way of making one real without the other.

What could I do?

Well, first things first: I had to try to get Aphros and Helios connected to Gemma's new land. At the moment, they were connected to it only through their connections with Gemma, the cord from Helios bright and gold, and Valley's cord now green instead of the deep black it had been, thanks to Aphros.

No wonder she'd been able to merge soulprints with us to save us when we were in the heart of the Valley. No wonder her hair repelled the shadows.

Wait, there was something in that.

"Scott!" I shouted.

He leaned close, replied—but I couldn't hear what he said over the raging wind and the need to concentrate fiercely on what was going on above our heads.

"The ward!" I shouted. "I need the unicorn ward!"

His knee bumped against mine as he moved. Stillness... And then the rough, wiry braid being wrapped around my wrist, knotted tightly in place.

"Thanks!"

Warm pressure around my arm.

Okay. I had to get the shadows away from the connection to the new Sanctuary—and then do something to make sure they wouldn't come back again, but that was problem two.

I had my road mastery, which could attract their attention, and I had the ward, which could repel them. Now to see if my harebrained, desperate idea would work.

Carefully, I fed a little trickle of my road mastery into the braid and felt it warm around my wrist.

"Gem!" I called, hoping she'd be able to understand me. "Imagine harder. I need the shadows practically real. And… this might hurt a bit."

I didn't hear her reply, but surely enough, the vision above us intensified, colours brightening, edges sharpening—and the shadows darkening where they climbed the connection between Gem and the vision.

Deep breath.

Keeping the tiny bit of road mastery connected with the braid, I sent the rest out above me, that weird, cellophane noise accompanying the movement. Closer, closer…

The shadows were climbing higher, drawing near to the new Sanctuary.

I moved faster.

Closer. Bit more. Nearly there. Not too close, or I wouldn't have space to get away.

There.

Now the painful bit.

I let the power *flow*, as though it was spilling out of me. Silver light flashed. Bells tinkled, and the smell of vintage roses appeared.

The shadows halted their climb, and I felt them staring.

Come on, I thought, vaguely aware that my body was panting and gasping.

My lungs hurt. So did my head, fire searing from behind my eyes down to the top of my spine.

Gritting my teeth, I forced more power out through my road mastery—and vomited.

Frogs. I hoped it had missed Scott and Gem. Probably, since I could distantly recognise the feel of Scott's arm around my shoulders.

Acid burned my throat and sinuses—but the silver light flashed again, the bells rang louder, and the shadows reversed direction and began leaping down the connection toward me.

I waited until they were just above Gem's head before I let my road mastery begin backing away.

The shadows followed, racing into Gemma's body.

She screamed.

Keep coming! I shouted at the shadows, flashing power through my road mastery again.

The silver light flared, the bells rang, the smell of roses filled the air—and I vomited again, like someone had turned me inside out.

Come on! I told them.

The leaders left Gemma behind and leapt at my road mastery.

I reeled it back toward me.

The shadows drew nearer—almost all of them had left Gemma now, space folding weirdly so that the distance between her and me seemed like halfway to forever.

My road mastery collided with my body.

I rocked, fighting for balance.

The last shadow left Gemma.

"Now!" I screamed through the roar of the wind, the nausea in my stomach, the fear, the adrenalin, the shadows leaping toward me like a train bearing down on me. "Imagine it fully, Gemma! Now!"

The vision snapped to full, glowing colour above us.

The shadows pivoted toward it.

"No!" I shouted, activating the ward in my hand. I retched again and the surreal feeling of seeing my body splayed out in front of me intensified.

Knives stabbed my belly; fire burned in my throat.

I forced my road mastery away from me again, dragging the power of the ward with it, dragging my own soulprint out of my body, the cellophane crackling of my road mastery moving tearing at my ears like it would make them bleed.

The shadows raced at me.

My road mastery leapt over them, my body gasping for air.

I stretched at the top of the leap—and there was Gemma's connection with the new Sanctuary. I wrapped the power of the ward around it, and sent one last immense burst of power toward it, the flashing silver light, tinkling bells, and rose scent of my own soulprint filling the air.

The shadows would get back up through that connection only over my literal dead body.

35

THE WARD'S POWER severed Gemma's connection with her imagined land.

As the two ends of the connection snapped away, I grabbed, hunting frantically for the green and the gold. Hurry, hurry… I was holding onto consciousness by a thread, my whole body pounding.

There, right there.

I latched onto the green and gold with my road mastery, dragged them upward…

And as Gemma's connection fell away, blasted by the unicorn ward so that no more shadows could follow, the strand of green and the strand of gold were left, still connected to the land above us.

I held them for as long as I could, supporting the connection—and as I fell away, my road mastery weak and faint and snapping back toward my body, relief washed over me: it was working. Helios and Aphros's connections to the land was strengthening, their power flowing into the land where it swirled around, strengthening further before returning to them.

At once, I saw how this connection would be able to sustain them; Helios wouldn't need to be connected to a human in order to maintain his body, because his connection with the land would do it.

My road mastery collided with my body. I reeled, landing flat on my back.

After a moment, my vision stopped spinning. "I'm okay," I croaked to Scott, who was feverishly checking for a pulse in my neck.

And it was true. I ached like nothing I'd ever felt before, and my stomach felt like it wouldn't settle for days—but I was okay.

And above us, Helios's gold power and Aphros's green power were merging and mixing, filling up the land with self-sustaining power.

And that was why there had been two of them, I realised, watching the green and gold powers swirling through the land, filling it from the dirt deep beneath the surface, all the way up to the tips of the grass, creeping up the trees, up the mountains, up, up, up until the land glowed. The two powers merged, blending into a unified spring-green glow, like sunshine through soft spring leaves; Sanctuary and the Valley were whole again, with two hearts that beat in unison to power this glorious, imaginary place.

Awe for the first creators filled me, and I stared up at the land in wonder. To have imagined all this alone, that first time, to have called Aphros and Helios into being to sustain the land...

I pressed my hands to my cheeks.

But there was still one thing left to deal with—the shadows. They swarmed hungrily around Gemma's feet, searching for a way in.

The lingering power of the unicorn ward I'd broken over her was holding them at bay for now, but they recognised her as the way into the new Sanctuary, and they were circling like sharks, and they weren't going to give up any time soon.

I could take Gemma away, just step off the roads into her new version of Sanctuary and leave the shadows behind.

But I couldn't leave them here. They'd break through eventually, just as they'd break through from wherever we trapped them.

But what was I going to do with them? Sure, Aphros's wards could hold them at bay, but if she hadn't been able to banish them completely before now, it seemed hardly likely that the wards could do it now.

I bounced the inside of my lip between my teeth. I was missing something.

The shadows were memories. Bad memories. The roads had shoved them aside, they'd grown...

I sighed. That was the key, of course. You couldn't just shove bad memories aside and hope they'd go away. Bad memories festered. You had to learn how to process them, how to let them be without letting them overpower you.

I'd learned that. I still wasn't great at it—like anything, it was a skill you had to practice—but with the police psychologist's help, I had enough skills under my belt to deal with my own dark memories without getting crushed.

I sighed again and pulled myself up into a sitting position, groaning as I met sore muscles I didn't know I had, shoulders heaving.

Scott wrapped one arm around me and drew me against him, helping me stay mostly upright.

In front of me, Gemma had collapsed forward over her folded legs. I reached out and coaxed her toward me, and she curled up with her arms cushioning her head in my lap. I twined my fingers through her hair.

Roads? I sent, exhausted and spent, but surrounded by my best friends in the whole wide world, both lending me whatever strength they had left.

Panic in my chest that wasn't mine.

Please, I said. *I can't destroy you. I don't know how, and even if I did, I wouldn't do it. But I can help you.*

Disbelief, a man scoffing, a woman sniffing scornfully.

Look. I tilted my head toward the newly made Sanctuary above me, still glowing, a spot of calm in the wind that roared like a tornado around us. *I can help you. I know how. I promise.*

Silence, empty of everything but the gale.

Please, I said. *Trust me.*

The wind died away with a snap so sharp my ears rang, and for a moment I shook my head against Scott's shoulder, wondering if the wind had really stopped or if I'd finally gone deaf.

But no: the raging winds were gone, and slowly my mind adjusted to the silence.

I took a deep breath. *This is hard,* I said, assuming the abrupt death of the wind was a good sign and that I had the roads' attention. *Really hard. You're going to have to actually look at the memories.*

Panic; frantic creatures, small and furry, fleeing madly through the dark, tiny, squeaky screams going with them.

Trust me, I said. *I know.* Visions of blood and shadow filled my mind: the shadows, chasing me through the Valley; the zombie trees, snatching at my shoulders, my arms, my hair, roots lifting to trip my feet; Georgia.

Usually, I breathed hard and imagined a waterfall washing them all away; this time, I opened myself up to the roads, slowly, hesitantly.

It recoiled. *I don't want it, I don't want it.*

Please, I said small-ly as my fingers clenched. Distantly, I felt Gemma detangle them from her hair and wrap them in her hands. *You don't have to take it. But please just look.*

The roads' attention came back around slowly, one tiny space at a time. *It hurts.*

Yeah, I said, feeling the panicked nausea well in my stomach. I pushed it down. *It does. It's awful, and it sucks, but—*I inhaled. *But you can't run from it. All you can do is learn to live with it.*

How? the roads begged. *How can you do that? It hurts so much.*

I stumbled as a reel of images flashed past, schoolyard bullying and a car crash victim and bodies in the wreckage of a building and more and more and on and on and on, every horrible, awful thing people had ever done to each other or experienced.

I heaved, but there was nothing left in my stomach to come up—nothing except a little more acid, its burn still less than the horror of the images.

I wiped my mouth with the back of my wrist, wiped my wrist off on the side of my formerly-blue shirt. *Yeah,* I gasped at the roads as Scott clutched my shoulders tighter. *Yeah, it's awful. But what's the alternative?*

The roads shoved the memories it had shown me away so hard I nearly fell. An unreal wall of brick slammed up in front of me, twice as tall as I was and climbing fast.

I reached out toward the vision that seemed so real, so close—and I touched the un-wall gently, just with my fingertips. *I know*, I said. *I know you want to run and hide. I know you just want to cut the memories loose, shut everyone off.* I'd done that for eight weeks over Christmas, mostly by force—but I hadn't exactly made an effort to make new friends, either. *But are you really happy that way?*

Yes. The shushing, multiple voices of the roads were petulant, like a toddler clinging to a point of view they knew was wrong out of sheer spite.

You can't lock yourself away, I said. Like Sanctuary, the real world would always call you back eventually; you couldn't stay hidden from it forever.

Images of the shadows. *We can lock* them *away. Make better rules, so no one will find them.*

I shook my head. *You know you can't. Rules can't keep you safe. They're important, good rules are great, but you can't rely on them, roads. Someone will break them eventually, and you can't keep running forever. The only thing that can keep you safe is you—and trusting someone to help you.*

Ideas whirled in my head about my own life, my own running—our family's running. Maybe, just maybe, I was talking to myself here too.

And maybe—just maybe—there was something I could do.

But I had to solve this problem first, or the other wouldn't matter; the shadows were circling around us now, and I wasn't getting out of this alive if I couldn't convince the roads to listen.

I held out my hand toward the wall in front of me. *Will you? Trust me? Let me help?* I waited, breath caught in my chest, eyes scrunching so tightly closed they hurt. *Please,* I thought to myself. *Please say yes.*

An exhalation; the sense of someone taking my hand. The wall vanished. *Show us.*

36

AND SO I did: for the first time in a long time, I let the memory of Georgia consume me.

The open-air train station bustled with commuters in the after-school rush, the smell of hot concrete and trains mingling with the hot chips a knot of students were noisily consuming further down the platform, their navy-blue blazers rounding their shoulders so they looked like a cluster of formally-attired gulls, licking salt from their fingers and laughing, eyes bright, smiles wide.

They must have been dripping with sweat in this late spring humidity—and indeed, the brown-haired boy cradling the butcher's paper package in one arm had thrown off his blazer, had it slung nonchalantly over his shoulder, and sweat had darkened his light-blue shirt—under his arms, over his back.

The chips smelled good regardless.

I stayed away from the boisterous group, my thumbs tucked into the straps of my backpack, heavy with the weight of my textbooks, and cast them little side glances, longing more for their hot chips than the sense of belonging they exuded.

I had my own friends, my own group, and even though I caught a different train home than any of them, even though they always decided what we were going to do without asking me—Grace especially—it didn't matter, because I didn't know any better, and they were my friends.

I shifted restlessly as a train took off in the opposite direction, hot air puffing against my face like an oven, and glanced at the count-down timer over our own platform. Six minutes until my train.

Six minutes was long enough to pee, right?

Right.

The crowd had thinned with the departure of that last train, and I didn't have to dodge anyone as I made my way back down the gum-stained platform to the awful, dingy toilet block.

I hated using train station toilets—but it was this, or hold for the forty minutes it took to get home.

I glanced around to make sure no one was watching, and used my skirt over my hand to protect me from the grime and germs as I twisted the handle of the toilet door.

Inside, white tiles about ten centimetres square lined the floor and the first foot of the walls—an attempt at something classy that fell way, way short when paired with dingy beige walls with cracked paint, covered in stains and festooned with cobwebs.

Used paper towels littered the floor, damp, scrunchy breeding grounds for disease, and someone had spilled something dark red all over the floor.

I clapped my hand over my mouth as I realised it looked like blood. I'd seen stalls before spattered inside with blood where some woman had clearly been having the period of her life, but this was next level again. Gross.

I hovered in the doorway, unsure if I really wanted to deal with this today.

Hold for forty minutes, or step over some disgusting woman's mess? They'd probably missed the sanitary bin and left a tampon lying on the floor, and it had seeped into a puddle of water or something—because that was an awful lot of blood.

Forty minutes. Eh.

I stepped forward—and my brain registered what was going on before my eyes or body did, because I hadn't even stopped moving when I started to scream, and by the time I stopped dead the scream had already ended, and I was backing up against the wall, hands over my mouth, my backpack crushed between me and the sink, tears stinging my eyes, gasping, stomach heaving—

Breathe, Edge, breathe, remember how to breathe, it isn't Anna, it isn't, it can't be Anna, she's at school, she's still at school, and look, that's not your uniform, it's close but it's not quite right and oh God above, please let this be a joke, this can't be real, she isn't dead, she isn't, she isn't, her *face*.

So much blood.

So much blood.

So much blood.

Screaming, high-pitched and painful, shrieking, and I was sobbing, sobbing, sobbing, and the roads around me screamed and writhed. *It hurts,* they cried. *No, it hurts, please stop!*

But I couldn't, I was there, and it was like the last four months had never happened, and there was Georgia right there, right now, in front of me, and I was shaking and I knew I was supposed to do something to back out of the memory, but I couldn't remember, it was too vivid, too real, she was *right. there.*

"Edge, Edge please, come on!"

"We're here, Edge, it's okay, we're here for you. We've got you."

Someone was holding me, rocking me.

Someone else was in my lap, clinging around my waist.

"Hush, Edge. It's okay. I know. I know. But I've got you."

"Please, Edge. Please come back to me!"

Stop! the roads screamed. *Please, we want you to stop!*

I hurt all over, inside and out. My road mastery felt faint, and ragged. My stomach was rolling in panic, my chest heaving.

But Gemma was here, and Scott, and they were holding me tight.

Around us, the shadows twined.

I forced myself to draw in a long, long breath to cut through the panic.

Please stop, the roads whimpered.

"Like this," I whispered to them, and slowly, slowly, one tiny, baby step at a time, I drew on the steps the police psychologist had taught me.

Acknowledge the memory. *I see you, Georgia.*

Locate it in my body. *My stomach heaving. Chest tight, gasping. Face and hands tight. Spine crawling.*

Take control of my body. *Deep breaths, long and slow. Relax the hands. Untense my face.*

Can't do much about the stomach or the spine, but breathe. Long and slow. Long and slow.

Separate my thoughts from the memory. *There's Georgia, over there.*

Here's me. Separate.

Still panicky, but separate.

I felt the roads watching, focusing intently on what I was doing.

Legitimise the fear. *Yep, totally rational to be terrified when you find a murdered body who looks like your sister.*

319

This is logic. This is a rational, normal response. There is nothing wrong with this response.

Reassure it. *I take this fear seriously. I can take the following steps to address it: stay with my friends in strange places. Keep our location secret. Stay in contact with the police. Let someone know where I'm going. Be on my phone to someone when I enter a strange place so if I get knocked out, someone will know. Use my road mastery to make sure no one dangerous is around.*

This is a legitimate fear. I have taken steps to address it.

I remembered how I'd felt when I'd defeated the shadows that first time—like finally, I'd taken control of something I was afraid of, like I'd stood up to it—and won.

I am calm, I told myself. *I am in control. I acknowledge this memory as a part of my identity. I acknowledge that I will never be rid of it, and that it will shape who I become. But memory?* I addressed the image of Georgia in the train station bathroom directly, as an image in my head, but separate and distinct from my own thoughts. *You are not in control. You have made me who I am*—and it had, in so, so many ways, I realised: because of this event, I had Gemma, and Scott, and Sanctuary; because of this, I had grown the courage to stand up for my friends, for my family, to battle the shadows, to fight for what I believed in; I'd learned that standing up for things meant making sacrifices, like my dad had, but that I was capable of defeating the darkness in the end.

Tears rolled down my cheeks.

You have made me who I am.

I wrapped one arm around Gemma in my lap, still hugging my waist, and my other arm around Scott, still holding me tight.

But you are not in charge.

In my mind's eye, I imagined a river, deep and clean and wide, and full of things like love, like friendship, like the people who were there for me over and over and over again, like the smell of Mum's chocolate-chip cookie soulprint, like the sound of Dad laughing, like pleasant dreams and Sanctuary and the smell of Aphros's soulprint, the way I'd felt when I'd realised Gemma was safe, the look in Scott's eyes when he'd realised for the first time that *he* was...

I let all of it spill into the river, and let the river wash over the image of Georgia in the bathroom, sweeping it away.

Around me, another river ran, silver and shining and barely visible to my sorely weakened road mastery—a river created by the roads, washing away the shadows.

Somehow, I knew that we wouldn't be seeing the shadows again—and that the next time I remembered Georgia's face, I'd thank her, because even though I'd much rather she be alive, it was because of her unintentional sacrifice that I was here—and that Anna was.

And while I couldn't skip back in time far enough to stop her dying, I could use the rest of my *future* time to make sure that she hadn't died for nothing.

Goodbye, I whispered as the rivers faded.

And the roads whispered back, *Goodbye*.

37

I BREATHED A deep sigh of relief as Scott capped the last of the vials and tossed it onto the thigh-high pile next to us. It landed with a clink that I barely noticed through the sensations of sandpaper against my fingertips, the feel of hot, tropical, summer sun beating down on me, and the smell and taste of the world's freshest, ripest, most perfect peach in my mouth, juice dribbling down my chin.

Carefully, I rolled all the sensations together, forcing them down with my road mastery, pressurising them, more and more and more until—

Pop.

The fleeting sensation of an orange-winged fairy before she vanished, presumably to reappear in Sanctuary.

"There," Scott said, dusting off his hands. The whole reviving had taken less than three seconds this time; it was amazing what more than a hundred repetitions of something in a short period of time did for your skills. "All done."

I slumped, aching all over.

It was done.

I had a strong suspicion that when we got back to Sanctuary, everything would be perfect: Gemma had done a stellar job of reimagining it, and after a brief rest and with Scott's help, I'd managed to bring every single fairy back alive—even Skye and Ambergris, who'd been taken by the shadows—and even Viri.

I figured everyone deserved a second chance. No one deserved the shadows—and no one deserved to die alone with their guilt, even if it was totally justified guilt.

"Awesome," I said wearily. "I'll take you back to Sanctuary now."

Scott narrowed his eyes. "I feel like there's a definite 'but' waiting at the end of that sentence."

I shrugged—more of a twitch than anything else, I was so bone-tired. "No but. I'll drop you off, and then there's something else I need to do real quick before I join you."

He opened his mouth, but I waved at him to shush.

"Please. Just, don't argue, okay? I have to do this."

He squinted suspiciously at me some more, but nodded. "Okay. Fine. But if you're not back, like, three minutes after I am, I'm coming to find you."

"You can't get on the roads by yourself," I said, grabbing his hand and preparing to twist.

"I don't care," he said, squeezing my hand gently. "I'd find you anyway. I'd never stop looking till I found you, if I thought that you were in danger."

I rolled my eyes. "I'm not doing anything dangerous."

"You're on the roads and you're exhausted. That's like, like, driving home at three a.m. after a party."

"First," I said, "you sound like my parents. And second, when have you ever been to a party that lasted until three a.m., not to mention had to drive anywhere afterwards?"

He shrugged. "I'm imagining, right? It's the theme of the day. Plus," he added, sobering, "I can actually drive. Mum used to make me drive her down to the store sometimes. You know. When she was too, um…" He scuffed his feet against the ground. "Well, you know. When she couldn't drive herself."

I stared at him, horrified. "That's awful."

He shrugged again. "So look, you have three minutes, is all I'm saying, Miss Time Traveller. And then I'm going to assume you're in trouble, and I will find you."

I squeezed his hand back gently. "Yeah," I said. "I know."

And before he could keep staring intently at me, I twisted, popping us out right on the beach in Sanctuary. Immediately, I let go of his hand and twisted back again, reaching for the roads.

Scott grabbed after me, but it wasn't a proper entry point to the roads, and I was the only one who could get through. I smiled a tiny bit as I felt the ghost of his grip on my hand. Three minutes, or he'd tear the world apart to save me.

Deep breath.

This time, as I twisted, I felt the fog of the roads try to come with me.

The image of a puppy, sitting square-upright, desperate to be helpful; a child, bringing slightly bruised and mangled wildflowers in from a garden with pride and delight.

Can you take me to them? I sent, along with a picture of the people I meant.

A pause, and then agreement, heads nodding vigorously—the puppy, also nodding, its tongue lolling to one side. *Yes.*

I twisted again, letting the fog follow me. It hissed out into the world ahead of me, and I watched as everything froze.

But this had to be the wrong place, surely: I'd expected to come out in the city—one of them, anyway—where I could see what the men were up to. Instead, I'd come out in the middle of the bush, gum trees with olive-green bark and some with white-

326

and-grey trunks and still others with black, rough skin; the smell of eucalyptus everywhere; tussocky grass beneath my feet, and twig-and-leaf matter, and scrubby, tiny-leafed bushes with little orange berries.

This is the wrong place, I told the roads, which were never far away from me, no matter where I was. I sent a picture of what I'd intended.

Heads nodding, so many of them, a whole auditorium full. *Yes, yes. Go on, go on.*

I shrugged—but I walked on, my road mastery protecting me from the time leak—just as it had done back at school when I'd felt Sanctuary descend on us.

My heart nearly stopped as I looked up from watching my step and saw three men just ahead. But they were held fast by the roads' fog, frozen in time, and even though my heart pounded wildly in my chest, I crept closer.

It stopped again as I realised what the men were doing: they weren't just standing around, staring aimlessly at the ground. There was a hole there, at their feet, a hole about four feet across, and—I swallowed hard—just deep enough to hide a curled up body in.

I pressed my eyes closed and steadied myself. *How does this help?* I asked the roads. *I don't even know where we are.*

A vision filled my mind of the bush around us, every hill picked out, every track, and I could see the main road winding back toward the city.

The sensation of a desperate-to-please puppy accompanied it, and I smiled.

Thanks, I said. *That's perfect.*

One more quick stop, and we'd be able to stop running—for good.

I twisted, and the bush disappeared.

38

I LANDED BACK in Sanctuary under the pines near the beach. Nothing looked the same. It was better.

Cool, fresh pine mingled with the salty smell of the sea, and a gentle breeze lifted the small, wispy hairs on my neck.

In front of me, the meadow stretched out like a thick, emerald rug, grass calf-high and crisp enough to crunch, smooth as velvet from the bottom of the slope to the top.

Down to my right, the wall around the entrance alcove gleamed in the dusk light, a jellybean-shaped pearl, the wall smooth and shining.

To my left at the top of the hill, the Lodge seemed to have grown by two or three storeys; now it sprawled *up* as much as it sprawled *out*, and living, breathing vines twined over it, their tiny white flowers twinkling so bright it seemed covered in fairy lights. I smiled. How appropriate.

Directly across from me, the stables had had a makeover, too: they too gleamed white in the low light, walls clean and fresh with wide breezy windows.

But what really made my heart skip were the trees behind the stable. The far end of the meadow was part of the border with the Valley, part you couldn't cross, part where the brush had always been thick and dense, the trees not sickly so much as unwelcoming, like a thorny hedge or a fence.

Only now, it was clear that it wasn't the Valley any longer, but simply an extension of Sanctuary: the underbrush had opened up, and the ashy trees grew tall and straight, tiny round leaves fluttering like confetti, ferns and baby plants swaying at their feet.

And beyond, where the sickly trees had been, twisted gum trees—still gnarled and worn but now smooth-barked and stain-free, friendly trunks with character and personality, waving kindly in the breeze.

And the mountains behind, blue-cast and wholesome, and the air smelled fresh and clean.

A bark.

I whirled around to see Veve bounding toward me from the Lodge, followed closely by the turquoise-blue, fluttering flash of Quoise's wings. I dashed toward her, and we met in the middle of the slope, me falling to my knees to hug Veve, Veve jumping manically around, stomping on my fingers, slurping at my cheek.

I laughed, and smeared the tears from my eyes.

Quoise caught up and launched herself at my neck, hugging me tight. I patted her on the back gently and grinned. "So you like it, then?" I said.

She gave a muffled, strangled sound that I took as a yes.

"You made it!" Gem and Scott joined us from the stables, Aphros following with Helios trailing behind.

"Yeah," I said, standing up.

"Where did you go?" Scott asked.

I ignored him and turned to Gemma. One world might be safe—but I still had to finish dealing with the other one. "How long do we have left?"

She blinked. "Oh. Yeah."

I smiled a little. I wasn't surprised that she'd forgotten about my home deadline in all the chaos. But I hadn't.

She checked her phone, and her face fell a little. "Thirty seconds over time." She glanced up at me. "I'm so sorry."

I laughed, and held out my hand for her. "You're going to have to hold onto her," I told Scott. "I have to take Veve." I wound my free hand through Veve's collar.

"But Edge, we're too late, what are you doing?"

"Roads," I said, grinning. "We'll be back soon," I told Aphros and Quoise and Helios. "I promise."

Helios bowed gravely. "You have done well, Emma Tanning," he said. "You have restored my home and my family to me. I thank you."

I softened, shoulders relaxing as I exhaled. "Yeah," I said. "You're welcome."

Then I grinned again. "Look after those babies, when you find them."

He tossed his head and flared his wings, nodding me away—and an instant later, I was twisting us off again, back to my own yard.

Bright sunshine washed over us, and the smells shifted to the concrete-and-oil smells of town mingling with the green, eucalypt smell of the bush.

Mum exhaled heavily. "You're back." Her gaze slipped to Veve, panting happily at my side. "You did it."

I nodded.

"Sanctuary?"

"Fixed," Gemma said.

Mum's shoulders relaxed a little. "Well done."

I closed my eyes. "Mum," I said. "Do you have your phone on you?"

"Of course. Why?"

I tried doing the maths in my head. I'd gotten it right. I *had* to have gotten it right.

Of course I had.

"You should be getting a phone call in a sec," I said.

Sure enough, her pocket began to trill. Brows lowered in confusion, she drew the phone out and answered it, turning away from us toward the house.

I bounced my inner lip between my teeth and tried to ignore my pulse thundering in my ear. Any minute now. Any minute.

Veve pulled away, and I let her go, the leather of her collar rough against my fingertips. She bounced toward Mum, gave her a sniff which Mum ignored, and went off to find her water.

Mum turned back to us, her eyes round. "It's the police," she stage-whispered, fingers over the microphone. "They've caught them. They think they've actually caught them. And not just them, but *him*, too. Emma, they *actually* think they've *got* him this time!"

Scott and Gemma were lost in a confusion of pronouns, but I knew exactly what she meant, and I could hardly stop myself cracking at the seams with relief. They'd done it. *I'd* done it. It was over.

"They couldn't tell us earlier," Mum said, voice thick with awe as she relayed the information she was receiving through the phone, "but they found a body a few weeks ago in the bush up in the Dandenongs thanks to an anonymous tip. It's taken them this long to finalise it all, but they have enough evidence to arrest them all in conjunction with that murder—and a couple more. We can stay," she said, eyes bright. "We don't have to run."

We'd have to wait and see if they could make the charges stick, but it was a start. A really, really good start.

I pressed my fingers over the grin blooming over my lips.

We'd done it. And now, we could finally stop running. For good.

EPILOGUE

THE DOORBELL RANG.

That doesn't sound exciting in and of itself—and it wasn't, not really. But as I left my cosy-warm bedroom and came out into the icy hall, where the pale, wintry light through the window by the door was dappling the tiles as the leafless trees danced in the breeze outside, I smiled. Veve stood woofing at the door, tail up like a flag, ears pricked.

Mum popped out of her bedroom, bouncing on her toes. "Can I try again?"

I laughed. "Sure," I said, and gestured to the door.

Mum pushed Veve gently aside with her knee and closed her eyes, resting her forehead against the door. "Navy blue," she said. "I hear rain, and... is that loud ticking, like a really big clock?"

"Anything else?" I prompted, even though I was already impressed; visiting Sanctuary hadn't boosted her skills dramatically like it had mine (likely she wasn't all that strong in the first place), but it had given her enough of a push that she could work on developing her road mastery with solid practice—and she was doing well. A month ago, she wouldn't have picked up on the ticking.

Mum inhaled loudly. "Is that... cinnamon?"

I nodded, face alight. "I think so."

She turned to me, beaming with pride.

I held out my fist for her to bump. "We'd better answer it," I added, gesturing at the door with my free hand.

"Oh. Yeah." Mum stepped aside so I could do the honours.

The deliveryman outside nodded. "Parcel." He hefted a small box at me.

I opened the screen just wide enough to grab the box—and not wide enough for Veve to push past—and juggled the box inside, tucking it under my arm so I could sign for it. "Thanks," I said.

He nodded again, and left.

The door closed behind me with a satisfying click, and I checked the addressee. "Anna," I told Mum. She nodded, and retreated to her bedroom to do whatever it was she'd been doing before the opportunity to practise her skills had arisen. "Anna!" I yelled down the hall. "Parcel!"

There was a muffled thumping and then, down the end of the hall, her door popped open, spilling the sound of dance-rhythm pop music into the house. "Here," she said.

I took it over to her. "I'm going to take Veve for a walk," I said as I handed over the box.

"Yeah, sure." She was already flipping the box over in her hands, looking for the return address. "Whatever." She withdrew, her door closing with a little snick. Immediately, it popped open again. "We're still on for this evening though, right?"

I made a confused face. "This evening? Nope, no idea what you're talking about. Totally forgotten."

She threw a sock at me and slammed her door.

I squeaked, hoping the sock was clean. "Meet me outside at five!" I shouted through the door. "Or I'm going without you again!"

She'd be there, of course. The way she'd lit up that time I'd taken her to the Valley was nothing compared to how she was now with the reimagined Sanctuary—especially now that Aphros was finally pregnant. It was that which had made Anna decide to aim for animal nursing next year, since she didn't have the grades to do vet science.

I stuck my tongue out at her door and headed outside.

I might have a date with Anna in Sanctuary this evening, but I had a prior engagement to deal with first.

Outside, the wintry air prickled my cheeks, and I inhaled deeply, relishing the feel of the fresh air deep in my lungs. Nowra didn't have a winter like Melbourne did, but this was a passable substitute.

"Hey, Edge!"

I whirled around. Gemma was on the footpath outside my front fence, bundled up to her chin with a thick, cream scarf under her coat and a cable-knit beanie over her dark hair. "Hi!" I called.

She let herself in through the gate, and Veve went ballistic, tucking her tail under her butt and spinning in mad, gleeful circles all around the yard. "Hi, Veve," Gem said as Veve finally quit and trotted back over to say hi. Gem tussled Veve's ears, then brushed her gloves on my arms to get rid of the brown fur. "Hi, Edgey." Her cheeks were flushed pink.

"It's not that cold," I said. I had a jacket, sure, but I'd come from Melbourne: this was *not* gloves-and-beanie weather.

"Shut up," she said.

"You two losers going to hang out in the backyard all day?"

We turned, and there was Scott, striding across the footpath in a frogging t-shirt, arms swinging like he owned the whole wide world, blonde hair spiked and tousled, grinning wide as the sea.

Gemma rolled her eyes. "No. Of course not."

"So where are we going?" he said, letting himself in—as though there was ever an option.

I grinned. Sanctuary was calling our names.

Gemma tucked her arms through ours, and Veve danced around us, and the corellas flew overhead with their screechy cries, and together with my best friends in the world, I twisted away from one home toward the other—toward Sanctuary.

THANK YOU!

Dear You,

Wow! I can't believe we made it all the way to the end! Thank you *so* much for taking the time to read this book, and presumably the whole series. If you made it this far, you are honestly amazing; it's readers like you who make writing worthwhile ☺

It was fun digging into the background of the characters some more, and I think all the Scott-fans out there should be pleased ;) If you're keen to know more about his background, keep an eye out for the short story "Another Kind of Hunger", which gives a (very short) glimpse into his life before Sanctuary—and before Emma. The short story is available in the Sanctuary Series bundle, and also as a standalone story in the Inklet series—

See www.inkprintpress.com/inklets for more details.

Again, thanks so much for joining me on this adventure! Here's to future stories, both yours and mine!

Love and unicorns,
Amy

FREE EBOOK

Thank you for buying this book!

When you buy an Inkprint Press book in print, we like to thank you by offering you the ebook for free. Please head to:

http://www.inkprintpress.com/books/books-by-genre/fantasy/sanctuary/when-worlds-collide/

and use the coupon WWCPRINT to download your free copy in both .mobi and .epub formats. (The coupon will only work once.)

SUPPORTERS

With thanks to my amazing Patreon supporters, Clare, Thea and Bethy <3

https://www.patreon.com/amylaurens

ACKNOWLEDGEMENTS

First thanks go to Clare, not only for dealing once again with my constantly fluid and always urgent deadlines, and not only for creating a GORGEOUS body to house my lil book, but also for her infinite patience with receiving sixty single-sentence emails a day in peak periods, for constant encouragement (hellooo, master enabler!), and for just generally being the absolute best friend a writer person could ask for. I don't deserve you. Truly.

And further people I do not deserve: Daimien (good golly, I know the house has been a trashfire this year, and your patience as I pick away as this writing thing trying to turn it into a career is magnificent) and Liana (honestly, it's a wonder your eyes are still attached to your head with the frequency with which you must roll them at me, wondering what harebrained scheme I have concocted next).

Significant thanks also to Kerryn, Bethany, and particularly Miles, who came back for multiple rounds, for their incredible generosity in proofreading. Your eyes are utterly invaluable in spotting all my horrendous typos, and I adore you immensely. <3

Wow. A whole trilogy. Thanks, God: we did it.

ABOUT THE AUTHOR

AMY LAURENS is an Australian author of fantasy fiction for all ages. She has never seen a fairy or travelled to Sanctuary (sadly), but she has definitely owned a Labrador almost exactly like Veve (though Amy's Labrador was yellow, not brown).

And while she's definitely not a Road Master (pity), her kids are pretty sure she has eyes in the back of her head and a sixth sense for spotting trouble. She hasn't told anyone this, but actually she has *two* sets of eyes in the back of her head—one because she's a mum, and one because she's a teacher.

You can find out more about Amy and her books at her website, www.amylaurens.com.

www.ingramcontent.com/pod-product-compliance
Lightning Source LLC
Chambersburg PA
CBHW030657120726
47905CB00001B/251